BEVERLY OF GRAUSTARK

Beverly.

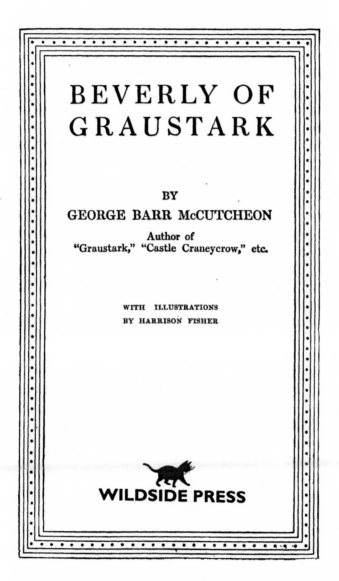

BEVERLY OF GRAUSTARK

BY

GEORGE BARR McCUTCHEON

Author of
"Graustark," "Castle Craneycrow," etc.

WITH ILLUSTRATIONS
BY HARRISON FISHER

WILDSIDE PRESS

Published by
Wildside Press, LLC
P.O. Box 301
Holicong, PA 18928-0301 USA
www.wildsidepress.com

Wildside Press Edition: MMIII

CONTENTS

CONTENTS

ILLUSTRATIONS

Beverly of Graustark

CHAPTER I

EAST OF THE SETTING SUN

AR off in the mountain lands, some-where to the east of the setting sun, lies the principality of Graustark, serene relic of rare old feudal days. The traveler reaches the little do-main after an arduous, sometimes perilous journey from the great European capitals, whether they be north or south or west — never east. He crosses great rivers and wide plains; he winds through fertile valleys and over barren pla-teaus; he twists and turns and climbs among sombre gorges and rugged mountains; he touches the cold clouds in one day and the placid warmth of the valley in the next. One does not go to Graustark for a pleasure jaunt. It is too far from the rest of the world and the ways are often dangerous because of the strife among the tribes of the intervening moun-tains. If one hungers for excitement and peril he finds it in the journey from the north or the south into the land of the Graustarkians. From Vienna

1

and other places almost directly west the way is not so full of thrills, for the railroad skirts the darkest of the dangerlands.

Once in the heart of Graustark, however, the traveler is charmed into dreams of peace and happiness and — paradise. The peasants and the poets sing in one voice and accord, their psalm being of never-ending love. Down in the lowlands and up in the hills, the simple worker of the soil rejoices that he lives in Graustark; in the towns and villages the humble merchant and his thrifty customer unite to sing the song of peace and contentment; in the palaces of the noble the same patriotism warms its heart with thoughts of Graustark, the ancient. Prince and pauper strike hands for the love of the land, while outside the great, heartless world goes rumbling on without a thought of the rare little principality among the eastern mountains.

In point of area, Graustark is but a mite in the great galaxy of nations. Glancing over the map of the world, one is almost sure to miss the infinitesimal patch of green that marks its location. One could not be blamed if he regarded the spot as a typographical or topographical illusion. Yet the people of this quaint little land hold in their hearts a love and a confidence that is not surpassed by any of the lordly monarchs who measure their patriotism by miles and millions. The Graustarkians are a sturdy, courageous race. From the faraway century when they fought themselves clear of the Tartar yoke, to this very hour, they have been warriors of might and valor. The

boundaries of their tiny domain were kept inviolate
for hundreds of years, and but one victorious foe had
come down to lay siege to Edelweiss, the capital.
Axphain, a powerful principality in the north, had
conquered Graustark in the latter part of the nineteenth century, but only after a bitter war in which
starvation and famine proved far more destructive
than the arms of the victors. The treaty of peace
and the indemnity that fell to the lot of vanquished
Graustark have been discoursed upon at length in at
least one history.

Those who have followed that history must know,
of course, that the reigning princess, Yetive, was married to a young American at the very tag-end of the
nineteenth century. This admirable couple met in
quite romantic fashion while the young sovereign was
traveling incognito through the United States of
America. The American, a splendid fellow named
Lorry, was so persistent in the subsequent attack
upon her heart, that all ancestral prejudices were
swept away and she became his bride with the full consent of her entranced subjects. The manner in which
he wooed and won this young and adorable ruler forms
a very attractive chapter in romance, although un-
mentioned in history. This being the tale of another
day, it is not timely to dwell upon the interesting
events which led up to the marriage of the Princess
Yetive to Grenfall Lorry. Suffice it to say that Lorry
won his bride against all wishes and odds and at the
same time won an endless love and esteem from the
people of the little kingdom among the eastern hills.

Two years have passed since that notable wedding in Edelweiss.

Lorry and his wife, the princess, made their home in Washington, but spent a few months of each year in Edelweiss. During the periods spent in Washington and in travel, her affairs in Graustark were in the hands of a capable, austere old diplomat — her uncle, Count Caspar Halfont. Princess Volga reigned as regent over the principality of Axphain. To the south lay the principality of Dawsbergen, ruled by young Prince Dantan, whose half brother, the deposed Prince Gabriel, had been for two years a prisoner in Graustark, the convicted assassin of Prince Lorenz, of Axphain, one time suitor for the hand of Yetive.

It was after the second visit of the Lorrys to Edelweiss that a serious turn of affairs presented itself. Gabriel had succeeded in escaping from his dungeon. His friends in Dawsbergen stirred up a revolution and Dantan was driven from the throne at Serros. On the arrival of Gabriel at the capital, the army of Dawsbergen espoused the cause of the Prince it had spurned and, three days after his escape, he was on his throne, defying Yetive and offering a price for the head of the unfortunate Dantan, now a fugitive in the hills along the Graustark frontier.

CHAPTER II

BEVERLY CALHOUN

AJOR GEORGE CALHOUN was a member of Congress from one of the southern states. His forefathers had represented the same commonwealth, and so, it was likely, would his descendants, if there is virtue in the fitness of things and the heredity of love. While intrepid frontiersmen were opening the trails through the fertile wilds west of the Alleghanies, a strong branch of the Calhoun family followed close in their footsteps. The major's great-grandfather saw the glories and the possibilities of the new territory. He struck boldly westward from the old revolutionary grounds, abandoning the luxuries and traditions of the Carolinas for a fresh, wild life of promise. His sons and daughters became solid stones in the foundation of a commonwealth, and his grandchildren are still at work on the structure. State and national legislatures had known the Calhouns from the beginning. Battlefields had tested their valor, and drawing-rooms had proved their gentility.

Major Calhoun had fought with Stonewall Jackson and won his spurs — and at the same time the heart and hand of Betty Haswell, the staunchest Confederate who ever made flags, bandages and prayers

5

for the boys in gray. When the reconstruction came
he went to Congress and later on became prominent in
the United States consular service, for years holding an important European post. Congress claimed
him once more in the early '90s, and there he is at this
very time.

Everybody in Washington's social and diplomatic
circles admired the beautiful Beverly Calhoun. According to his own loving term of identification, she
was the major's " youngest." The fair southerner
had seen two seasons in the nation's capital. Cupid,
standing directly in front of her, had shot his darts
ruthlessly and resistlessly into the passing hosts, and
masculine Washington looked humbly to her for the
balm that might soothe its pains. The wily god of
love was fair enough to protect the girl whom he
forced to be his unwilling, perhaps unconscious, ally.
He held his impenetrable shield between her heart
and the assaults of a whole army of suitors, high and
low, great and small. It was not idle rumor that said
she had declined a coronet or two, that the millions of
more than one American Midas had been offered to
her, and that she had dealt gently but firmly with a
score of hearts which had nothing but love, ambition
and poverty to support them in the conflict.

The Calhouns lived in a handsome home not far
from the residence of Mr. and Mrs. Grenfall Lorry.
It seemed but natural that the two beautiful young
women should become constant and loyal friends.
Women as lovely as they have no reason to be jealous.
It is only the woman who does not feel secure of her

personal charms that cultivates envy. At the home of Graustark's princess Beverly met the dukes and barons from the far east; it was in the warmth of the Calhoun hospitality that Yetive formed her dearest love for the American people.

Miss Beverly was neither tall nor short. She was of that divine and indefinite height known as medium; slender but perfectly molded; strong but graceful, an absolutely healthy young person whose beauty knew well how to take care of itself. Being quite heart-whole and fancy-free, she slept well, ate well, and enjoyed every minute of life. In her blood ran the warm, eager impulses of the south; hereditary love of ease and luxury displayed itself in every emotion; the perfectly normal demand upon men's admiration was as characteristic in her as it is in any daughter of the land whose women are born to expect chivalry and homage.

A couple of years in a New York "finishing school" for young ladies had served greatly to modify Miss Calhoun's colloquial charms. Many of her delightful "way down south" phrases and mannerisms were blighted by the cold, unromantic atmosphere of a seminary conducted by two ladies from Boston who were too old to marry, too penurious to love and too prim to think that other women might care to do both. There were times, however,— if she were excited or enthusiastic,— when pretty Beverly so far forgot her training as to break forth with a very attractive "yo' all," "suah 'nough," or "go 'long naow." And when the bands played "Dixie" she was not afraid to stand up and wave her handkerchief. The northerner who happened to be with her on such occasions usually found himself doing likewise before he could escape the infection.

Miss Calhoun's face was one that painters coveted deep down in their artistic souls. It never knew a dull instant; there was expression in every lineament, in every look; life, genuine life, dwelt in the mobile countenance that turned the head of every man and woman who looked upon it. Her hair was dark-brown and abundant; her eyes were a deep gray and looked eagerly from between long lashes of black; her lips were red and ever willing to smile or turn plaintive as occasion required; her brow was broad and fair, and her frown was as dangerous as a smile. As to her age, if the major admitted, somewhat indiscreetly, that all his children were old enough to vote, her mother, with the reluctance born in women, confessed that she was past twenty, so a year or two either way will determine Miss Beverly's age, so far as the telling of this story is concerned. Her eldest brother — Keith Calhoun (the one with the congressional heritage) — thought she was too young to marry, while her second brother, Dan, held that she soon would be too old to attract men with matrimonial intentions. Lucy, the only sister, having been happily wedded for ten years, advised her not to think of marriage until she was old enough to know her own mind.

Toward the close of one of the most brilliant seasons the Capital had ever known, less than a fortnight before Congress was to adjourn, the wife of Grenfall

Lorry received the news which spread gloomy disappointment over the entire social realm. A dozen receptions, teas and balls were destined to lose their richest attraction, and hostesses were in despair. The princess had been called to Graustark.

Beverly Calhoun was miserably unhappy. She had heard the story of Gabriel's escape and the consequent probability of a conflict with Axphain. It did not require a great stretch of imagination to convince her that the Lorrys were hurrying off to scenes of intrigue, strife and bloodshed, and that not only Graustark but its princess was in jeopardy.

Miss Calhoun's most cherished hopes faded with the announcement that trouble, not pleasure, called Yetive to Edelweiss. It had been their plan that Beverly should spend the delightful summer months in Graustark, a guest at the royal palace. The original arrangements of the Lorrys were hopelessly disturbed by the late news from Count Halfont. They were obliged to leave Washington two months earlier than they intended, and they could not take Beverly Calhoun into danger-ridden Graustark. The contemplated visit to St. Petersburg and other pleasures had to be abandoned, and they were in tears.

Yetive's maids were packing the trunks, and Lorry's servants were in a wild state of haste preparing for the departure on Saturday's ship. On Friday afternoon, Beverly was naturally where she could do the most good and be of the least help — at the Lorrys'. Self-confessedly, she delayed the preparations. Respectful maidservants and respectful menservants came often to the princess's boudoir to ask questions, and Beverly just as frequently made tearful resolutions to leave the household in peace — if such a hullaballoo could be called peace. Callers came by the dozen, but Yetive would see no one. Letters, telegrams and telephone calls almost swamped her secretary; the footman and the butler fairly gasped under the strain of excitement. Through it all the two friends sat despondent and alone in the drear room that once had been the abode of pure delight. Grenfall Lorry was off in town closing up all matters of business that could be despatched at once. The princess and her industrious retinue were to take the evening express for New York and the next day would find them at sea.

"I know I shall cry all summer," vowed Miss Calhoun, with conviction in her eyes. "It's just too awful for anything." She was lying back among the cushions of the divan and her hat was the picture of cruel neglect. For three solid hours she had stubbornly withstood Yetive's appeals to remove her hat, insisting that she could not trust herself to stay more than a minute or two. "It seems to me, Yetive, that your jailers must be very incompetent or they wouldn't have let loose all this trouble upon you," she complained.

"Prince Gabriel is the very essence of trouble," confessed Yetive, plaintively. "He was born to annoy people, just like the evil prince in the fairy tales."

"I wish we had him over here," the American girl answered stoutly. "He wouldn't be such a trouble,

I'm sure. We don't let small troubles worry us very long, you know."

"But he's dreadfully important over there, Beverly; that's the difficult part of it," said Yetive, solemnly. "You see, he is a condemned murderer."

"Then, you ought to hang him or electrocute him or whatever it is that you do to murderers over there," promptly spoke Beverly.

"But, dear, you don't understand. He won't permit us either to hang or to electrocute him, my dear. The situation is precisely the reverse, if he is correctly quoted by my uncle. When Uncle Caspar sent an envoy to inform Dawsbergen respectfully that Graustark would hold it personally responsible if Gabriel were not surrendered, Gabriel himself replied: 'Graustark be hanged!'"

"How rude of him, especially when your uncle was so courteous about it. He must be a very disagreeable person," announced Miss Calhoun.

"I am sure you wouldn't like him," said the princess. "His brother, who has been driven from the throne — and from the capital, in fact — is quite different. I have not seen him, but my ministers regard him as a splendid young man."

"Oh, how I hope he may go back with his army and annihilate that old Gabriel!" cried Beverly, frowning fiercely.

"Alas," sighed the princess, "he hasn't an army, and besides he is finding it extremely difficult to keep from being annihilated himself. The army has gone over to Prince Gabriel."

"Pooh!" scoffed Miss Calhoun, who was thinking of the enormous armies the United States can produce at a day's notice. "What good is a ridiculous little army like his, anyway? A battalion from Fort Thomas could beat it to —— "

"Don't boast, dear," interrupted Yetive, with a wan smile. "Dawsbergen has a standing army of ten thousand excellent soldiers. With the war reserves she has twice the available force I can produce."

"But your men are so brave," cried Beverly, who had heard their praises sung.

"True, God bless them; but you forget that we must attack Gabriel in his own territory. To recapture him means a perilous expedition into the mountains of Dawsbergen, and I am sorely afraid. Oh, dear, I hope he'll surrender peaceably!"

"And go back to jail for life?" cried Miss Calhoun. "It's a good deal to expect of him, dear. I fancy it's much better fun kicking up a rumpus on the outside than it is kicking one's toes off against an obdurate stone wall from the inside. You can't blame him for fighting a bit."

"No — I suppose not," agreed the princess, miserably. "Gren is actually happy over the miserable affair, Beverly. He is full of enthusiasm and positively aching to be in Graustark — right in the thick of it all. To hear him talk, one would think that Prince Gabriel has no show at all. He kept me up till four o'clock this morning telling me that Dawsbergen didn't know what kind of a snag it was going up against. I have a vague idea what he means by that;

his manner did not leave much room for doubt. He also said that we would jolt Dawsbergen off the map. It sounds encouraging, at least, doesn't it?"

"It sounds very funny for you to say those things," admitted Beverly, "even though they come second-hand. You were not cut out for slang."

"Why, I'm sure they are all good English words," remonstrated Yetive. "Oh, dear, I wonder what they are doing in Graustark this very instant. Are they fighting or —— "

"No; they are merely talking. Don't you know, dear, that there is never a fight until both sides have talked themselves out of breath? We shall have six months of talk and a week or two of fight, just as they always do nowadays."

"Oh, you Americans have such a comfortable way of looking at things," cried the princess. "Don't you ever see the serious side of life?"

"My dear, the American always lets the other fellow see the serious side of life," said Beverly.

"You wouldn't be so optimistic if a country much bigger and more powerful than America happened to be the other fellow."

"It did sound frightfully boastful, didn't it? It's the way we've been brought up, I reckon,— even we southerners who know what it is to be whipped. The idea of a girl like me talking about war and trouble and all that! It's absurd, isn't it?"

"Nevertheless, I wish I could see things through those dear gray eyes of yours. Oh, how I'd like to have you with me through all the months that are to come. You would be such a help to me — such a joy. Nothing would seem so hard if you were there to make me see things through your brave American eyes." The princess put her arms about Beverly's neck and drew her close.

"But Mr. Lorry possesses an excellent pair of American eyes," protested Miss Beverly, loyally and very happily.

"I know, dear, but they are a man's eyes. Somehow, there is a difference, you know. I wouldn't dare cry when he was looking, but I could boo-hoo all day if you were there to comfort me. He thinks I am very brave — and I'm not," she confessed, dismally.

"Oh, I'm an awful coward," explained Beverly, consolingly. "I think you are the bravest girl in all the world," she added. "Don't you remember what you did at — " and then she recalled the stories that had come from Graustark ahead of the bridal party two years before. Yetive was finally obliged to place her hand on the enthusiastic visitor's lips.

"Peace," she cried, blushing. "You make me feel like a-a — what is it you call her — a dime-novel heroine?"

"A yellow-back girl? Never!" exclaimed Beverly, severely.

Visitors of importance in administration circles came at this moment and the princess could not refuse to see them. Beverly Calhoun reluctantly departed, but not until after giving a promise to accompany the Lorrys to the railway station.

＊ ＊ ＊ ＊ ＊ ＊ ＊ ＊

The trunks had gone to be checked, and the household was quieter than it had been in many days. There was an air of depression about the place that had its inception in the room upstairs where sober-faced Halkins served dinner for a not over-talkative young couple.

" It will be all right, dearest," said Lorry, divining his wife's thoughts as she sat staring rather soberly straight ahead of her. " Just as soon as we get to Edelweiss, the whole affair will look so simple that we can laugh at the fears of to-day. You see, we are a long way off just now."

" I am only afraid of what may happen before we get there, Gren," she said, simply. He leaned over and kissed her hand, smiling at the emphasis she unconsciously placed on the pronoun.

Beverly Calhoun was announced just before coffee was served, and a moment later was in the room. She stopped just inside the door, clicked her little heels together and gravely brought her hand to " salute." Her eyes were sparkling and her lips trembled with suppressed excitement.

" I think I can report to you in Edelweiss next month, general," she announced, with soldierly dignity. Her hearers stared at the picturesque recruit, and Halkins so far forgot himself as to drop Mr. Lorry's lump of sugar upon the table instead of into the cup.

" Explain yourself, sergeant! " finally fell from Lorry's lips. The eyes of the princess were beginning to take on a rapturous glow.

" May I have a cup of coffee, please, sir? I've been so excited I couldn't eat a mouthful at home." She gracefully slid into the chair Halkins offered, and broke into an ecstatic giggle that would have resulted in a court-martial had she been serving any commander but Love.

With a plenteous supply of Southern idioms she succeeded in making them understand that the major had promised to let her visit friends in the legation at St. Petersburg in April a month or so after the departure of the Lorrys.

" He wanted to know where I'd rather spend the Spring — Washin'ton or Lexin'ton, and I told him St. Petersburg. We had a terrific discussion and neither of us ate a speck at dinner. Mamma said it would be all right for me to go to St. Petersburg if Aunt Josephine was still of a mind to go, too. You see, Auntie was scared almost out of her boots when she heard there was prospect of war in Graustark, just as though a tiny little war like that could make any difference away up in Russia — hundreds of thousands of miles away — " (with a scornful wave of the hand) — " and then I just made Auntie say she'd go to St. Petersburg in April — a whole month sooner than she expected to go in the first place — and —— "

" You dear, dear Beverly! " cried Yetive, rushing joyously around the table to clasp her in her arms.

" And St. Petersburg really isn't a hundred thousand miles from Edelweiss," cried Beverly, gaily.

" It's much less than that," said Lorry, smiling.

" But you surely don't expect to come to Edelweiss if we are fighting. We couldn't think of letting you do that, you know. Your mother would never —— "

" My mother wasn't afraid of a much bigger war than yours can ever hope to be," cried Beverly, resentfully. " You can't stop me if I choose to visit Graustark."

" Does your father know that you contemplate such a trip? " asked Lorry, returning her handclasp and looking doubtfully into the swimming blue eyes of his wife.

" No, he doesn't," admitted Beverly, a trifle aggressively.

" He could stop you, you know," he suggested. Yetive was discreetly silent.

" But he won't know anything about it," cried Beverly triumphantly.

" I could tell him, you know," said Lorry.

" No, you *couldn't* do anything so mean as that," announced Beverly. " You're not that sort."

CHAPTER III

ON THE ROAD FROM BALAK

 PONDEROUS coach lumbered slowly, almost painfully, along the narrow road that skirted the base of a mountain. It was drawn by four horses, and upon the seat sat two rough, unkempt Russians, one holding the reins, the other lying back in a lazy doze. The month was June and all the world seemed soft and sweet and joyous. To the right flowed a turbulent mountain stream, boiling savagely with the alien waters of the flood season. Ahead of the creaking coach rode four horsemen, all heavily armed; another quartette followed some distance in the rear. At the side of the coach an officer of the Russian mounted police was riding easily, jangling his accoutrements with a vigor that disheartened at least one occupant of the vehicle. The windows of the coach doors were lowered, permitting the fresh mountain air to caress fondly the face of the young woman who tried to find comfort in one of the broad seats. Since early morn she had struggled with the hardships of that seat, and the late afternoon found her very much out of patience. The opposite seat was the resting place of a substantial colored woman and a stupendous pile of

18

bags and boxes. The boxes were continually toppling over and the bags were forever getting under the feet of the once placid servant, whose face, quite luckily, was much too black to reflect the anger she was able, otherwise, through years of practice, to conceal.

"How much farther have we to go, lieutenant?" asked the girl on the rear seat, plaintively, even humbly. The man was very deliberate with his English. He had been recommended to her as the best linguist in the service at Radovitch, and he had a reputation to sustain.

"It another hour is but yet," he managed to inform her, with a confident smile.

"Oh, dear," she sighed, "a whole hour of this!"

"We soon be dar, Miss Bev'ly; jes' yo' mak' up yo' mine to res' easy-like, an' we — " but the faithful old colored woman's advice was lost in the wrathful exclamation that accompanied another dislodgment of bags and boxes. The wheels of the coach had dropped suddenly into a deep rut. Aunt Fanny's growls were scarcely more potent than poor Miss Beverly's moans.

"It is getting worse and worse," exclaimed Aunt Fanny's mistress, petulantly. "I'm black and blue from head to foot, aren't you, Aunt Fanny?"

"Ah cain' say as to de blue, Miss Bev'ly. Hit's a mos' monstrous bad road, sho 'nough. Stay up dar, will yo'!" she concluded, jamming a bag into an upper corner.

Miss Calhoun, tourist extraordinary, again consulted the linguist in the saddle. She knew at the outset that the quest would be hopeless, but she could think of no better way to pass the next hour than to extract a mite of information from the officer.

"Now for a good old chat," she said, beaming a smile upon the grizzled Russian. "Is there a decent hotel in the village?" she asked.

They were on the edge of the village before she succeeded in finding out all that she could, and it was not a great deal, either. She learned that the town of Balak was in Axphain, scarcely a mile from the Graustark line. There was an eating and sleeping house on the main street, and the population of the place did not exceed three hundred.

When Miss Beverly awoke the next morning, sore and distressed, she looked back upon the night with a horror that sleep had been kind enough to interrupt only at intervals. The wretched hostelry lived long in her secret catalogue of terrors. Her bed was not a bed; it was a torture. The room, the table, the — but it was all too odious for description. Fatigue was her only friend in that miserable hole. Aunt Fanny had slept on the floor near her mistress's cot, and it was the good old colored woman's grumbling that awoke Beverly. The sun was climbing up the mountains in the east, and there was an air of general activity about the place. Beverly's watch told her that it was past eight o'clock.

"Good gracious!" she exclaimed. "It's nearly noon, Aunt Fanny. Hurry along here and get me up. We must leave this abominable place in ten minutes." She was up and racing about excitedly.

"Befo' breakfas'?" demanded Aunt Fanny weakly.

"Goodness, Aunt Fanny, is that all you think about?"

"Well, honey, yo' all be thinkin' moughty serious 'bout breakfas' 'long to'ahds 'leben o'clock. Dat li'l tummy o' yourn 'll be pow'ful mad 'cause yo' didn'—— "

"Very well, Aunt Fanny, you can run along and have the woman put up a breakfast for us and we'll eat it on the road. I positively refuse to eat another mouthful in that awful dining-room. I'll be down in ten minutes."

She was down in less. Sleep, no matter how hard-earned, had revived her spirits materially. She pronounced herself ready for anything; there was a wholesome disdain for the rigors of the coming ride through the mountains in the way she gave orders for the start. The Russian officer met her just outside the entrance to the inn. He was less English than ever, but he eventually gave her to understand that he had secured permission to escort her as far as Ganlook, a town in Graustark not more than fifteen miles from Edelweiss and at least two days from Balak. Two competent Axphainian guides had been retained, and the party was quite ready to start. He had been warned of the presence of brigands in the wild mountainous passes north of Ganlook. The Russians could go no farther than Ganlook because of a royal edict from Edelweiss forbidding the nearer approach of armed forces. At that town, however, he was sure she easily could obtain an escort of Graustarkian soldiers.

As the big coach crawled up the mountain road and further into the oppressive solitudes, Beverly Calhoun drew from the difficult lieutenant considerable information concerning the state of affairs in Graustark. She had been eagerly awaiting the time when something definite could be learned. Before leaving St. Petersburg early in the week she was assured that a state of war did not exist. The Princess Yetive had been in Edelweiss for six weeks. A formal demand was framed soon after her return from America, requiring Dawsbergen to surrender the person of Prince Gabriel to the authorities of Graustark. To this demand there was no definite response, Dawsbergen insolently requesting time in which to consider the proposition. Axphain immediately sent an envoy to Edelweiss to say that all friendly relations between the two governments would cease unless Graustark took vigorous steps to recapture the royal assassin. On one side of the unhappy principality a strong, overbearing princess was egging Graustark on to fight, while on the other side an equally aggressive people defied Yetive to come and take the fugitive if she could. The poor princess was between two ugly alternatives, and a struggle seemed inevitable. At Balak it was learned that Axphain had recently sent a final appeal to the government of Graustark, and it was no secret that something like a threat accompanied the message.

Prince Gabriel was in complete control at Serros and was disposed to laugh at the demands of his late captors. His half-brother, the dethroned Prince Dantan, was still hiding in the fastnesses of the hills, protected by a small company of nobles, and there was no hope that he ever could regain his crown. Gabriel's power over the army was supreme. The general public admired Dantan, but it was helpless in the face of circumstances.

"But why should Axphain seek to harass Graustark at this time?" demanded Beverly Calhoun, in perplexity and wrath. "I should think the brutes would try to help her."

"There is an element of opposition to the course the government is taking," the officer informed her in his own way, "but it is greatly in the minority. The Axphainians have hated Graustark since the last war, and the princess despises this American. It is an open fact that the Duke of Mizrox leads the opposition to Princess Volga, and she is sure to have him beheaded if the chance affords. He is friendly to Graustark and has been against the policy of his princess from the start."

"I'd like to hug the Duke of Mizrox," cried Beverly, warmly. The officer did not understand her, but Aunt Fanny was scandalized.

"Good Lawd!" she muttered to the boxes and bags.

As the coach rolled deeper and deeper into the rock-shadowed wilderness, Beverly Calhoun felt an undeniable sensation of awe creeping over her. The brave, impetuous girl had plunged gaily into the proj-

ect which now led her into the deadliest of uncer-
tainties, with but little thought of the consequences.

The first stage of the journey by coach had been
good fun. They had passed along pleasant roads,
through quaint villages and among interesting people,
and progress had been rapid. The second stage had
presented rather terrifying prospects, and the third
day promised even greater vicissitudes. Looking from
the coach windows out upon the quiet, desolate gran-
deur of her surroundings, poor Beverly began to ap-
preciate how abjectly helpless and alone she was. Her
companions were ugly, vicious-looking men, any one
of whom could inspire terror by a look. She had en-
trusted herself to the care of these strange creatures
in the moment of inspired courage and now she was
constrained to regret her action. True, they had
proved worthy protectors as far as they had gone,
but the very possibilities that lay in their power were
appalling, now that she had time to consider the
situation.

The officer in charge had been recommended as a
trusted servant of the Czar; an American consul had
secured the escort for her direct from the frontier
patrol authorities. Men high in power had vouched
for the integrity of the detachment, but all this was
forgotten in the mighty solitude of the mountains.
She was beginning to fear her escort more than she
feared the brigands of the hills.

Treachery seemed printed on their backs as they
rode ahead of her. The big officer was ever polite and
alert, but she was ready to distrust him on the slight-

est excuse. These men could not help knowing that she was rich, and it was reasonable for them to suspect that she carried money and jewels with her. In her mind's eye she could picture these traitors rifling her bags and boxes in some dark pass, and then there were other horrors that almost petrified her when she allowed herself to think of them.

Here and there the travelers passed by rude cots where dwelt woodmen and mountaineers, and at long intervals a solitary but picturesque horseman stood aside and gave them the road. As the coach penetrated deeper into the gorge, signs of human life and activity became fewer. The sun could not send his light into this shadowy tomb of granite. The rattle of the wheels and the clatter of the horses' hoofs sounded like a constant crash of thunder in the ears of the tender traveler, a dainty morsel among hawks and wolves.

There was an unmistakable tremor in her voice when she at last found heart to ask the officer where they were to spend the night. It was far past noon and Aunt Fanny had suggested opening the lunch-baskets. One of the guides was called back, the leader being as much in the dark as his charge.

" There is no village within twenty miles," he said, " and we must sleep in the pass."

Beverly's voice faltered. " Out here in all this awful —— " Then she caught herself quickly. It came to her suddenly that she must not let these men see that she was apprehensive. Her voice was a trifle shrill and her eyes glistened with a strange new light as she went on, changing her tack completely: "How romantic! I've often wanted to do something like this."

The officer looked bewildered, and said nothing. Aunt Fanny was speechless. Later on, when the lieutenant had gone ahead to confer with the guides about the suspicious actions of a small troop of horsemen they had seen, Beverly confided to the old negress that she was frightened almost out of her boots, but that she'd die before the men should see a sign of cowardice in a Calhoun. Aunt Fanny was not so proud and imperious. It was with difficulty that her high-strung young mistress suppressed the wails that long had been under restraint in Aunt Fanny's huge and turbulent bosom.

"Good Lawd, Miss Bev'ly, dey'll chop us all to pieces an' take ouah jewl'ry an' money an' clo'es and ev'ything else we done got about us. Good Lawd, le's tu'n back, Miss Bev'ly. We ain' got no mo' show out heah in dese mountings dan a —— "

"Be still, Aunt Fanny!" commanded Beverly, with a fine show of courage. "You must be brave. Don't you see we can't turn back? It's just as dangerous and a heap sight more so. If we let on we're not one bit afraid they'll respect us, don't you see, and men never harm women whom they respect."

"Umph!" grunted Aunt Fanny, with exaggerated irony.

"Well, they never do!" maintained Beverly, who was not at all sure about it. "And they look like real nice men — honest men, even though they have such awful whiskers."

"Dey's de wust trash Ah eveh did see," exploded Aunt Fanny.

"Sh! Don't let them hear you," whispered Beverly.

In spite of her terror and perplexity, she was compelled to smile. It was all so like the farce comedies one sees at the theatre.

As the officer rode up, his face was pale in the shadowy light of the afternoon and he was plainly very nervous.

"What is the latest news from the front?" she inquired cheerfully.

"The men refuse to ride on," he exclaimed, speaking rapidly, making it still harder for her to understand. "Our advance guard has met a party of hunters from Axphain. They insist that you — 'the fine lady in the coach' — are the Princess Yetive, returning from a secret visit to St. Petersburg, where you went to plead for assistance from the Czar."

Beverly Calhoun gasped in astonishment. It was too incredible to believe. It was actually ludicrous, She laughed heartily. "How perfectly absurd."

"I am well aware that you are not the Princess Yetive," he continued emphatically; "but what can I do; the men won't believe me. They swear they have been tricked and are panic-stricken over the situation. The hunters tell them that the Axphain authorities, fully aware of the hurried flight of the Princess through these wilds, are preparing to intercept her. A large detachment of soldiers are already across the Graustark frontier. It is only a question of time before the ' red legs ' will be upon them. I have assured them that their beautiful charge is not the Princess, but an American girl, and that there is no mystery about the coach and escort. All in vain. The Axphain guides already feel that their heads are on the block; while as for the Cossacks, not even my dire threats of the awful anger of the White Czar, when he finds they have disobeyed his commands, will move them."

" Speak to your men once more, sir, and promise them big purses of gold when we reach Ganlook. I have no money or valuables with me; but there I can obtain plenty," said Beverly, shrewdly thinking it better that they should believe her to be without funds.

The cavalcade had halted during this colloquy. All the men were ahead conversing sullenly and excitedly with much gesticulation. The driver, a stolid creature, seemingly indifferent to all that was going on, alone remained at his post. The situation, apparently dangerous, was certainly most annoying. But if Beverly could have read the mind of that silent figure on the box, she would have felt slightly relieved, for he was infinitely more anxious to proceed than even she; but from far different reasons. He was a Russian convict, who had escaped on the way to Siberia. Disguised as a coachman he was seeking life and safety in Graustark, or any out-of-the-way place. It mattered little to him where the escort concluded to

go. He was going ahead. He dared not go back —
he must go on.

At the end of half an hour, the officer returned; all
hope had gone from his face. "It is useless!" he
cried out. "The guides refuse to proceed. See!
They are going off with their countrymen! We are
lost without them. I do not know what to do. We
cannot get to Ganlook; I do not know the way, and
the danger is great. Ah! Madam! Here they come!
The Cossacks are going back."

As he spoke, the surly mutineers were riding slowly
towards the coach. Every man had his pistol on
the high pommel of the saddle. Their faces wore
an ugly look. As they passed the officer, one of them,
pointing ahead of him with his sword, shouted savagely, "Balak!"

It was conclusive and convincing. They were deserting her.

"Oh, oh, oh! The cowards!" sobbed Beverly
in rage and despair. "I must go on! Is it possible
that even such men would leave —— "

She was interrupted by the voice of the officer, who,
raising his cap to her, commanded at the same time
the driver to turn his horses and follow the escort to
Balak.

"What is that?" demanded Beverly in alarm.

From far off came the sound of firearms. A dozen
shots were fired, and reverberated down through the
gloomy pass ahead of the coach.

"They are fighting somewhere in the hills in front
of us," answered the now frightened officer. Turn-

ing quickly, he saw the deserting horsemen halt, listen a minute, and then spur their horses. He cried out sharply to the driver, " Come, there! Turn round! We have no time to lose! "

With a savage grin, the hitherto motionless driver hurled some insulting remark at the officer, who was already following his men, now in full flight down the road, and settling himself firmly on the seat, taking a fresh grip of the reins, he yelled to his horses, at the same time lashing them furiously with his whip, and started the coach ahead at a fearful pace. His only thought was to get away as far as possible from the Russian officer, then deliberately desert the coach and its occupants and take to the hills.

CHAPTER IV

THE RAGGED RETINUE

HOROUGHLY mystified by the action of the driver and at length terrified by the pace that carried them careening along the narrow road, Beverly cried out to him, her voice shrill with alarm. Aunt Fanny was crouching on the floor of the coach, between the seats, groaning and praying.

"Stop! Where are you going?" cried Beverly, putting her head recklessly through the window. If the man heard her he gave no evidence of the fact. His face was set forward and he was guiding the horses with a firm, unquivering hand. The coach rattled and bounded along the dangerous way hewn in the side of the mountain. A misstep or a false turn might easily start the clumsy vehicle rolling down the declivity on the right. The convict was taking desperate chances, and with a cool, calculating brain, prepared to leap to the ground in case of accident and save himself, without a thought for the victims inside.

"Stop! Turn around!" she cried in a frenzy. "We shall be killed. Are you crazy?"

By this time they had struck a descent in the road
and were rushing along at breakneck speed into
oppressive shadows that bore the first imprints of
night. Realizing at last that her cries were falling
upon purposely deaf ears, Beverly Calhoun sank
back into the seat, weak and terror-stricken. It was
plain to her that the horses were not running away,
for the man had been lashing them furiously. There
was but one conclusion: he was deliberately taking
her farther into the mountain fastnesses, his purpose
known only to himself. A hundred terrors presented
themselves to her as she lay huddled against the side
of the coach, her eyes closed tightly, her tender body
tossed furiously about with the sway of the vehicle.
There was the fundamental fear that she would be
dashed to death down the side of the mountain, but
apart from this her quick brain was evolving all sorts
of possible endings — none short of absolute disaster.

Even as she prayed that something might intervene to check the mad rush and to deliver her from
the horrors of the moment, the raucous voice of the
driver was heard calling to his horses and the pace
became slower. The awful rocking and the jolting
grew less severe, the clatter resolved itself into a broken
rumble, and then the coach stopped with a mighty
lurch.

Dragging herself from the corner, poor Beverly
Calhoun, no longer a disdainful heroine, gazed piteously out into the shadows, expecting the murderous
blade of the driver to meet her as she did so. Pauloff
had swung from the box of the coach and was peer-

ing first into the woodland below and then upon the
rocks to the left.   He wore the expression of a man
trapped and seeking means of escape.   Suddenly he
darted behind the coach, almost brushing against
Beverly's hat as he passed the window.   She opened
her lips to call to him, but even as she did so he
took to his heels and raced back over the road they
had traveled so precipitously.

Overcome by surprise and dismay, she only could
watch the flight in silence.   Less than a hundred feet
from where the coach was standing he turned to the
right and was lost among the rocks.   Ahead, four
horses, covered with sweat, were panting and heaving
as if in great distress after their mad run.   Aunt
Fanny was still moaning and praying by turns in
the bottom of the carriage.   Darkness was settling
down upon the pass, and objects a hundred yards
away were swallowed by the gloom.   There was no
sound save the blowing of the tired animals and the
moaning of the old negress.   Beverly realized with a
sinking heart that they were alone and helpless in the
mountains with night upon them.

She never knew where the strength and courage
came from, but she forced open the stubborn coach-
door and scrambled to the ground, looking frantically
in all directions for a single sign of hope.   In the
most despairing terror she had ever experienced, she
started toward the lead horses, hoping against hope
that at least one of her men had remained faithful.

A man stepped quietly from the inner side of the
road and advanced with the uncertain tread of one

who is overcome by amazement. He was a stranger, and wore an odd, uncouth garb. The failing light told her that he was not one of her late protectors. She shrank back with a faint cry of alarm, ready to fly to the protecting arms of hopeless Aunt Fanny if her uncertain legs could carry her. At the same instant another ragged stranger, then two, three, four, or five, appeared as if by magic, some near her, others approaching from the shadows.

"Who — who in heaven's name are you?" she faltered. The sound of her own voice in a measure restored the courage that had been paralyzed. Unconsciously this slim sprig of southern valor threw back her shoulders and lifted her chin. If they were brigands they should not find her a cringing coward. After all, she was a Calhoun.

The man she had first observed stopped near the horses' heads and peered intently at her from beneath a broad and rakish hat. He was tall and appeared to be more respectably clad than his fellows, although there was not one who looked as though he possessed a complete outfit of wearing apparel.

"Poor wayfarers, may it please your highness," replied the tall vagabond, bowing low. To her surprise he spoke in very good English; his voice was clear, and there was a tinge of polite irony in the tones. "But all people are alike in the mountains. The king and the thief, the princess and the jade live in the common fold," and his hat swung so low that it touched the ground.

"I am powerless. I only implore you to take

"Who—who in heaven's name are you?" she
faltered.

what valuables you may find and let us proceed un-
harmed —— " she cried, rapidly, eager to have it
over.

"Pray, how can your highness proceed? You
have no guide, no driver, no escort," said the man,
mockingly. Beverly looked at him appealingly,
utterly without words to reply. The tears were well-
ing to her eyes and her heart was throbbing like that
of a captured bird. In after life she was able to
picture in her mind's eye all the details of that tab-
leau in the mountain pass — the hopeless coach, the
steaming horses, the rakish bandit, and his picturesque
men, the towering crags, and a mite of a girl facing
the end of everything.

"Your highness is said to be brave, but even your
wonderful courage can avail nothing in this instance," said the leader, pleasantly. "Your escort
has fled as though pursued by something stronger
than shadows; your driver has deserted; your horses
are half-dead; you are indeed, as you have said, powerless. And you are, besides all these, in the clutches
of a band of merciless cutthroats."

"Oh," moaned Beverly, suddenly leaning against
the fore wheel, her eyes almost starting from her head.
The leader laughed quietly — yes, good-naturedly.
"Oh, you won't — you won't kill us?" She had time
to observe that there were smiles on the faces of all the
men within the circle of light.

"Rest assured, your highness," said the leader,
leaning upon his rifle-barrel with careless grace, "we
intend no harm to you. Every man you meet in

Graustark is not a brigand, I trust, for your sake.
We are simple hunters, and not what we may seem.
It is fortunate that you have fallen into honest hands.
There is someone in the coach?" he asked, quickly
alert. A prolonged groan proved to Beverly that
Aunt Fanny had screwed up sufficient courage to look
out of the window.

"My old servant," she half whispered. Then, as
several of the men started toward the door: "But
she is old and wouldn't harm a fly. Please, please
don't hurt her."

"Compose yourself; she is safe," said the leader.
By this time it was quite dark. At a word from
him two or three men lighted lanterns. The picture was more weird than ever in the fitful glow.
"May I ask, your highness, how do you intend to
reach Edelweiss in your present condition. You
cannot manage those horses, and besides, you do not
know the way."

"Aren't you going to rob us?" demanded Beverly,
hope springing to the surface with a joyful bound.
The stranger laughed heartily, and shook his head.

"Do we not look like honest men?" he cried, with
a wave of his hand toward his companions. Beverly
looked dubious. "We live the good, clean life of
the wilderness. Out-door life is necessary for our
health. We could not live in the city," he went on
with grim humor. For the first time, Beverly noticed
that he wore a huge black patch over his left eye, held
in place by a cord. He appeared more formidable
than ever under the light of critical inspection.

"I am very much relieved," said Beverly, who was not at all relieved. "But why have you stopped us in this manner?"

"Stopped you?" cried the man with the patch. "I implore you to unsay that, your highness. Your coach was quite at a standstill before we knew of its presence. You do us a grave injustice."

"It's very strange," muttered Beverly, somewhat taken aback.

"Have you observed that it is quite dark?" asked the leader, putting away his brief show of indignation.

"Dear me; so it is!" cried she, now able to think more clearly.

"And you are miles from an inn or house of any kind," he went on. "Do you expect to stay here all night?"

"I'm — I'm not afraid," bravely shivered Beverly.

"It is most dangerous."

"I have a revolver," the weak little voice went on.

"Oho! What is it for?"

"To use in case of emergency."

"Such as repelling brigands who suddenly appear upon the scene?"

"Yes."

"May I ask why you did not use it this evening?"

"Because it is locked up in one of my bags — I don't know just which one — and Aunt Fanny has the key," confessed Beverly.

The chief of the "honest men" laughed again, a clear, ringing laugh that bespoke supreme confidence in his right to enjoy himself.

"And who is Aunt Fanny?" he asked, covering his patch carefully with his slouching hat.

"My servant. She's colored."

"Colored?" he asked in amazement. "What do you mean?"

"Why, she's a negress. Don't you know what a colored person is?"

"You mean she is a slave — a black slave?"

"We don't own slaves any mo' — more." He looked more puzzled than ever — then at last, to satisfy himself, walked over and peered into the coach. Aunt Fanny set up a dismal howl; an instant later Sir Honesty was pushed aside, and Miss Calhoun was anxiously trying to comfort her old friend through the window. The man looked on in silent wonder for a minute, and then strode off to where a group of his men stood talking.

"Is yo' daid yit, Miss Bev'ly — is de end came?" moaned Aunt Fanny. Beverly could not repress a smile.

"I am quite alive, Auntie. These men will not hurt us. They are *very nice* gentlemen." She uttered the last observation in a loud voice and it had its effect, for the leader came to her side with long strides.

"Convince your servant that we mean no harm, your highness," he said eagerly, a new deference in his voice and manner. "We have only the best of motives in mind. True, the hills are full of lawless fellows and we are obliged to fight them almost daily, but you have fallen in with honest men — very nice

gentlemen, I trust.   Less than an hour ago we put a
band of robbers to flight —— "

"I heard the shooting," cried Beverly.   "It was
that which put my escort to flight."

"They could not have been soldiers of Graustark,
then, your highness," quite gallantly.

"They were Cossacks, or whatever you call them.
But, pray, why do you call me ' your highness ' ? "
demanded Beverly.   The tall leader swept the ground
with his hat once more.

"All the outside world knows the Princess Yetive —
why not the humble mountain man?   You will pardon
me, but every man in the hills knows that you are
to pass through on the way from St. Petersburg to
Ganlook.   We are not so far from the world, after
all, we rough people of the hills.   We know that your
highness left St. Petersburg by rail last Sunday and
took to the highway day before yesterday, because the
floods had washed away the bridges north of Axphain.
Even the hills have eyes and ears."

Beverly listened with increasing perplexity.   It
was true that she had left St. Petersburg on Sunday;
that the unprecedented floods had stopped all railway
traffic in the hills, compelling her to travel for many
miles by stage, and that the whole country was con-
fusing her in some strange way with the Princess
Yetive.   The news had evidently sped through
Axphain and the hills with the swiftness of fire.   It
would be useless to deny the story; these men would
not believe her.   In a flash she decided that it would
be best to pose for the time being as the ruler of

Graustark. It remained only for her to impress upon Aunt Fanny the importance of this resolution.

"What wise old hills they must be," she said, with evasive enthusiasm. "You cannot expect me to admit, however, that I am the princess," she went on.

"It would not be just to your excellent reputation for tact if you did so, your highness," calmly spoke the man. "It is quite as easy to say that you are not the princess as to say that you are, so what matters, after all? We reserve the right, however, to do homage to the queen who rules over these wise old hills. I offer you the humble services of myself and my companions. We are yours to command."

"I am very grateful to find that you are not brigands, believe me," said Beverly. "Pray tell me who you are, then, and you shall be sufficiently rewarded for your good intentions."

"I? Oh, your highness, I am Baldos, the goat-hunter, a poor subject for reward at your hands. I may as well admit that I am a poacher, and have no legal right to the prosperity of your hills. The only reward I can ask is forgiveness for trespassing upon the property of others."

"You shall receive pardon for all transgressions. But you must get me to some place of safety," said Beverly, eagerly.

"And quickly, too, you might well have added," he said, lightly. "The horses have rested, I think, so with your permission we may proceed. I know of a place where you may spend the night comfortably and be refreshed for the rough journey to-morrow."

"To-morrow? How can I go on? I am alone,"
she cried, despairingly.

"Permit me to remind you that you are no longer
alone. You have a ragged following, your highness,
but it shall be a loyal one. Will you re-enter the
coach? It is not far to the place I speak of, and I
myself will drive you there. Come, it is getting late,
and your retinue, at least, is hungry."

He flung open the coach door, and his hat swept
the ground once more. The light of a lantern played
fitfully upon his dark, gaunt face, with its gallant
smile and ominous patch. She hesitated, fear entering
her soul once more. He looked up quickly and saw the
indecision in her eyes, the mute appeal.

"Trust me, your highness," he said, gravely, and
she allowed him to hand her into the coach.

A moment later he was upon the driver's box, reins
in hand. Calling out to his companions in a language strange to Beverly, he cracked the whip, and
once more they were lumbering over the wretched
road. Beverly sank back into the seat with a deep
sigh of resignation.

"Well, I'm in for it," she thought. "It doesn't
matter whether they are thieves or angels, I reckon
I'll have to take what comes. He doesn't look very
much like an angel, but he looked at me just now as if
he thought I were one. Dear me, I wish I were back
in Washin'ton!"

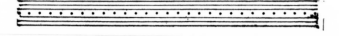

CHAPTER V.

THE INN OF THE HAWK AND RAVEN

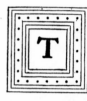WO of the men walked close beside the door, one of them bearing a lantern. They conversed in low tones and in a language which Beverly could not understand. After awhile she found herself analyzing the garb and manner of the men. She was saying to herself that here were her first real specimens of Graustark peasantry, and they were to mark an ineffaceable spot in her memory. They were dark, strong-faced men of medium height, with fierce, black eyes and long black hair. As no two were dressed alike, it was impossible to recognize characteristic styles of attire. Some were in the rude, baggy costumes of the peasant as she had imagined him; others were dressed in the tight-fitting but dilapidated uniforms of the soldiery, while several were in clothes partly European and partly Oriental. There were hats and fezzes and caps, some with feathers in the bands, others without. The man nearest the coach wore the dirty gray uniform of an army officer, full of holes and rents, while another strode along in a

pair of baggy yellow trousers and a dusty London
dinner jacket. All in all, it was the motliest band of
vagabonds she had ever seen. There were at least
ten or a dozen in the party. While a few carried
swords, all lugged the long rifles and crooked daggers
of the Tartars.

"Aunt Fanny," Beverly whispered, suddenly moving to the side of the subdued servant, "where is my
revolver?" It had come to her like a flash that a
subsequent emergency should not find her unprepared. Aunt Fanny's jaw dropped, and her eyes were
like white rings in a black screen.

"Good Lawd — wha — what fo', Miss Bev'ly — "

"Sh! Don't call me Miss Bev'ly. Now, just you
pay 'tention to me and I'll tell you something queer.
Get my revolver right away, and don't let those men
see what you are doing." While Aunt Fanny's trembling fingers went in search of the firearm, Beverly
outlined the situation briefly but explicitly. The old
woman was not slow to understand. Her wits sharp-
ened by fear, she grasped Beverly's instructions with
astonishing avidity.

"Ve'y well, yo' highness," she said with fine reverence, "Ah'll p'ocuah de bottle o' pepp'mint fo' yo'
if yo' jes don' mine me pullin' an' haulin' 'mongst dese
boxes. Mebbe yo' all 'druther hab de gingeh?"
With this wonderful subterfuge as a shield she dug
slyly into one of the bags and pulled forth a revolver.
Under ordinary circumstances she would have been
mortally afraid to touch it, but not so in this emer-

gency. Beverly shoved the weapon into the pocket
of her gray traveling jacket.

" I feel much better now, Aunt Fanny," she said,
and Aunt Fanny gave a vast chuckle.

" Yas, ma'am, indeed,— yo' highness," she agreed,
suavely.

The coach rolled along for half an hour, and then
stopped with a sudden jolt. An instant later the
tall driver appeared at the window, his head uncov-
ered. A man hard by held a lantern.

" *Qua vandos ar deltanet, yos serent,*" said the
leader, showing his white teeth in a triumphant smile.
His exposed eye seemed to be glowing with pleasure
and excitement.

" What? " murmured Beverly, hopelessly. A puzzled expression came into his face. Then his smile
deepened and his eye took on a knowing gleam.

" Ah, I see," he said, gaily, " your highness prefers
not to speak the language of Graustark. Is it necessary for me to repeat in English? "

" I really wish you would," said Beverly, catching
her breath. " Just to see how it sounds, you know."

" Your every wish shall be gratified. I beg to inform you that we have reached the Inn of the Hawk
and Raven. This is where we dwelt last night. To-
morrow we, too, abandon the place, so our fortunes
may run together for some hours, at least. There
is but little to offer you in the way of nourishment,
and there are none of the comforts of a palace. Yet
princesses can no more be choosers than beggars when
the fare's in one pot. Come, your highness, let me

conduct you to the guest chamber of the Inn of the Hawk and Raven."

Beverly took his hand and stepped to the ground, looking about in wonder and perplexity.

" I see no inn," she murmured apprehensively.

" Look aloft, your highness. That great black canopy is the roof; we are standing upon the floor, and the dark shadows just beyond the circle of light are the walls of the Hawk and Raven. This is the largest tavern in all Graustark. Its dimensions are as wide as the world itself."

" You mean that there is no inn at all? " the girl cried in dismay.

" Alas, I must confess it. And yet there is shelter here. Come with me. Let your servant follow." He took her by the hand, and led her away from the coach, a ragged lantern-bearer preceding. Beverly's little right hand was rigidly clutching the revolver in her pocket. It was a capacious pocket, and the muzzle of the weapon bored defiantly into a timid powder-rag that lay on the bottom. The little leather purse from which it escaped had its silver lips opened as if in a broad grin of derision, reveling in the plight of the chamois. The guide's hand was at once firm and gentle, his stride bold, yet easy. His rakish hat, with its aggressive red feather, towered a full head above Beverly's Parisian violets.

" Have you no home at all — no house in which to sleep? " Beverly managed to ask.

" I live in a castle of air," said he, waving his hand gracefully. " I sleep in the house of my fathers."

" You poor fellow," cried Beverly, pityingly.   He laughed and absently patted the hilt of his sword.

She heard the men behind them turning the coach into the glen through which they walked carefully. Her feet fell upon a soft, grassy sward and the clat· ter of stones was now no longer heard.   They were among the shadowy trees, gaunt trunks of enormous size looming up in the light of the lanterns.   Unconsciously her thoughts went over to the Forest of Arden and the woodland home of Rosalind, as she had imagined it to be.   Soon there came to her ears the swish of waters, as of some turbulent river hurrying by.   Instinctively she drew back and her eyes were set with alarm upon the black wall of night ahead. Yetive had spoken more than once of this wilderness. Many an unlucky traveler had been lost forever in its fastnesses.

" It is the river, your highness.   There is no danger.   I will not lead you into it," he said, a trifle roughly.   " We are low in the valley and there are marshes yonder when the river is in its natural bed. The floods have covered the low grounds, and there is a torrent coming down from the hills.   Here we are, your highness.   This is the Inn of the Hawk and Raven."

He bowed and pointed with his hat to the smouldering fire a short distance ahead.   They had turned a bend in the overhanging cliff, and were very close to the retreat before she saw the glow.

The fire was in the open air and directly in front of a deep cleft in the rocky background.   Judging

by the sound, the river could not be more than two
hundred feet away. Men came up with lanterns and
others piled brush upon the fire. In a very short
time the glen was weirdly illuminated by the dancing
flames. From her seat on a huge log, Beverly was
thus enabled to survey a portion of her surroundings.
The overhanging ledge of rock formed a wide, deep
canopy, underneath which was perfect shelter. The
floor seemed to be rich, grassless loam, and here and
there were pallets of long grass, evidently the couches
of these homeless men. All about were huge trees,
and in the direction of the river the grass grew higher
and then gave place to reeds. The foliage above was
so dense that the moon and stars were invisible. There
was a deathly stillness in the air. The very loneliness
was so appalling that Beverly's poor little heart was
in a quiver of dread. Aunt Fanny, who sat near by,
had not spoken since leaving the coach, but her eyes
were expressively active.

The tall leader stood near the fire, conversing with
half a dozen of his followers. Miss Calhoun's eyes
finally rested upon this central figure in the strange
picture. He was attired in a dark-gray uniform
that reminded her oddly of the dragoon choruses
in the comic operas at home. The garments, while
torn and soiled, were well-fitting. His shoulders were
broad and square, his hips narrow, his legs long and
straight. There was an air of impudent grace about
him that went well with his life and profession.
Surely, here was a careless freelance upon whom life
weighed lightly, while death " stood afar off " and

despaired. The light of the fire brought his gleaming face into bold relief, for his hat was off. Black and thick was his hair, rumpled and apparently uncared for. The face was lean, smooth and strong, with a devil-may-care curve at the corners of the mouth. Beverly found herself lamenting the fact that such an interesting face should be marred by an ugly black patch, covering she knew not what manner of defect. As for the rest of them, they were a grim company. Some were young and beardless, others were old and grizzly, but all were active, alert and strong. The leader appeared to be the only one in the party who could speak and understand the English language. As Beverly sat and watched his virile, mocking face, and studied his graceful movements, she found herself wondering how an ignorant, homeless wanderer in the hills could be so poetic and so cultured as this fellow seemed to be.

Three or four men, who were unmistakably of a lower order than their companions, set about preparing a supper. Others unhitched the tired horses and led them off toward the river. Two dashing young fellows carried the seat-cushions under the rocky canopy and constructed an elaborate couch for the "Princess." The chief, with his own hands, soon began the construction of a small chamber in this particular corner of the cave, near the opening. The walls of the chamber were formed of carriage robes and blankets, cloaks and oak branches.

"The guest chamber, your highness," he said, approaching her with a smile at the conclusion of his work.

" It has been most interesting to watch you," she said, rising.

" And it has been a delight to interest you," he responded. " You will find seclusion there, and you need see none of us until it pleases you."

She looked him fairly in the eye for a moment, and then impulsively extended her hand. He clasped it warmly, but not without some show of surprise.

" I am trusting you implicitly," she said.

" The knave is glorified," was his simple rejoinder. He conducted her to the improvised bed-chamber, Aunt Fanny following with loyal but uncertain tread. " I regret, your highness, that the conveniences are so few. We have no landlady except Mother Earth, no waiters, no porters, no maids, in the Inn of the Hawk and Raven. This being a men's hotel, the baths are on the river-front. I am having water brought to your apartments, however, but it is with deepest shame and sorrow that I confess we have no towels."

She laughed so heartily that his face brightened perceptibly, whilst the faces of his men turned in their direction as though by concert.

" It is a typical mountain resort, then," she said. " I think I can manage very well if you will fetch my bags to my room, sir."

" By the way, will you have dinner served in your room? " very good-humoredly.

" If you don't mind, I'd like to eat in the public

dining-room," said she. A few minutes later Beverly was sitting upon one of her small trunks and Aunt Fanny was laboriously brushing her dark hair.

"It's very jolly being a princess," murmured Miss Calhoun. She had bathed her face in one of the leather buckets from the coach, and the dust of the road had been brushed away by the vigorous lady-in-waiting.

"Yas, ma'am, Miss — yo' highness, hit's monstrous fine fo' yo', but whar is Ah goin' to sleep? Out yondah, wif all dose scalawags?" said Aunt Fanny, rebelliously.

"You shall have a bed in here, Aunt Fanny," said Beverly.

"Dey's de queeres' lot o' tramps Ah eveh did see, an' Ah wouldn' trust 'em 's fer as Ah could heave a brick house."

"But the leader is such a very courteous gentleman," remonstrated Beverly.

"Yas, ma'am; he mussa came f'm Gawgia or Kaintuck," was Aunt Fanny's sincere compliment.

The pseudo-princess dined with the vagabonds that night. She sat on the log beside the tall leader, and ate heartily of the broth and broiled goatmeat, the grapes and the nuts, and drank of the spring water which took the place of wine and coffee and cordial. It was a strange supper amid strange environments, but she enjoyed it as she had never before enjoyed a meal. The air was full of romance and danger, and her imagination was enthralled. Everything was so new and unreal that she scarcely could believe herself awake. The world seemed to have gone back to the days of Robin Hood and his merry men.

" You fare well at the Inn of the Hawk and Raven," she said to him, her voice tremulous with excitement. He looked mournfully at her for a moment and then smiled naively.

" It is the first wholesome meal we have had in two days," he replied.

" You don't mean it! "

" Yes. We were lucky with the guns to-day. Fate was kind to us — and to you, for we are better prepared to entertain royalty to-day than at any time since I have been in the hills of Graustark."

" Then you have not always lived in Graustark? "

" Alas, no, your highness. I have lived elsewhere."

" But you were born in the principality? "

" I am a subject of its princess in heart from this day forth, but not by birth or condition. I am a native of the vast domain known to a few of us as Circumstance," and he smiled rather recklessly.

" You are a poet, a delicious poet," cried Beverly, forgetting herself in her enthusiasm.

" Perhaps that is why I am hungry and unshorn. It had not occurred to me in that light. When you are ready to retire, your highness," he said, abruptly rising, " we shall be pleased to consider the Inn of the Hawk and Raven closed for the night. Having feasted well, we should sleep well. We have a hard day before us. With your consent, I shall place my couch of grass near your door. I am the porter. You have but to call if anything is desired."

She was tired, but she would have sat up all night rather than miss any of the strange romance that had been thrust upon her. But Sir Red-feather's suggestion savored of a command and she reluctantly made her way to the flapping blanket that marked the entrance to the bed-chamber. He drew the curtain aside, swung his hat low and muttered a soft good-night.

"May your highness's dreams be pleasant ones!" he said.

"Thank you," said she, and the curtain dropped impertinently. "That was very cool of him, I must say," she added, as she looked at the wavering door.

When she went to sleep, she never knew; she was certain that her eyes were rebellious for a long time and that she wondered how her gray dress would look after she had slept in it all night. She heard low singing as if in the distance, but after a while the stillness became so intense that its pressure almost suffocated her. The rush of the river grew louder and louder and there was a swishing sound that died in her ears almost as she wondered what it meant. Her last waking thoughts were of the "black-patch" poet. Was he lying near the door?

She was awakened in the middle of the night by the violent flapping of her chamber door. Startled, she sat bolt upright and strained her eyes to pierce the mysterious darkness. Aunt Fanny, on her bed of grass, stirred convulsively, but did not awake. The blackness of the strange chamber was broken ever and anon by faint flashes of light from without, and she lived through long minutes of terror before it dawned upon her that a thunderstorm was brewing. The wind was rising, and the night seemed agog with excitement. Beverly crept from her couch and felt her way to the fluttering doorway. Drawing aside the blanket she peered forth into the night, her heart jumping with terror. Her highness was very much afraid of thunder and lightning.

The fire in the open had died down until naught remained but a few glowing embers. These were blown into brilliancy by the wind, casting a steady red light over the scene. There was but one human figure in sight. Beside the fire stood the tall wanderer. He was hatless and coatless, and his arms were folded across his chest. Seemingly oblivious to the approach of the storm, he stood staring into the heap of ashes at his feet. His face was toward her, every feature plainly distinguishable in the faint glow from the fire. To her amazement the black patch was missing from the eye; and, what surprised her almost to the point of exclaiming aloud, there appeared to be absolutely no reason for its presence there at any time. There was no mark or blemish upon or about the eye; it was as clear and penetrating as its fellow, darkly gleaming in the red glow from below. Moreover, Beverly saw that he was strikingly handsome — a strong, manly face. The highly imaginative southern girl's mind reverted to the first portraits of Napoleon she had seen.

Suddenly he started, threw up his head and looking up to the sky uttered some strange words. Then he

strode abruptly toward her doorway. She fell back
breathless. He stopped just outside, and she knew
that he was listening for sounds from within. After
many minutes she stealthily looked forth again. He
was standing near the fire, his back toward her, looking
off into the night.

The wind was growing stronger; the breezes fanned
the night into a rush of shivery coolness. Constant
flickerings of lightning illuminated the forest, trans-
forming the tree-tops into great black waves. Tall
reeds along the river bank began to bend their tops,
to swing themselves gently to and from the wind. In
the lowlands down from the cave " will o' the wisps "
played tag with " Jack o' the lanterns," merrily scam-
pering about in the blackness, reminding her of the
revellers in a famous Brocken scene. Low moans
grew out of the havoc, and voices seemed to speak in
unintelligible whispers to the agitated twigs and
leaves. The secrets of the wind were being spread
upon the records of the night; tales of many climes
passed through the ears of Nature.

From gentle undulations the marshland reeds swept
into lower dips, danced wilder minuets, lashed each
other with infatuated glee, mocking the whistle of
the wind with an angry swish of their tall bodies.
Around the cornices of the Inn of the Hawk and
Raven scurried the singing breezes, reluctant to leave
a playground so pleasing to the fancy. Soon the
night became a cauldron, a surging, hissing, roaring
receptacle in which were mixing the ingredients of
disaster. Night-birds flapped through the moaning

tree-tops, in search of shelter; reeds were flattened to the earth, bowing to the sovereignty of the wind; clouds roared with the rumble of a million chariots, and then the sky and the earth met in one of those savage conflicts that make all other warfare seem as play.

As Beverly sank back from the crash, she saw him throw his arms aloft as though inviting the elements to mass themselves and their energy upon his head. She shrieked involuntarily and he heard the cry above the carnage. Instantly his face was turned in her direction.

"Help! Help!" she cried. He bounded toward the swishing robes and blankets, but his impulse had found a rival in the blast. Like a flash the walls of the guest chamber were whisked away, scuttling off into the night or back into the depths of the cavern. With the deluge came the man. From among the stifling robes he snatched her up and bore her away, she knew not whither.

CHAPTER VI

THE HOME OF THE LION

AY all storms be as pleasant as this one!" she heard someone say, with a merry laugh. The next instant she was placed soundly upon her feet. A blinding flash of lightning revealed Baldos, the goat-hunter, at her side, while a dozen shadowy figures were scrambling to their feet in all corners of the Hawk and Raven. Someone was clutching her by the dress at the knees. She did not have to look down to know that it was Aunt Fanny.

"Goodness!" gasped the princess, and then it was pitch dark again. The man at her side called out a command in his own language, and then turned his face close to hers.

"Do not be alarmed. We are quite safe now. The royal bed-chamber has come to grief, however, I am sorry to say. What a fool I was not to have foreseen all this! The storm has been brewing since midnight," he was saying to her.

"Isn't it awful?" cried Beverly, between a moan and a shriek.

"They are trifles after one gets used to them,"

56

he said. " I have come to be quite at home in the
tempest. There are other things much more annoying, I assure your highness. We shall have lights in
a moment." Even as he spoke, two or three lanterns
began to flicker feebly.

" Be quiet, Aunt Fanny; you are not killed at all,"
commanded Beverly, quite firmly.

" De house is suah to blow down, Miss — yo' highness," groaned the trusty maidservant. Beverly
laughed bravely but nervously with the tall goat-
hunter. He at once set about making his guest comfortable and secure from the effects of the tempest,
which was now at its height. Her couch of cushions
was dragged far back into the cavern and the rescued
blankets, though drenched, again became a screen.

" Do you imagine that I'm going in there while
this storm rages? " Beverly demanded, as the work
progressed.

" Are you not afraid of lightning? Most young
women are."

" That's the trouble. I am afraid of it. I'd much
rather stay out here where there is company. You
don't mind, do you? "

" Paradise cannot be spurned by one who now feels
its warmth for the first time," said he, gallantly.
" Your fear is my delight. Pray sit upon our throne.
It was once a humble carriage pail of leather, but now
it is exalted. Besides, it is much more comfortable
than some of the gilded chairs we hear about."

" You are given to irony, I fear," she said, observing a peculiar smile on his lips.

" I crave pardon, your highness," he said, humbly.
" The heart of the goat-hunter is more gentle than
his wit. I shall not again forget that you are a
princess and I the veriest beggar."

" I didn't mean to hurt you!" she cried, in contrition, for she was a very poor example of what a
princess is supposed to be.

" There is no wound, your highness," he quickly
said. With a mocking grace that almost angered her,
he dropped to his knee and motioned for her to be
seated. She sat down suddenly, clapping her hands
to her ears and shutting her eyes tightly. The
crash of thunder that came at that instant was the
most fearful of all, and it was a full minute before
she dared to lift her lids again. He was standing
before her, and there was genuine compassion in his
face. " It's terrible," he said. " Never before have
I seen such a storm. Have courage, your highness;
it can last but little longer."

" Goodness!" said the real American girl, for want
of something more expressive.

" Your servant has crept into your couch, I fear.
Shall I sit here at your feet? Perhaps you may feel
a small sense of security if I —— "

" Indeed, I want you to sit there," she cried. He
forthwith threw himself upon the floor of the cave, a
graceful, respectful guardian. Minutes went by
without a word from either. The noise of the storm
made it impossible to speak and be heard. Scattered
about the cavern were his outstretched followers,
doubtless asleep once more in all this turmoil. With

the first lull in the war of the elements, Beverly gave
utterance to the thought that long had been struggling for release.

"Why do you wear that horrid black patch over
your eye?" she asked, a trifle timidly. He muttered
a sharp exclamation and clapped his hand to his eye.
For the first time since the beginning of their strange
acquaintanceship Beverly observed downright confusion in this debonair knight of the wilds.

"It has — has slipped off ——" he stammered,
with a guilty grin. His merry insolence was gone,
his composure with it. Beverly laughed with keen
enjoyment over the discomfiture of the shame-faced
vagabond.

"You can't fool me," she exclaimed, shaking her
finger at him in the most unconventional way. "It
was intended to be a disguise. There is absolutely
nothing the matter with your eye."

He was speechless for a moment, recovering himself.
Wisdom is conceived in silence, and he knew this.
Vagabond or gentleman, he was a clever actor.

"The eye is weak, your highness, and I cover it
in the daytime to protect it from the sunlight," he
said, coolly.

"That's all very nice, but it looks to be quite as
good as the other. And what is more, sir, you are not
putting the patch over the same eye that wore it when
I first saw you. It was the left eye at sunset. Does
the trouble transfer after dark?"

He broke into an honest laugh and hastily moved
the black patch across his nose to the left eye.

"I was turned around in the darkness, that's all," he said, serenely. "It belongs over the left eye, and I am deeply grateful to you for discovering the error."

"I don't see any especial reason why you should wear it after dark, do you? There is no sunlight, I'm sure."

"I am dazzled, nevertheless," he retorted.

"Fiddlesticks!" she said. "This is a cave, not a drawing-room."

"In other words, I am a lout and not a courtier," he smiled. "Well, a lout may look at a princess. We have no court etiquette in the hills, I am sorry to say."

"That was very unkind, even though you said it most becomingly," she protested. "You have called this pail a throne. Let us also imagine that you are a courtier."

"You punish me most gently, your highness. I shall not forget my manners again, believe me." He seemed thoroughly subdued.

"Then I shall expect you to remove that horrid black thing. It is positively villainous. You look much better without it."

"Is it an edict or a compliment?" he asked with such deep gravity that she flushed.

"It is neither," she answered. "You don't have to take it off unless you want to——"

"In either event, it is off. You were right. It serves as a partial disguise. I have many enemies and the black patch is a very good friend."

" How perfectly lovely," cried Beverly. " Tell me all about it. I adore stories about feuds and all that."

" Your husband is an American. He should be able to keep you well entertained with blood-and-thunder stories," said he.

" My hus — What do you — Oh, yes!" gasped Beverly. " To be sure. I didn't hear you, I guess. That was rather a severe clap of thunder, wasn't it? "

" Is that also a command? "

" What do you mean? "

" There was no thunderclap, you know."

" Oh, wasn't there? " helplessly.

" The storm is quite past. There is still a dash of rain in the air and the wind may be dying hard, but aside from that I think the noise is quite subdued."

" I believe you are right. How sudden it all was."

" There are several hours between this and dawn, your highness, and you should try to get a little more sleep. Your cushions are dry and —— "

" Very well, since you are so eager to get rid of —— " began Beverly, and then stopped, for it did not sound particularly regal. " I should have said, you are very thoughtful. You will call me if I sleep late? "

" We shall start early, with your permission. It is forty miles to Ganlook, and we must be half way there by nightfall."

" Must we spend another night like this? " cried Beverly, dolefully.

" Alas, I fear you must endure us another night. I

am afraid, however, we shall not find quarters as comfortable as these of the Hawk and Raven."

" I didn't mean to be ungrateful and — er — snippish," she said, wondering if he knew the meaning of the word.

" No? " he said politely, and she knew he did not — whereupon she felt distinctly humbled.

" You know you speak such excellent English," she said irrelevantly.

He bowed low. As he straightened his figure, to his amazement, he beheld an agonizing look of horror on her face; her eyes riveted on the mouth of the cavern. Then, there came an angrier sound, unlike any that had gone before in that night of turmoil.

" Look there! Quick! "

The cry of terror from the girl's palsied lips, as she pointed to something behind him, awoke the mountain man to instant action. Instinctively, he snatched his long dagger from its sheath and turned quickly. Not twenty feet from them a huge cat-like beast stood half crouched on the edge of the darkness, his long tail switching angrily. The feeble light from the depth of the cave threw the long, water-soaked visitor into bold relief against the black wall beyond. Apparently, he was as much surprised as the two who glared at him, as though frozen to the spot. A snarling whine, a fierce growl, indicated his fury at finding his shelter — his lair occupied.

" My God! A mountain lion! Ravone! Franz! To me! " he cried hoarsely, and sprang before her shouting loudly to the sleepers.

A score of men, half awake, grasped their weapons
and struggled to their feet in answer to his call. The
lion's gaunt body shot through the air. In two
bounds, he was upon the goat-hunter. Baldos stood
squarely and firmly to meet the rush of the maddened
beast, his long dagger poised for the death-dealing
blow.

" Run ! " he shouted to her.

Beverly Calhoun had fighting blood in her veins.
Utterly unconscious of her action, at the time, she
quickly drew the little silver-handled revolver from
the pocket of her gown. As man, beast and knife
came together, in her excitement she fired recklessly
at the combatants without any thought of the immi-
nent danger of killing her protector. There was a wild
scream of pain from the wounded beast, more pistol
shots, fierce yells from the excited hunters, the rush
of feet and then the terrified and almost frantic girl
staggered and fell against the rocky wall. Her wide
gray eyes were fastened upon the writhing lion and
the smoking pistol was tightly clutched in her hand.

It had all occurred in such an incredible short space
of time that she could not yet realize what had happened.

Her heart and brain seemed paralyzed, her limbs
stiff and immovable. Like the dizzy whirl of a ka-
leidoscope, the picture before her resolved itself into
shape.

The beast was gasping his last upon the rocky floor,
the hilt of the goat hunter's dagger protruding from
his side. Baldos, supported by two of his men, stood

above the savage victim, his legs covered with blood.
The cave was full of smoke and the smell of powder.
Out of the haze she began to see the light of understanding. Baldos alone was injured. He had stood
between her and the rush of the lion, and he had
saved her, at a cost she knew not how great.

"Oh, the blood!" she cried hoarsely. "Is it —
is it — are you badly hurt?" She was at his side,
the pistol falling from her nervous fingers.

"Don't come nea me; I'm all right," he cried
quickly.

"Take care — your dress —— "

"Oh, I'm so glad to hear you speak! Never mind
the dress! You are torn to pieces! You must be
frightfully hurt. Oh, isn't it terrible — horrible!
Aunt Fanny! Come here this minute!"

Forgetting the beast and throwing off the paralysis
of fear, she pushed one of the men away and grasped
the arm of the injured man. He winced perceptibly
and she felt something warm and sticky on her hands.
She knew it was blood, but it was not in her to shrink
at a moment like this.

"Your arm, too!" she gasped. He smiled,
although his face was white with pain. "How brave
you were! You might have been — I'll never forget
it — never! Don't stand there, Aunt Fanny! Quick!
Get those cushions for him. He's hurt."

"Good Lawd!" was all the old woman could say,
but she obeyed her mistress.

"It was easier than it looked, your highness,"
murmured Baldos. "Luck was with me. The knife

went to his heart. I am merely scratched. His leap was short, but he caught me above the knees with his claws. Alas, your highness, these trousers of mine were bad enough before, but now they are in shreds. What patching I shall have to do! And you may well imagine we are short of thread and needles and thimbles ——"

"Don't jest, for heaven's sake! Don't talk like that. Here! Lie down upon these cushions and ——"

"Never! Desecrate the couch of Graustark's ruler? I, the poor goat-hunter? I'll use the lion for a pillow and the rock for an operating table. In ten minutes my men can have these scratches dressed and bound — in fact, there is a surgical student among them, poor fellow. I think I am his first patient. Ravone, attend me."

He threw himself upon the ground and calmly placed his head upon the body of the animal.

"I insist upon your taking these cushions," cried Beverly.

"And I decline irrevocably." She stared at him in positive anger. "Trust Ravone to dress these trifling wounds, your highness. He may not be as gentle, but he is as firm as any princess in all the world."

"But your arm?" she cried. "Didn't you say it was your legs? Your arm is covered with blood, too. Oh, dear me, I'm afraid you are frightfully wounded."

"A stray bullet from one of my men struck me

there, I think. You know there was but little time for aiming ——"

"Wait! Let me think a minute! Good heavens!" she exclaimed with a start. Her eyes were suddenly filled with tears and there was a break in her voice. "I shot you! Don't deny it — don't! It is the right arm, and your men could not have hit it from where they stood. Oh, oh, oh!"

Baldos smiled as he bared his arm. "Your aim was good," he admitted. "Had not my knife already been in the lion's heart, your bullet would have gone there. It is my misfortune that my arm was in the way. Besides, your highness, it has only cut through the skin — and a little below, perhaps. It will be well in a day or two. I am sure you will find your bullet in the carcass of our lamented friend, the probable owner of this place."

Ravone, a hungry-looking youth, took charge of the wounded leader, while her highness retreated to the farthest corner of the cavern. There she sat and trembled while the wounds were being dressed. Aunt Fanny bustled back and forth, first unceremoniously pushing her way through the circle of men to take observations, and then reporting to the impatient girl. The storm had passed and the night was still, except for the rush of the river; raindrops fell now and then from the trees, glistening like diamonds as they touched the light from the cavern's mouth. It was all very dreary, uncanny and oppressive to poor Beverly. Now and then she caught herself sobbing, more out of shame and humiliation than in sadness,

for had she not shot the man who stepped between
her and death? What must he think of her?

"He says yo' all 'd betteh go to baid, Miss Bev —
yo' highness," said Aunt Fanny after one of her
trips.

"Oh, he does, does he?" sniffed Beverly. "I'll
go to bed when I please. Tell him so. No, no —
don't do it, Aunt Fanny! Tell him I'll go to bed
when I'm sure he is quite comfortable, not before."

"But he's jes' a goat puncheh er a ——"

"He's a man, if there ever was one. Don't let
me hear you call him a goat puncher again. How
are his legs?" Aunt Fanny was almost stunned by
this amazing question from her ever-decorous mistress.
"Why don't you answer? Will they have to be cut
off? Didn't you see them?"

"Fo' de Lawd's sake, missy, co'se Ah did, but yo'
all kindeh susprise me. Dey's p'etty bad skun up,
missy; de hide's peeled up consid'ble. But hit ain'
dang'ous,— no, ma'am. Jes' skun, 'at's all."

"And his arm — where I shot him?"

"Puffec'ly triflin', ma'am,— yo' highness. Cobwebs 'd stop de bleedin' an' Ah tole 'em so, but 'at
felleh couldn' un'stan' me. Misteh what's-his-name,
he says something to de docteh, an' den dey goes afteh
de cobwebs, suah 'nough. 'Tain' bleedin' no mo',
missy. He's mostes' neah doin' ve'y fine. Co'se, he
cain' walk fo' sev'l days wiv dem laigs o' his'n,
but ——"

"Then, in heaven's name, how are we to get to
Edelweiss?"

" He c'n ride, cain't he? Wha's to hindeh him? "

" Quite right. He shall ride inside the coach. Go and see if I can do anything for him."

Aunt Fanny returned in a few minutes.

" He says yo'll do him a great favoh if yo' jes' go to baid. He sends his 'spects an' hopes yo' slumbeh won' be distubbed ag'in."

" He's a perfect brute! " exclaimed Beverly, but she went over and crawled under the blankets and among the cushions the wounded man had scorned.

CHAPTER VII

SOME FACTS AND FANCIES

 HERE was a soft, warm, yellow glow to the world when Beverly Calhoun next looked upon it. The sun from his throne in the mountain tops was smiling down upon the valley the night had ravaged while he was on the other side of the earth. The leaves of the trees were a softer green, the white of the rocks and the yellow of the road were of a gentler tint; the brown and green reeds were proudly erect once more.

The stirring of the mountain men had awakened Aunt Fanny, and she in turn called her mistress from the surprisingly peaceful slumber into which perfect health had sent her not so many hours before. At the entrance to the improvised bedchamber stood buckets of water from the spring.

"We have very thoughtful chambermaids," remarked Beverly while Aunt Fanny was putting her hair into presentable shape. "And an energetic cook," she added as the odor of broiled meat came to her nostrils.

" Ah cain' see nothin' o' dat beastes, Miss Beverly
— an' — Ah — Ah got mah suspicions," said Aunt
Fanny, with sepulchral despair in her voice.

" They've thrown the awful thing into the river,"
concluded Beverly.

" Dey's cookin' hit!" said Aunt Fanny solemnly.

" Good heaven, no!" cried Beverly. " Go and see,
this minute. I wouldn't eat that catlike thing for the
whole world." Aunt Fanny came back a few minutes
later with the assurance that they were roasting goat
meat. The skin of the midnight visitor was stretched
upon the ground not far away.

" And how is he?" asked Beverly, jamming a hat
pin through a helpless bunch of violets.

" He's ve'y 'spectably skun, yo' highness."

" I don't mean the animal, stupid."

" Yo' mean 'at Misteh Goat man? He's settin' up
an' chattin' as if nothin' happened. He says to me
'at we staht on ouah way jes' as soon as yo' all eats
yo' b'eakfus'. De hosses is hitched up an'——"

" Has everybody else eaten? Am I the only one
that hasn't?" cried Beverly.

" 'Ceptin' me, yo' highness. Ah'm as hungry as a
poah man's dawg, an'——"

" And he is being kept from the hospital because
I am a lazy, good-for-nothing little — Come on, Aunt
Fanny; we haven't a minute to spare. If he looks
very ill, *we* do without breakfast."

But Baldos was the most cheerful man in the party.
He was sitting with his back against a tree, his right

arm in a sling of woven reeds, his black patch set
upon the proper eye.

"You will pardon me for not rising," he said
cheerily, "but, your highness, I am much too awkward this morning to act as befitting a courtier in the
presence of his sovereign. You have slept well?"

"Too well, I fear. So well, in fact, that you have
suffered for it. Can't we start at once?" She was
debating within herself whether it would be quite
good form to shake hands with the reclining hero.
In the glare of the broad daylight he and his followers looked more ragged and famished than before, but
they also appeared more picturesquely romantic.

"When you have eaten of our humble fare, your
highness, — the last meal at the Hawk and Raven."

"But I'm not a bit hungry."

"It is very considerate of you, but equally unreasonable. You must eat before we start."

"I can't bear the thought of your suffering when
we should be hurrying to a hospital and competent
surgeons." He laughed gaily. "Oh, you needn't
laugh. I know it hurts. You say we cannot reach
Ganlook before to-morrow? Well, we can't stop here
a minute longer than we — Oh, thank you!" A
ragged servitor had placed a rude bowl of meat and
some fruit before her.

"Sit down here, your highness, and prepare yourself for a long fast. We may go until nightfall without food. The game is scarce and we dare not venture
far into the hills."

Beverly sat at his feet and daintily began the opera-tion of picking a bone with her pretty fingers and teeth. " I am sorry we have no knives and forks," he apologized.

" I don't mind," said she. " I wish you would remove that black patch."

" Alas, I must resume the hated disguise. A chance enemy might recognize me:"

" Your — your clothes have been mended," she remarked with a furtive glance at his long legs. The trousers had been rudely sewed up and no bandages were visible. " Are you — your legs terribly hurt? "

" They are badly scratched, but not seriously. The bandages are skilfully placed," he added, seeing her look of doubt. " Ravone is a genius."

" Well, I'll hurry," she said, blushing deeply. Goat-hunter though he was and she a princess, his eyes gleamed with the joy of her beauty and his heart thumped with a most unruly admiration. " You were very, very brave last night," she said at last — and her rescuer smiled contentedly.

She was not long in finishing the rude but wholesome meal, and then announced her readiness to be on the way. With the authority of a genuine princess she commanded him to ride inside the coach, gave incomprehensible directions to the driver and to the escort, and would listen to none of his protestations. When the clumsy vehicle was again in the highway and bumping over the ridges of flint, the goat-hunter was beside his princess on the rear seat, his feet upon the opposite cushions near Aunt Fanny, a well-arranged bridge of boxes and bags providing support for his long legs.

" We want to go to a hospital," Beverly had said to the driver, very much as she might have spoken had she been in Washington. She was standing bravely beside the forewheel, her face flushed and eager. Baldos, from his serene position on the cushions, watched her with kindling eyes. The grizzled driver grinned and shook his head despairingly. " Oh, pshaw! You don't understand, do you? Hospital — h-o-s-p-i-t-a-l," she spelt it out for him, and still he shook his head. Others in the motley retinue were smiling broadly.

" Speak to him in your own language, your highness, and he will be sure to understand," ventured the patient.

" I am speaking in my — I mean, I prefer to speak in English. Please tell him to go to a hospital," she said confusedly. Baldos gave a few jovial instructions, and then the raggedest courtier of them all handed Beverly into the carriage with a grace that amazed her.

" You are the most remarkable goat-hunters I have ever seen," she remarked in sincere wonder.

" And you speak the most perfect English I've ever heard," he replied.

" Oh, do you really think so? Miss Grimes used to say I was hopeless. You know I had a — a tutor," she hastily explained. " Don't you think it strange we've met no Axphain soldiers? " she went on, changing the subject abruptly.

" We are not yet out of the woods," he said.

" That was a purely American aphorism," she cried, looking at him intently. " Where did you learn all your English? "

" I had a tutor," he answered easily.

" You are a very odd person," she sighed. " I don't believe that you are a goat-hunter at all."

" If I were not a goat-hunter I should have starved long ago," he said. " Why do you doubt me? "

" Simply because you treat me one moment as if I were a princess, and the next as if I were a child. Humble goat-hunters do not forget their station in life."

" I have much to learn of the deference due to queens," he said.

" That's just like ' The Mikado ' or ' Pinafore,' " she exclaimed. " I believe you are a comic-opera brigand or a pirate chieftain, after all."

" I am a lowly outcast," he smiled.

" Well, I've decided to take you into Edelweiss and ——"

" Pardon me, your highness," he said firmly. " That cannot be. I shall not go to Edelweiss."

" But I command you ——"

" It's very kind of you, but I cannot enter a hospital — not even at Ganlook. I may as well confess that I am a hunted man and that the instructions are to take me dead or alive."

" Impossible! " she gasped, involuntarily shrinking from him.

" I have wronged no man, yet I am being hunted

down as though I were a beast," he said, his face
turning haggard for the moment. "The hills of
Graustark, the plateaus of Axphain and the valleys
of Dawsbergen are alive with men who are bent on
ending my unhappy but inconvenient existence. It
would be suicide for me to enter any' one of your
towns or cities. Even you could not protect me,
I fear."

"This sounds like a dream. Oh, dear me, you
don't look like a hardened criminal," she cried.

"I am the humble leader of a faithful band who
will die with me when the time comes. We are not
criminals, your highness. In return for what service
I may have performed for you, I implore you to
question me no further. Let me be your slave up to'
the walls of Ganlook, and then you may forget
Baldos, the goat-hunter."

"I never can forget you," she cried, touching his
injured arm gently. "Will you forget the one who
gave you this wound?"

"It is a very gentle wound, and I love it so that
I pray it may never heal." She looked away suddenly.

"Tell me one thing," she said, a mist coming over
her eyes. "You say they are hunting you to the
death. Then — then your fault must be a grievous
one. Have you — have you killed a man?" she added
hastily. He was silent for a long time.

"I fear I have killed more than one man," he said
in low tones. Again she shrank into the corner of
the coach. "History says that your father was a

brave soldier and fought in many battles," he went on.

"Yes," she said, thinking of Major George Calhoun.

"He killed men then, perhaps, as I have killed them," he said.

"Oh, my father never killed a man!" cried Beverly, in devout horror.

"Yet Graustark reveres his mighty prowess on the field of battle," said he, half laconically.

"Oh," she murmured, remembering that she was now the daughter of Yetive's father. "I see. You are not a — a — a mere murderer, then?"

"No. I have been a soldier — that is all."

"Thank heaven!" she murmured, and was no longer afraid of him. "Would — would a pardon be of any especial benefit to you?" she asked, wondering how far her influence might go with the Princess Yetive.

".It is beyond your power to help me," he said gravely. She was silent, but it was the silence of deep reflection. "Your highness left the castle ten days ago," he said, dismissing himself as a subject for conversation. "Have you kept in close communication with Edelweiss during that time?"

"I know nothing of what is going on there," she said, quite truthfully. She only knew that she had sent a message to the Princess Yetive, apprising her of her arrival in St. Petersburg and of her intention to leave soon for the Graustark capital.

"Then you do not know that Mr. Lorry is still on the Dawsbergen frontier in conference with representatives from Serros. He may not return for a week, so Colonel Quinnox brings back word."

" It's news to me," murmured Beverly.

" You do not seem to be alarmed," he ventured. " Yet I fancy it is not a dangerous mission, although Prince Gabriel is ready to battle at a moment's notice."

" I have the utmost confidence in Mr. Lorry," said Beverly, with proper pride.

" Baron Dangloss, your minister of police, is in these mountains watching the operations of Axphain scouts and spies."

" Is he? You are very well posted, it seems."

" Moreover, the Axphainians are planning to attack Ganlook upon the first signal from their ruler. I do not wish to alarm your highness, but we may as well expect trouble before we come to the Ganlook gates. You are known to be in the pass, and I am certain an effort will be made to take possession of your person."

" They wouldn't dare!" she exclaimed. " Uncle Sam would annihilate them in a week."

" Uncle Sam? Is he related to your Aunt Fanny? I'm afraid he could do but little against Volga's fighting men," he said, with a smile.

" They'd soon find out who Uncle Sam is if they touch me," she threatened grandly. He seemed puzzled, but was too polite to press her for explanations. " But, he is a long way off and couldn't do much if we were suddenly attacked from ambush, could he? What would they do to me if I were taken, as you suggest?" she was more concerned than she appeared to be.

"With you in their hands, Graustark would be utterly helpless. Volga could demand anything she liked, and your ministry would be forced to submit."

"I really think it would be a capital joke on the Princess Volga," mused Beverly reflectively. He did not know what she meant, but regarded her soft smile as the clear title to the serenity of a princess.

She sank back and gave herself over to the complications that were likely to grow out of her involuntary deception. The one thing which worried her more than all others was the fear that Yetive might not be in Edelweiss. According to all reports, she had lately been in St. Petersburg and the mere fact that she was supposed to be traveling by coach was sufficient proof that she was not at her capital. Then there was, of course, the possibility of trouble on the road with the Axphain scouts, but Beverly enjoyed the optimism of youth and civilization.

Baldos, the goat-hunter, was dreamily thinking of the beautiful young woman at his side and of the queer freak Fortune had played in bringing them together. As he studied her face he could not but lament that marriage, at least, established a barrier between her and the advances his bold heart might otherwise be willing to risk. His black hair straggled down over his forehead and his dark eyes — the patch had been surreptitiously lifted — were unusually pensive.

"It is strange that you live in Graustark and have not seen its princess — before," she said, laying groundwork for enquiry concerning the acts and whereabouts of the real princess.

"May it please your highness, I have not lived long in Graustark. Besides, it is said that half the people of Ganlook have never looked upon your face."

"I'm not surprised at that. The proportion is much smaller than I imagined. I have not visited Ganlook, strange as it may seem to you."

"One of my company fell in with some of your guards from the Ganlook garrison day before yesterday. He learned that you were to reach that city within forty-eight hours. A large detachment of men has been sent to meet you at Labbot."

"Oh, indeed," said Beverly, very much interested.

"They must have been misinformed as to your route — or else your Russian escort decided to take you through by the lower and more hazardous way. It was our luck that you came by the wrong road. Otherwise we should not have met each other — and the lion," he said, smiling reflectively.

"Where is Labbot?" asked she, intent upon the one subject uppermost in her mind.

"In the mountains many leagues north of this pass. Had you taken that route instead of this, you would by this time have left Labbot for the town of Erros, a half-day's journey from Ganlook. Instead of vagabonds, your escort would have been made up of loyal soldiers, well-fed, well-clad, and well satisfied with themselves, at least."

"But no braver, no truer than my soldiers of fortune." she said earnestly. "By the way, are you informed as to the state of affairs in Dawsbergen?"

"Scarcely as well as your highness must be," he replied.

"The young prince — what's his name?" she paused, looking to him for the name.

"Dantan?"

"Yes, that's it. What has become of him? I am terribly interested in him."

"He is a fugitive, they say."

"They haven't captured him, then? Good! I am so glad."

Baldos exhibited little or no interest in the fresh topic.

"It is strange you should have forgotten his name," he said wearily.

"Oh, I do so many ridiculous things!" complained Beverly, remembering who she was supposed to be. "I have never seen him, you know," she added.

"It is not strange, your highness. He was educated in England and had seen but little of his own country when he was called to the throne two years ago. You remember, of course, that his mother was an Englishwoman — Lady Ida Falconer."

"I — I think I have heard some of his history — a very little, to be sure," she explained lamely.

"Prince Gabriel, his half brother, is the son of Prince Louis the Third by his first wife, who was a Polish countess. After her death, when Gabriel was two years old, the prince married Lady Ida. Dantan is their son. He has a sister — Candace, who is but nineteen years of age."

" I am ashamed to confess that you know so much more about my neighbors than I," she said.

" I lived in Dawsbergen for a little while, and was ever interested in the doings of royalty. That is a poor man's privilege, you know."

" Prince Gabriel must be a terrible man," cried Beverly, her heart swelling with tender thoughts of the exiled Dantan and his little sister.

" You have cause to know," said he shortly, and she was perplexed until she recalled the stories of Gabriel's misdemeanors at the court of Edelweiss.

" Is Prince Dantan as handsome as they say he is? " she asked.

" It is entirely a matter of opinion," he replied. " I, for one, do not consider him at all prepossessing."

The day went on, fatiguing, distressing in its length and its happenings. Progress was necessarily slow, the perils of the road increasing as the little cavalcade wound deeper and deeper into the wilderness. There were times when the coach fairly crawled along the edge of a precipice, a proceeding so hazardous that Beverly shuddered as if in a chill. Aunt Fanny slept serenely most of the time, and Baldos took to dreaming with his eyes wide open. Contrary to her expectations, the Axphainians did not appear, and if there were robbers in the hills they thought better than to attack the valorous-looking party. It dawned upon her finally that the Axphainians were guarding the upper route and not the one over which she was traveling. Yetive doubtless was approaching Ganlook over the northern pass, pro-

vided the enemy had not been encountered before
Labbot was reached. Beverly soon found herself fear-
ing for the safety of the princess, a fear which at last
became almost unendurable.

Near nightfall they came upon three Graustark
shepherds and learned that Ganlook could not be
reached before the next afternoon. The tired, hungry
travelers spent the night in a snug little valley
through which a rivulet bounded onward to the river
below. The supper was a scant one, the foragers having poor luck in the hunt for food. Daybreak saw
them on their way once more. Hunger and dread had
worn down Beverly's supply of good spirits; she was
having difficulty in keeping the haggard, distressed
look from her face. Her tender, hopeful eyes were not
so bold or so merry as on the day before; cheerfulness
cost her an effort, but she managed to keep it fairly
alive. Her escort, wretched and half-starved, never
forgot the deference due to their charge, but strode
steadily on with the doggedness of martyrs. At times
she was impelled to disclose her true identity, but dis-
cretion told her that deception was her best safeguard.

Late in the afternoon of the second day the front
axle of the coach snapped in two, and a tedious delay
of two hours ensued. Baldos was strangely silent and
subdued. It was not until the misfortune came that
Beverly observed the flushed condition of his face.
Involuntarily and with the compassion of a true
woman she touched his hand and brow. They were
burning-hot. The wounded man was in a high fever.
He laughed at her fears and scoffed at the prospect

of blood-poisoning and the hundred other possibilities that suggested themselves to her anxious brain.

"We are close to Ganlook," he said, with the setting of the sun. " Soon you may be relieved of your tiresome, cheerless company, your highness."

"You are going to a physician," she said, resolutely, alive and active once more, now that the worst part of the journey was coming to an end. " Tell that man to drive in a gallop all the rest of the way!"

CHAPTER VIII.

THROUGH THE GANLOOK GATES

Y this time they were passing the queer little huts that marked the outskirts of a habitable community. These were the homes of shepherds, hunters and others whose vocations related especially to the mountains. Farther on there were signs of farming interests; the homes became more numerous and more pretentious in appearance. The rock-lined gorge broadened into a fertile valley; the road was smooth and level, a condition which afforded relief to the travelers. Ravone had once more dressed the wounds inflicted by the lion; but he was unable to provide anything to subdue the fever. Baldos was undeniably ill. Beverly, between her exclamations of joy and relief at being in sight of Ganlook, was profuse in her expressions of concern for the hero of the Hawk and Raven. The feverish gleam in his dark eyes and the pain that marked his face touched her deeply. Suffering softened his lean, sun-browned features, obliterating the mocking lines that had impressed her so unfavorably at the outset. She was saying to herself that he was hand-

84

some after a most unusual cast; it was an unforgetable face.

"Your highness," he said earnestly, after she had
looked long and anxiously at his half-closed eyes, "we
are within an hour of Ganlook. It will be dark before
we reach the gates, I know, but you have nothing to
fear during the rest of the trip. Franz shall drive
you to the sentry post and turn over the horses to your
own men. My friends and I must leave you at the
end of the mountain road. We are —— "

"Ridiculous!" she cried. "I'll not permit it!
You must go to a hospital."

"If I enter the Ganlook gates it will be the same
as entering the gates of death," he protested.

"Nonsense! You have a fever or you wouldn't
talk like that. I can promise you absolute security."

"You do not understand, your highness."

"Nevertheless, you are going to a hospital," she
firmly said. "You would die out here in the wilds, so
what are the odds either way? Aunt Fanny, *will* you
be careful? Don't you know that the least movement
of those bags hurts him?"

"Please, do not mind me, your highness. I am
doing very well," he said, smiling.

The coach brought up in front of a roadside inn.
While some of the men were watering the horses others
gathered about its open window. A conversation in a
tongue utterly incomprehensible to Beverly took place
between Baldos and his followers. The latter seemed
to be disturbed about something, and there was no mis-
taking the solicitous air with which they regarded

their leader. The pseudo-princess was patient as long as possible and then broke into the discussion.

" What do they want? " she demanded in English.

" They are asking for instructions," he answered.

" Instruct them to do as I bid," she said. " Tell them to hurry along and get you a doctor; that's all."

Evidently his friends were of the same opinion, for after a long harangue in which he was obdurate to the last, they left the carriage and he sank back with a groan of dejection.

" What is it? " she anxiously demanded.

" They also insist that I shall go to a surgeon," he said hopelessly. His eyes were moist and he could not meet her gaze. She was full of exultation. " They have advised me to put myself under your protection, shameless as that may seem to a man. You and you alone have the power to protect me if I pass beyond the walls of Ganlook."

" I? " she cried, all a-flutter.

" I could not thrust my head into the jaws of death unless the princess of Graustark were there to stay their fury. Your royal hand alone can turn aside the inevitable. Alas, I am helpless and know not what to do."

Beverly Calhoun sat very straight and silent beside the misguided Baldos. After all, it was not within her power to protect him. She was not the princess and she had absolutely no influence in Ganlook. The authorities there could not be deceived as had been these ignorant men of the hills. If she led him into the city it was decidedly probable that she might be taking him to his death. She only could petition, not command. Once at Yetive's side she was confident she could save the man who had done so much for her, but Ganlook was many miles from Edelweiss, and there was no assurance that intervention could be obtained in time. On the other hand, if he went back to the hills he was likely to die of the poisonous fever. Beverly was in a most unhappy state of mind. If she confessed to him that she was not the princess, he would refuse to enter the gates of Ganlook, and be perfectly justified in doing so.

"But if I should fail?" she asked, at last, a shiver rushing over her and leaving her cold with dread.

"You are the only hope, your highness. You had better say farewell to Baldos and let him again seek the friendly valley," said he wearily. "We can go no farther. The soldiers must be near, your highness. It means capture if we go on. I cannot expose my friends to the dangers. Let me be put down here, and do you drive on to safety. I shall fare much better than you think, for I am young and strong and —— "

"No! I'll risk it," she cried. "You must go into the city. Tell them so and say that I will protect you with my own life and honor."

Fever made him submissive; her eyes gave him confidence; her voice soothed his fears, if he possessed them. Leaning from the window, he called his men together. Beverly looked on in wonder as these strange men bade farewell to their leader. Many of them were weeping, and most of them kissed his hand.

There were broken sentences, tear-choked promises, anxious inquiries, and the parting was over.

" Where are they going? " Beverly whispered, as they moved away in the dusk.

" Back into the mountains to starve, poor fellows. God be kind to them, God be good to them," he half sobbed, his chin dropping to his breast. He was trembling like a leaf.

" Starve? " she whispered. " Have they no money? "

" We are penniless," came in muffled tones from the stricken leader.

Beverly leaned from the window and called to the departing ones. Ravone and one other reluctantly approached. Without a word she opened a small traveling bag and drew forth a heavy purse. This she pressed into the hand of the student. It was filled with Graustark gavvos, for which she had exchanged American gold in Russia.

" God be with you," she fervently cried. He kissed her hand, and the two stood aside to let the coach roll on into the dusky shadows that separated them from the gates of Ganlook, old Franz still driving — the only one of the company left to serve his leader to the very end.

" Well, we have left them," muttered Baldos, as though to himself. " I may never see them again — never see them again. God, how true they have been ! "

" I shall send for them the moment I get to Ganlook

and I'll promise pardons for them all," she cried
rashly, in her compassion.

"No!" he exclaimed fiercely. "You are not to disturb them. Better that they should starve."

Beverly was sufficiently subdued. As they drew
nearer the city gates her heart began to fail her. This
man's life was in her weak, incapable hands and the
time was nearing when she must stand between him and
disaster.

"Where are these vaunted soldiers of yours?" he
suddenly asked, infinite irony in his voice.

"My soldiers?" she said faintly.

"Isn't it rather unusual that, in time of trouble and
uncertainty, we should be able to approach within a
mile of one of your most important cities without even
so much as seeing a soldier of Graustark?"

She felt that he was scoffing, but it mattered little
to her.

"It is a bit odd, isn't it?" she agreed.

"Worse than that, your highness."

"I shall speak to Dangloss about it," she said
serenely, and he looked up in new surprise. Truly,
she was an extraordinary princess.

Fully three-quarters of an hour passed before the
coach was checked. Beverly, looking from the windows, had seen the lighted windows of cottages growing closer and closer together. The barking of roadside dogs was the only sound that could be heard above
the rattle of the wheels. It was too dark inside the
coach to see the face of the man beside her, but something told her that he was staring intently into the

night, alert and anxious. The responsibility of her position swooped down upon her like an avalanche as she thought of what the next few minutes were to bring forth. It was the sudden stopping of the coach and the sharp commands from the outside that told her probation was at an end. She could no longer speculate; it was high time to act.

"The outpost," came from Baldos, in strained tones.

"Perhaps they won't know us — you, I mean," she whispered.

"Baron Dangloss knows everybody," he replied bitterly.

"What a horrid old busy-body he —— " she started to say, but thought better of it.

A couple of lanterns flashed at the window, almost blinding her. Aunt Fanny groaned audibly, but the figure of Baldos seemed to stiffen with defiance. Uniformed men peered into the interior with more rudeness and curiosity than seemed respectful to a princess, to say the least. They saw a pretty, pleading face, with wide gray eyes and parted lips, but they did not bow in humble submission as Baldos had expected. One of the men, evidently in command, addressed Beverly in rough but polite tones. It was a question that he asked, she knew, but she could not answer him, for she could not understand him.

"What do you want?" she put in English, with a creditable display of dignity.

"He does not speak English, your highness," vol·

unteered Baldos, in a voice so well disguised that it startled her. The officer was staring blankly at her.

"Every officer in my army should and must learn to speak English," she said, at her wits' end. "I decline to be questioned by the fellow. Will you talk to him in my stead?"

"I, your highness?" he cried in dismay.

"Yes. Tell him who we are and ask where the hospital is," she murmured, sinking back with the air of a queen, but with the inward feeling that all was lost.

"But I don't speak your language well," he protested.

"You speak it beautifully," she said. Baldos leaned forward painfully and spoke to the officer in the Graustark tongue.

"Don't you know your princess?" he demanded, a trifle harshly. The man's eyes flew wide open in an instant and his jaw dropped.

"Th — the princess?" he gasped.

"Don't stare like that, sir. Direct us to the main gate at once, or you will have cause to regret your slowness."

"But the princess was — is coming by the northern pass," mumbled the man. "The guard has gone out to meet her and —— " Baldos cut him off shortly with the information that the princess, as he could see, had come by the lower pass and that she was eager to reach a resting-place at once. The convincing tone of the speaker and the regal indifference of the lady had full effect upon the officer, who had never seen her highness. He fell back with a deep obeisance, and gave a few bewildered commands to his men. The coach moved off, attended by a party of foot-soldiers, and Beverly breathed her first sigh of relief.

"You did it beautifully," she whispered to Baldos, and he was considerably puzzled by the ardor of her praise. "Where are we going now?" she asked.

"Into the city, your highness," he answered. It was beginning to dawn upon him that she was amazingly ignorant and inconsequential for one who enjoyed the right to command these common soldiers. Her old trepidation returned with this brief answer. Something told her that he was beginning to mistrust her at last. After all, it meant everything to him and so little to her.

When the coach halted before the city gates she was in a dire state of unhappiness. In the darkness she could feel the reproachful eyes of old Aunt Fanny searching for her abandoned conscience.

"Ask if Baron Dangloss is in Ganlook, and, if he is, command them to take me to him immediately," she whispered to Baldos, a sudden inspiration seizing her. She would lay the whole matter before the great chief of police, and trust to fortune. Her hand fell impulsively upon his and, to her amazement, it was as cold as ice. "What is the matter?" she cried in alarm.

"You trusted me in the wilds, your highness," he said tensely; "I am trusting you now." Before she could reply the officer in charge of the Ganlook gates appeared at the coach window. There were lights on all sides. Her heart sank like lead. It would be a miracle if she passed the gates unrecognized.

" I must see Baron Dangloss at once," she cried in English, utterly disdaining her instructions to Baldos.

" The baron is engaged at present and can see no one," responded the good-looking young officer in broken English.

" Where is he? " she demanded nervously.

" He is at the home of Colonel Goaz, the commandant. What is your business with him? "

" It is with him and not with you, sir," she said, imperious once more. " Conduct me to him immediately."

" You cannot enter the gates unless you ―― "

" Insolence! " exclaimed Baldos. " Is this the way, sir, in which you address the princess? Make way for her."

" The princess! " gasped the officer. Then a peculiar smile overspread his face. He had served three years in the Castle Guard at Edelweiss! There was a long pause fraught with disaster for Beverly. " Yes, perhaps it is just as well that we conduct her to Baron Dangloss," he said at last. The deep meaning in his voice appealed only to the unhappy girl. " There shall be no further delay, *your highness!* " he added mockingly. A moment later the gates swung open and they passed through. Beverly alone knew that they were going to Baron Dangloss under heavy guard, virtually as prisoners. The man knew her to be an impostor and was doing only his duty.

There were smiles of derision on the faces of the soldiers when Beverly swept proudly between the files

and up the steps leading to the commandant's door,
but there were no audible remarks. Baldos followed,
walking painfully but defiantly, and Aunt Fanny
came last with the handbag. The guards grinned
broadly as the corpulent negress waddled up the steps.
The young officer and two men entered the door with
the wayfarers, who were ordered to halt in the hallway.

"Will your highness come with me?" said the officer, returning to the hall after a short absence. There
was unmistakable derision in his voice and palpable
insolence in his manner. Beverly flushed angrily.
"Baron Dangloss is very *curious* to see you," he
added, with a smile. Nevertheless, he shrank a bit
beneath the cold gleam in the eyes of the impostor.

"You will remain here," she said, turning to Baldos
and the negress. "And you will have nothing whatever to say to this very important young man." The
"important young man" actually chuckled.

"Follow me, your most royal highness," he said,
preceding her through the door that opened into the
office of the commandant. Baldos glared after them
in angry amazement.

"Young man, some day and *soon* you will be a
much wiser soldier and, in the ranks," said Beverly
hotly. The smile instantly receded from the insolent
fellow's face, for there was a world of prophecy in
the way she said it. Somehow, he was in a much more
respectful humor when he returned to the hall and
stood in the presence of the tall, flushed stranger with
the ragged uniform.

A short, fierce little man in the picturesque uniform of a Graustark officer arose as Beverly entered the office. His short beard bristled as though it were concealing a smile, but his manner was polite, even deferential. She advanced fearlessly toward him, a wayward smile struggling into her face.

"I daresay you know I am not the princess," she said composedly. Every vestige of fear was gone now that she had reached the line of battle. The doughty baron looked somewhat surprised at this frank way of opening the interview.

"I am quite well aware of it," he said politely.

"They say you know everyone, Baron Dangloss," she boldly said. "Pray, who am I?"

The powerful official looked at the smiling face for a moment, his bushy eyebrows contracting ever so slightly. There was a shameless streak of dust across her cheek, but there was also a dimple there that appealed to the grim old man. His eyes twinkled as he replied, with fine obsequiousness:

"You are Miss Beverly Calhoun, of Washington."

CHAPTER IX

THE REDOUBTABLE DANGLOSS

 EVERLY'S eyes showed her astonishment. Baron Dangloss courteously placed a chair for her and asked her to be seated.

"We were expecting you, Miss Calhoun," he explained. "Her royal highness left St. Petersburg but a few hours after your departure, having unfortunately missed you."

"You don't mean to say that the princess tried to find me in St. Petersburg?" cried Beverly, in wonder and delight.

"That was one of the purposes of her visit," said he brusquely.

"Oh, how jolly!" cried she, her gray eyes sparkling. The grim old captain was startled for the smallest fraction of a minute, but at once fell to admiring the fresh, eager face of the visitor.

"The public at large is under the impression that she visited the Czar on matters of importance," he said, with a condescending smile.

"And it really was of no importance at all, that's what you mean?" she smiled back securely.

96

"Your message informing her highness of your presence in St. Petersburg had no sooner arrived than she set forth to meet you in that city, much against the advice of her counsellors. I will admit that she had other business there but it could have waited. You see, Miss Calhoun, it was a great risk at this particular time. Misfortune means disaster now. But Providence was her friend. She arrived safely in Ganlook not an hour since."

"Really? Oh, Baron Dangloss, where is she?" excitedly cried the American girl.

"For the night she is stopping with the Countess Rallowitz. A force of men, but not those whom you met at the gates, has just been dispatched at her command to search for you in the lower pass. You took the most dangerous road, Miss Calhoun, and I am amazed that you came through in safety."

"The Russians chose the lower pass, I know not why. Of course, I was quite ignorant. However, we met neither brigands nor soldiers, Axphain or Graustark. I encountered nothing more alarming than a mountain lion. And that, Baron Dangloss, recalls me to the sense of a duty I have been neglecting. A poor wanderer in the hills defended me against the beast and was badly wounded. He must be taken to a hospital at once, sir, where he may have the proper care."

Whereupon, at his request, she hurriedly related the story of that trying journey through the mountains, not forgetting to paint the courage of Baldos in most glowing colors. The chief was deeply interested in

the story of the goat-hunter and his party. There
was an odd gleam of satisfaction in his eyes, but she
did not observe it.

"You *will* see that he has immediate attention,
won't you?" she implored in the end.

"He shall have our deepest consideration," promised he.

"You know I am rather interested, because I shot
him, just as if it were not enough that his legs were
being torn by the brute at the time. He ought not
to walk, Baron Dangloss. If you don't mind, I'd
suggest an ambulance," she hurried on glibly. He
could not conceal the smile that her eagerness inspired. "Really, he is in a serious condition. I think
he needs some quinine and whiskey, too, and —— "

"He shall have the *best* of care," interrupted the
captain. "Leave him to me, Miss Calhoun."

"Now, let me tell you something," said she, after
due reflection. "You must not pay any attention to
what he says. He is liable to be delirious and talk in
a terrible sort of way. You know delirious people
never talk rationally." She was loyally trying to protect Baldos, the hunted, against any incriminating
statements he might make.

"Quite right, Miss Calhoun," said the baron
very gravely.

"And now, I'd like to go to the princess," said
Beverly, absolutely sure of herself. "You know we
are great friends, she and I."

"I have sent a messenger to announce your arrival.

She will expect you." Beverly looked about the room in perplexity.

" But there has been no messenger here," she said.

" He left here some minutes before you came. I knew who it was that came knocking at our gates, even though she traveled as Princess Yetive of Graustark."

" And, oh! that reminds me, Baron Dangloss, Baldos still believes me to be the princess. Is it necessary to — to tell him the truth about me? Just at present, I mean? I'm sure he'll rest much easier if he doesn't know differently."

" So far as I am concerned, Miss Calhoun, he shall always regard you as a queen," said Dangloss gallantly.

" Thank you. It's very nice of you to —— "

A man in uniform entered after knocking at the door of the room. He saluted his superior and uttered a few words in his own language.

" Her royal highness is awaiting you at the home of the countess, Miss Calhoun. A detail of men will escort you and your servant to her place."

" Now, please, Baron Dangloss," pleaded Beverly at the door, " be nice to him. You know it hurts him to walk. Can't you have him carried in? "

" If he will consent," said he quietly. Beverly hurried into the outer room, after giving the baron a smile he never forgot. Baldos looked up eagerly, anxiously.

" It's all right," she said in low tones, pausing for a moment beside his chair. " Don't get up! Good-bye. I'll come to see you to-morrow. Don't be in the least disturbed. Baron Dangloss has his instructions." Impulsively giving him her hand which he respectfully raised to his lips, she followed Aunt Fanny and was gone.

Almost immediately Baldos was requested to present himself before Baron Dangloss in the adjoining room. Refusing to be carried in, he resolutely strode through the door and stood before the grim old captain of police, an easy, confident smile on his face. The black patch once more covered his eye with defiant assertiveness.

"They tell me you are Baldos, a goat-hunter," said Baron Dangloss, eyeing him keenly.

"Yes."

"And you were hurt in defending one who is of much consequence in Graustark. Sit down, my good fellow." Baldos' eyes gleamed coldly for an instant. Then he sank into a chair. "While admitting that you have done Graustark a great service, I am obliged to tell you that I, at least, know you to be other than what you say. You are not a goat-hunter, and Baldos is not your name. Am I not right?"

"You have had instructions from your sovereign, Baron Dangloss. Did they include a command to cross-question me?" asked Baldos haughtily. Dangloss hesitated for a full minute.

"They did not. I take the liberty of inquiring on my own responsibility."

"Very well, sir. Until you have a right to question me, I am Baldos and a goat-hunter. I think I am here to receive surgical treatment."

" You decline to tell me anything concerning yourself? "

" Only that I am injured and need relief."

" Perhaps I know more about you than you suspect, sir."

" I am not in the least interested, Baron Dangloss, in what you know. The princess brought me into Ganlook, and I have her promise of help and protection while here. That is all I have to say, except that I have implicit faith in her word."

Dangloss sat watching him in silence for some time. No one but himself knew what was going on in that shrewd, speculative mind. At length he arose and approached the proud fellow in rags.

" You have earned every consideration at our hands. My men will take you to the hospital and you shall have the best of care. You have served our princess well. To-morrow you may feel inclined to talk more freely with me, for I am your friend, Baldos."

" I am grateful for that, Baron Dangloss," said the other simply. Then he was led away and a comfortable cot in the Ganlook hospital soon held his long, feverish frame, while capable hands took care of his wounds. He did not know it, but two fully armed soldiers maintained a careful guard outside his door under instructions from the head of the police. Moreover, a picked detail of men sallied forth into the lower pass in search of the goat-hunter's followers.

In the meantime Beverly was conducted to the home of the Countess Rallowitz. Her meeting with the princess was most affectionate. There were tears, laughter and kisses. The whole atmosphere of the place suggested romance to the eager American girl. Downstairs were the royal guards; in the halls were attendants; all about were maidservants and obsequious lackeys, crowding the home of the kindly countess. At last, comfortable and free from the dust of travel, the two friends sat down to a dainty meal.

" Oh, I am so delighted," murmured Beverly for the hundredth time.

" I'm appalled when I think of the dangers you incurred in coming to me. No one but a very foolish American girl could have undertaken such a trip as this. Dear me, Beverly, I should have died if anything dreadful had happened to you. Why did you do it? " questioned the princess. And then they laughed joyously.

" And you went all the way to St. Petersburg to meet me, you dear, dear Yetive," cried Beverly, so warmly that the attentive servant forgot his mask of reverence.

" Wasn't it ridiculous of me? I know Gren would have forbidden it if he had been in Edelweiss when I started. And, more shame to me, the poor fellow is doubtless at the conference with Dawsbergen, utterly ignorant of my escapade. You should have heard the ministry — er — ah —— " and the princess paused for an English word.

" Kick? " Beverly supplied.

"Yes. They objected violently. And, do you know, I was finally compelled to issue a private edict to restrain them from sending an appeal to Grenfall away off there on the frontier. Whether or no, my uncle insisted that he should be brought home, a three-days' journey, in order that he might keep me from going to St. Petersburg. Of course, they could not disobey my edict, and so poor Gren is none the wiser, unless he has returned from the conference. If he has, I am sure he is on the way to Ganlook at this very minute."

"What a whimsical ruler you are," cried Beverly. "Upsetting everything sensible just to rush off hundreds of miles to meet me. And Axphain is trying to capture you, too! Goodness, you must love me!"

"Oh, but I *did* have a trifling affair of state to lay before the Czar, my dear. To-morrow we shall be safe and sound in the castle and it will all be very much worth while. You see, Beverly, dear, even princesses enjoy a diversion now and then. One wouldn't think anything of this adventure in the United States; it is the environment that makes it noticeable. Besides, you traveled as a princess. How did you like it?"

And then the conversation related particularly to the advantages of royalty as viewed from one side and the disadvantages as regarded from another. For a long time Beverly had been wondering how she should proceed in the effort to secure absolute clemency for Baldos. As yet she had said nothing to Yetive of her promise to him, made while she was a princess.

"At any rate, I'm sure the goat-hunters would not

have been so faithful and true if they had not believed me to be a princess," said Beverly, paving the
way. "You haven't a man in your kingdom who
could be more chivalrous than Baldos."

"If he is that kind of a man, he would treat any
woman as gently."

"You should have heard him call me 'your highness,'" cried Beverly. "He will loathe me if he ever
learns that I deceived him."

"Oh, I think he deceived himself," spoke Yetive
easily. "Besides, you look as much like a princess
as I."

"There is something I want to speak very seriously
about to you, Yetive," said Beverly, making ready
for the cast. "You see, he did not want to enter Ganlook with me, but I insisted. He had been so brave
and gallant, and he was suffering so intensely. It
would have been criminal in me to leave him out there
in the wilderness, wouldn't it?"

"It would have been heartless."

"So I just made him come along. That was right,
wasn't it? That's what you would have done, no matter who he was or what his objections might have been.
Well, you see, it's this way, Yetive: he is some sort of
a fugitive — not a criminal, you know — but just
some one they are hunting for, I don't know why. He
wouldn't tell me. That was perfectly right, if he felt
that way, wasn't it?"

"And he had fought a lion in your defense," sup-
plemented Yetive, with a schoolgirl's ardor.

"And I had shot him in the arm, too," added Beverly. "So of course, I just had to be reasonable. In order to induce him to come with me to a hospital, I was obliged to guarantee perfect safety to him. His men went back to the hills, all except old Franz, the driver. Now, the trouble is this, Yetive: I am *not* the princess and I cannot redeem a single promise I made to him. He is helpless, and if anything goes wrong with him he will hate me forever."

"No; he will hate *me*, for I am the princess and he is none the wiser."

"But he will be told that his princess was Beverly Calhoun, a supposedly nice American girl. Don't you see how awkward it will be for me? Now, Yetive, darling, what I wish you to do is to write a note, order or edict or whatever it is to Baron Dangloss, commanding him to treat Baldos as a patient and not as a prisoner; and that when he is fully recovered he is to have the privilege of leaving Ganlook without reservation."

"But he may be a desperate offender against the state, Beverly," plaintively protested Yetive. "If we only knew what he is charged with!"

"I'm afraid it's something dreadfully serious," admitted Beverly gloomily. "He doesn't look like the sort of man who would engage in a petty undertaking. I'll tell you his story, just as he told it to me," and she repeated the meagre confessions of Baldos.

"I see no reason why we should hesitate," said the princess. "By his own statement, he is not a desperate criminal. You did quite right in promising him protection, dear, and I shall sustain you. Do you want to play the princess to Baldos a little longer? "

" I should love it," cried Beverly, her eyes sparkling.

" Then I shall write the order to Dangloss at once. Oh, dear, I have forgotten, I have no official seal here."

" Couldn't you seal it with your ring? " suggested Beverly. " Oh, I have it! Send for Baron Dangloss and have him witness your signature. He can't get away from that, you see, and after we reach Edelweiss, you can fix up a regular edict, seal and all," cried the resourceful American girl.

Ink and paper were sent for and the two conspirators lent their wisdom to the task of preparing an order for the salvation of Baldos, the fugitive. The order read:

To Baron Jasto Dangloss, Commanding the Civic and Military Police of Graustark:

" You are hereby informed that Baldos, the man who entered the city with Miss Calhoun, is not to be regarded as a prisoner now or hereafter. He is to be given capable medical and surgical attention until fully recovered, when he is to be allowed to go his way in peace unquestioned.

" Also, he is to be provided with suitable wearing apparel and made comfortable in every way.

" Also, the members of his party, now in the hills (whose names are unknown to me), are to be accorded every protection. Franz, the driver, is to have his freedom if he desires it.

" And from this edict there is no recourse until its abatement by royal decree.

" Yetive."

" There," said the princess, affixing her signature.

" I think that will be sufficient." Then she rang for a servant. " Send to Baron Dangloss and ask him to come here at once."

Fifteen minutes later the chief of police stood in the presence of the eager young interpreters of justice.

" I want you to witness my signature, Baron Dangloss," said the princess after the greetings.

" Gladly," said the officer.

" Well, here is where I signed," said Yetive, handing him the paper. " I don't have to write my name over again, do I? "

" Not at all," said the baron gallantly. And he boldly signed his name as a witness.

" They wouldn't do that in the United States," murmured Beverly, who knew something about red tape at Washington.

" It is a command to you, baron," said Yetive, handing him the document with a rare smile. He read it through slowly. Then he bit his lip and coughed. " What is the matter, baron? " asked Yetive, still smiling.

" A transitory emotion, your highness, that is all," said he; but his hand trembled as he folded the paper.

CHAPTER X

INSIDE THE CASTLE WALLS

RIGHT and early the next morning, the party was ready for the last of the journey to Edelweiss. Less than twenty miles separated Ganlook from the capital, and the road was in excellent condition. Beverly Calhoun, tired and contented, had slept soundly until aroused by the princess herself. Their rooms adjoined each other, and when Yetive, shortly after daybreak, stole into the American girl's chamber, Beverly was sleeping so sweetly that the intruder would have retreated had it not been for the boisterous shouts of stable-boys in the courtyard below the windows. She hurried to a window and looked out upon the gray-cloaked morning. Postillions and stable-boys were congregated near the gates, tormenting a ragged old man who stood with his back against one of the huge posts. In some curiosity, she called Beverly from her slumbers, urging the sleepy one to hasten to the window.

" Is this one of your friends from the wilderness? " she asked.

"It's Franz!" cried Beverly, rubbing her pretty eyes. Then she became thoroughly awake. "What are they doing to him? Who are those ruffians?" she demanded indignantly.

"They are my servants, and —— "

"Shame on them! The wretches! What has old Franz done that they should —— Call to them! Tell 'em you'll cut their heads off if they don't stop. He's a dear old fellow in spite of his rags, and he —— "

The window-sash flew open and the tormentors in the court below were astonished by the sound of a woman's voice, coming, as it were, from the clouds. A dozen pairs of eyes were turned upward; the commotion ended suddenly. In the window above stood two graceful, white-robed figures. The sun, still far below the ridge of mountains, had not yet robbed the morning of the gray, dewy shadows that belong to five o'clock.

"What are you doing to that poor old man?" cried Yetive, and it was the first time any of them had seen anger in the princess's face. They slunk back in dismay. "Let him alone! You, Gartz, see that he has food and drink, and without delay. Report to me later on, sir, and explain, if you can, why you have conducted yourselves in so unbecoming a manner." Then the window was closed and the princess found herself in the warm arms of her friend.

"I couldn't understand a word you said, Yetive, but I knew you were giving it to them hot and heavy. Did you see how nicely old Franz bowed to you? Goodness, his head almost touched the ground."

" He was bowing to you, Beverly. You forgot that you are the princess to him."

" Isn't that funny? I had quite forgotten it — the poor old goose."

Later, when the coaches and escort were drawn up in front of the Rallowitz palace ready for the start, the princess called the chief postillion, Gartz, to the step of her coach.

" What was the meaning of the disturbance I witnessed this morning? " she demanded.

Gartz hung his head. " We thought the man was crazy, your highness. He had been telling us such monstrous lies," he mumbled.

" Are you sure they were lies? "

" Oh, quite sure, your highness. They were laughable. He said, for one thing, that it was he who drove your highness's coach into Ganlook last evening, when everybody knows that I had full charge of the coach and horses."

" You are very much mistaken, Gartz," she said, distinctly. He blinked his eyes.

" Your highness," he gasped, " you surely remember —— "

" Enough, sir. Franz drove the princess into Ganlook last night. He says so himself, does he not? "

" Yes, your highness," murmured poor Gartz.

" What more did he say to you? "

" He said he had come from his master, who is in the hospital, to inquire after your health and to bear his thanks for the kindnesses you have secured for him. He says his master is faring well and is satisfied to remain where he is. Also, he said that his master was sending him back into the mountains to assure his friends that he is safe and to bear a certain message of cheer to them, sent forth by the princess. It was all so foolish and crazy, your highness, that we could but jibe and laugh at the poor creature."

" It is you who have been foolish, sir. Send the old man to me."

" He has gone, your highness," in frightened tones.

" So much the better," said the princess, dismissing him with a wave of the hand. Gartz went away in a daze, and for days he took every opportunity to look for other signs of mental disorder in the conduct of his mistress, at the same time indulging in speculation as to his own soundness of mind.

Ganlook's population lined the chief thoroughfare, awaiting the departure of the princess, although the hour was early. Beverly peered forth curiously as the coach moved off. The quaint, half-oriental costumes of the townspeople, the odd little children, the bright colors, the perfect love and reverence that shone in the faces of the multitude impressed her deeply. She was never to forget that picturesque morning. Baron Dangloss rode beside the coach until it passed through the southern gates and into the countryside. A company of cavalrymen acted as escort. The bright red trousers and top-boots, with the deep-blue jackets, reminded Beverly more than ever of the operatic figures she had seen so often at home. There was a fierce, dark cast to the faces of these soldiers, however, that removed any suggestion of play. The girl was in ecstasies. Everything about her appealed to the romantic side of her nature; everything seemed so unreal and so like the story-book. The princess smiled lovingly upon the throngs that lined the street; there was no man among them who would not have laid down his life for the gracious ruler.

" Oh, I love your soldiers," cried Beverly warmly.

" Poor fellows, who knows how soon they may be called upon to face death in the Dawsbergen hills? " said Yetive, a shadow crossing her face.

Dangloss was to remain in Ganlook for several days, on guard against manifestations by the Axphainians. A corps of spies and scouts was working with him, and couriers were ready to ride at a moment's notice to the castle in Edelweiss. Before they parted, Beverly extracted a renewal of his promise to take good care of Baldos. She sent a message to the injured man, deploring the fact that she was compelled to leave Ganlook without seeing him as she had promised. It was her intention to have him come to Edelweiss as soon as he was in a condition to be removed. Captain Dangloss smiled mysteriously, but he had no comment to make. He had received his orders and was obeying them to the letter.

" I wonder if Grenfall has heard of my harum-scarum trip to St. Petersburg," reflected Yetive, making herself comfortable in the coach after the gates and the multitudes were far behind.

" I'll go you a box of chocolate creams that we

meet him before we get to Edelweiss," ventured Beverly.

"Agreed," said the princess.

"Don't say 'agreed,' dear. 'Done' is the word," corrected the American girl airily.

Beverly won. Grenfall Lorry and a small company of horsemen rode up in furious haste long before the sun was in mid-sky. An attempt to depict the scene between him and his venturesome wife would be a hopeless task. The way in which his face cleared itself of distress and worry was a joy in itself. To use his own words, he breathed freely for the first time in hours. "The American" took the place of the officer who rode beside the coach, and the trio kept up an eager, interesting conversation during the next two hours.

It was a warm, sleepy day, but all signs of drowsiness disappeared with the advent of Lorry. He had reached Edelweiss late the night before, after a three days' ride from the conference with Dawsbergen. At first he encountered trouble in trying to discover what had become of the princess. Those at the castle were aware of the fact that she had reached Ganlook safely and sought to put him off with subterfuges. He stormed to such a degree, however, that their object failed. The result was that he was off for Ganlook with the earliest light of day.

Regarding the conference with Prince Gabriel's representatives, he had but little to say. The escaped murderer naturally refused to surrender and was to all appearances quite firmly established in power once more.   Lorry's only hope was that the reversal of feeling in Dawsbergen might work ruin for the prince. He was carrying affairs with a high hand, dealing vengeful blows to the friends of his half-brother and encouraging a lawlessness that sooner or later must prove his undoing.   His representatives at the conference were an arrogant, law-defying set of men who laughed scornfully at every proposal made by the Graustarkians.

" We told them that if he were not surrendered to our authorities inside of sixty days we would declare war and go down and take him," concluded " The American."

" Two months," cried Yetive.   " I don't understand."

"There was method in that ultimatum.   Axphain, of course, will set up a howl, but we can forestall any action the Princess Volga may undertake.   Naturally, one might suspect that we should declare war at once, inasmuch as he must be taken sooner or later. But here is the point: before two months have elapsed the better element of Dawsbergen will be so disgusted with the new dose of Gabriel that it will do anything to avert a war on his account.   We have led them to believe that Axphain will lend moral, if not physical, support to our cause.   Give them two months in which to get over this tremendous hysteria, and they'll find their senses.   Gabriel isn't worth it, you see, and down in their hearts they know it.   They really loved young Dantan, who seems to be a devil of a good fellow.   I'll wager my head that in six weeks they'll be wishing he were back on the throne again. And just to think of it, Yetive, dear, you were off there in the very heart of Axphain, risking everything," he cried, wiping the moisture from his brow.

"It is just eleven days since I left Edelweiss, and I have had a lovely journey," she said, with one of her rare smiles. He shook his head gravely, and she resolved in her heart never to give him another such cause for alarm.

"And in the meantime, Mr. Grenfall Lorry, you are blaming me and hating me and all that for being the real cause of your wife's escapade," said Beverly Calhoun plaintively. "I'm awfully sorry. But, you must remember one thing, sir; I did not put her up to this ridiculous trip. She did it of her own free will and accord. Besides, I am the one who met the lion and almost got devoured, not Yetive, if you please."

"I'll punish you by turning you over to old Count Marlanx, the commander of the army in Graustark," said Lorry, laughingly. "He's a terrible ogre, worse than any lion."

"Heaven pity you, Beverly, if you fall into his clutches," cried Yetive. "He has had five wives and survives to look for a sixth. You see how terrible it would be."

"I'm not afraid of him," boasted Beverly, but there came a time when she thought of those words with a shudder.

"By the way, Yetive, I have had word from Harry Anguish. He and the countess will leave Paris this

week, if the baby's willing, and will be in Edelweiss
soon.   You don't know how it relieves me to know that
Harry will be with us at this time."

Yetive's eyes answered his enthusiasm.   Both had
a warm and grateful memory of the loyal service
which the young American had rendered his friend
when they had first come to Graustark in quest of
the princess; and both had a great regard for his wife,
the Countess Dagmar, who, as Yetive's lady in waiting, had been through all the perils of those exciting
days with them.

As they drew near the gates of Edelweiss, a large
body of horsemen rode forth to meet them.   The
afternoon was well on the way to night, and the air
of the valley was cool and refreshing, despite the rays
of the June sun.

"Edelweiss at last," murmured Beverly, her face
aglow.   "The heart of Graustark.   Do you know
that I have been brushing up on my grammar?   I
have learned the meaning of the word 'Graustark,'
and it seems so appropriate.   *Grau* is gray, hoary,
old; *stark* is strong.   Old and strong — isn't it,
dear?"

"And here rides the oldest and strongest man in
all Graustark — the Iron Count of Marlanx," said
Yetive, looking down the road.   "See — the strange
gray man in front there is our greatest general, our
craftiest fighter, our most heartless warrior.   Does
he not look like the eagle or the hawk?"

A moment later the parties met, and the newcomers
swung into line with the escort.   Two men rode up

to the carriage and saluted. One was Count Marlanx, the other Colonel Quinnox, of the Royal Guard. The count, lean and gray as a wolf, revealed rows of huge white teeth in his perfunctory smile of welcome, wnile young Quinnox's face fairly beamed with honest joy. In the post that he held, he was but following in the footsteps of his forefathers. Since history began in Graustark, a Quinnox had been in charge of the castle guard.

The " Iron Count," as he sometimes was called, was past his sixtieth year. For twenty years he had been in command of the army. One had but to look at his strong, sardonic face to know that he was a fearless leader, a savage fighter. His eyes were black, piercing and never quiet; his hair and close-cropped beard were almost snow-white; his voice was heavy and without a vestige of warmth. Since her babyhood Yetive had stood in awe of this grim old warrior. It was no uncommon thing for mothers to subdue disobedient children with the threat to give them over to the " Iron Count." " Old Marlanx will get you if you're not good," was a household phrase in Edelweiss. He had been married five times and as many times had he been left a widower. If he were disconsolate in any instance, no one had been able to discover the fact. Enormously rich, as riches go in Graustark, he had found young women for his wives who thought only of his gold and his lands in the trade they made with Cupid. It was said that without exception they died happy. Death was a joy. The fortress overlooking the valley to the south was no more rugged and unyielding than the man who made his home within its walls.   He lived there from choice and it was with his own money that he fitted up the commandant's quarters in truly regal style.   Power was more to him than wealth, though he enjoyed both.

Colonel Quinnox brought news from the castle. Yetive's uncle and aunt, the Count and Countess Halfont, were eagerly expecting her return, and the city was preparing to manifest its joy in the most exuberant fashion.   As they drew up to the gates the shouts of the people came to the ears of the travelers. Then the boom of cannon and the blare of bands broke upon the air, thrilling Beverly to the heart.   She wondered how Yetive could be so calm and unmoved in the face of all this homage.

Past the great Hotel Regengetz and the Tower moved the gay procession, into the broad stretch of boulevard that led to the gates of the palace grounds. The gates stood wide open and inviting.   Inside was Jacob Fraasch, the chief steward of the grounds, with his men drawn up in line; upon the walls the sentries came to parade rest; on the plaza the Royal band was playing as though by inspiration.   Then the gates closed behind the coach and escort, and Beverly Calhoun was safe inside the castle walls.   The "Iron Count" handed her from the carriage at the portals of the palace, and she stood as one in a dream.

CHAPTER XI

THE ROYAL COACH OF GRAUSTARK

HE two weeks following Beverly Calhoun's advent into the royal household were filled with joy and wonder for her. Daily she sent glowing letters to her father, mother and brothers in Washington, elaborating vastly upon the paradise into which she had fallen. To her highly emotional mind, the praises of Graustark had been but poorly sung. The huge old castle, relic of the feudal days, with its turrets and bastions and portcullises, impressed her with a never-ending sense of wonder. Its great halls and stairways, its chapel, the throne-room, and the armor-closet; its underground passages and dungeons all united to fill her imaginative soul with the richest, rarest joys of romance. Simple American girl that she was, unused to the rigorous etiquette of royalty, she found embarrassment in the first confusion of events, but she was not long in recovering her poise.

Her apartments were near those of the Princess Yetive. In the private intercourse enjoyed by these young women, all manner of restraint was abandoned

119

by the visitor and every vestige of royalty slipped
from the princess.   Count Halfont and his adorable
wife, the Countess Yvonne, both of whom had grown
old in the court, found the girl and her strange servant a source of wonder and delight.

Some days after Beverly's arrival there came to the
castle Harry Anguish and his wife, the vivacious
Dagmar.   With them came the year-old cooing babe
who was to overthrow the heart and head of every
being in the household, from princess down.   The
tiny Dagmar became queen at once, and no one disputed her rule.

Anguish, the painter, became Anguish, the strate-
gist and soldier.   He planned with Lorry and the
ministry, advancing some of the most hair-brained
projects that ever encouraged discussion in a solemn
conclave.   The staid, cautious ministers looked upon
him with wonder, but so plausible did he made his
proposals appear that they were forced to consider
them seriously.   The old Count of Marlanx held him
in great disdain, and did not hesitate to expose his
contempt.   This did not disturb Anguish in the least,
for he was as optimistic as the sunshine.   His plan
for the recapture of Gabriel was ridiculously improbable, but it was afterwards seen that had it been
attempted much distress and delay might actually
have been avoided.

Yetive and Beverly, with Dagmar and the baby,
made merry while the men were in council.   Their
mornings were spent in the shady park surrounding
the castle, their afternoons in driving, riding and

walking. Oftentimes the princess was barred from these simple pleasures by the exigencies of her position. She was obliged to grant audiences, observe certain customs of state, attend to the charities that came directly under her supervision, and confer with the nobles on affairs of weight and importance. Beverly delighted in the throne-room and the underground passages; they signified more to her than all the rest. She was shown the room in which Lorry had foiled the Viennese who once tried to abduct Yetive. The dungeon where Gabriel spent his first days of confinement, the Tower in which Lorry had been held a prisoner, and the monastery in the clouds were all places of unusual interest to her.

Soon the people of the city began to recognize the fair American girl who was a guest in the castle, and a certain amount of homage was paid to her. When she rode or drove in the streets, with her attendant soldiers, the people bowed as deeply and as respectfully as they did to the princess herself, and Beverly was just as grand and gracious as if she had been born with a sceptre in her hand.

The soft moonlight nights charmed her with a sense of rapture never known before. With the castle brilliantly illuminated, the halls and drawing-rooms filled with gay courtiers, the harpists at their posts, the military band playing in the parade ground, the balconies and porches offering their most inviting allurements, it is no wonder that Beverly was entranced. War had no terrors for her. If she thought of it at all, it was with the fear that it might dis-

turb the dream into which she had fallen.   True, there
was little or nothing to distress the most timid in these
first days.   The controversy between the principali-
ties was at a standstill, although there was not an hour
in which preparations for the worst were neglected.
To Beverly Calhoun, it meant little when sentiment
was laid aside; to Yetive and her people this probable war with Dawsbergen meant everything.

Dangloss, going back and forth between Edelweiss
and the frontier north of Ganlook, where the best of
the police and secret service watched with the sleepless eyes of the lynx, brought unsettling news to the
ministry.   Axphain troops were engaged in the
annual maneuvers just across the border in their own
territory.   Usually these were held in the plains near
the capital, and there was a sinister significance in
the fact that this year they were being carried on in
the rough southern extremity of the principality,
within a day's march of the Graustark line, fully two
months earlier than usual.   The doughty baron reported that foot, horse and artillery were engaged in
the drills, and that fully 8,000 men were massed in
the south of Axphain.   The fortifications of Ganlook,
Labbot and other towns in northern Graustark were
strengthened with almost the same care as those in
the south, where conflict with Dawsbergen might first
be expected.   General Marlanx and his staff rested
neither day nor night.   The army of Graustark was
ready.   Underneath the castle's gay exterior there
smouldered the fire of battle, the tremor of defiance.

Late one afternoon Beverly Calhoun and Mrs.

Anguish drove up in state to the Tower, wherein sat Dangloss and his watchdogs. The scowl left his face as far as nature would permit and he welcomed the ladies warmly.

" I came to ask about my friend, the goat-hunter," said Beverly, her cheeks a trifle rosier than usual.

" He is far from an amiable person, your highness," said the officer. When discussing Baldos he never failed to address Beverly as " your highness." " The fever is gone and he is able to walk without much pain, but he is as restless as a witch. Following instructions, I have not questioned him concerning his plans, but I fancy he is eager to return to the hills."

" What did he say when you gave him my message? " asked Beverly.

" Which one, your highness? " asked he, with tantalizing density.

" Why, the suggestion that he should come to Edelweiss for better treatment," retorted Beverly severely.

" He said he was extremely grateful for your kind offices, but he did not deem it advisable to come to this city. He requested me to thank you in his behalf and to tell you that he will never forget what you have done for him."

" And he refuses to come to Edelweiss? " irritably demanded Beverly.

" Yes, your highness. You see, he still regards himself with disfavor, being a fugitive. It is hardly fair to blame him for respecting the security of the hills."

" I hoped that I might induce him to give up his

old life and engage in something perfectly honest, although, mind you, Baron Dangloss, I do not question his integrity in the least. He should have a chance to prove himself worthy, that's all. This morning I petitioned Count Marlanx to give him a place in the Castle Guard."

" My dear Miss Calhoun, the princess has —— " began the captain.

" Her highness has sanctioned the request," interrupted she.

" And the count has promised to discover a vacancy," said Dagmar, with a smile that the baron understood perfectly well.

" This is the first time on record that old Marlanx has ever done anything to oblige a soul save himself. It is wonderful, Miss Calhoun. What spell do you Americans cast over rock and metal that they become as sand in your fingers? " said the baron, admiration and wonder in his eyes.

" You dear old flatterer," cried Beverly, so warmly that he caught his breath.

" I believe that you can conquer even that stubborn fellow in Ganlook," he said, fumbling with his glasses. " He is the most obstinate being I know, and yet in ten minutes you could bring him to terms, I am sure. He could not resist you."

" He still thinks I am the princess? "

" He does, and swears by you."

" Then, my mind is made up. I'll go to Ganlook and bring him back with me, willy-nilly. He is too good a man to be lost in the hills. Good-bye, Baron

Dangloss. Thank you ever and ever so much. Oh, yes; will you write an order delivering him over to me? The hospital people may be — er — disobliging, you know."

" It shall be in your highness's hands this evening."

The next morning, with Colonel Quinnox and a small escort, Beverly Calhoun set off in one of the royal coaches for Ganlook, accompanied by faithful Aunt Fanny. She carried the order from Baron Dangloss and a letter from Yetive to the Countess Rallowitz, insuring hospitality over night in the northern town. Lorry and the royal household entered merrily into her project, and she went away with the godspeeds of all. The Iron Count himself rode beside her coach to the city gates, an unheard-of condescension.

" Now, you'll be sure to find a nice place for him in the castle guard, won't you, Count Marlanx? " she said at the parting, her hopes as fresh as the daisy in the dew, her confidence supreme. The count promised faithfully, even eagerly. Colonel Quinnox, trained as he was in the diplomacy of silence, could scarcely conceal his astonishment at the conquest of the hard old warrior.

Although the afternoon was well spent before Beverly reached Ganlook, she was resolved to visit the obdurate patient at once, relying upon her resourcefulness to secure his promise to start with her for Edelweiss on the following morning. The coach delivered her at the hospital door in grand style. When the visitor was ushered into the snug little ante-

room of the governor's office, her heart was throbbing
and her composure was undergoing a most unusual
strain.   It annoyed her to discover that the approaching contact with an humble goat-hunter was giving
her such unmistakable symptoms of perturbation.

From an upstairs window in the hospital the con-
valescent but unhappy patient witnessed her approach
and arrival.   His sore, lonely heart gave a bound of
joy, for the days had seemed long since her departure.

He had had time to think during these days, too.
Turning over in his mind all of the details in connection with their meeting and their subsequent intercourse, it began to dawn upon him that she might not
be what she assumed to be.   Doubts assailed him, suspicions grew into amazing forms of certainty.   There
were times when he laughed sardonically at himself for
being taken in by this strange but charming young
woman, but through it all his heart and mind were
being drawn more and more fervently toward her.
More than once he called himself a fool and more
than once he dreamed foolish dreams of her — princess
or not.   Of one thing he was sure: he had come to
love the adventure for the sake of what it promised
and there was no bitterness beneath his suspicions.

Arrayed in clean linen and presentable clothes, pale
from indoor confinement and fever, but once more the
straight and strong cavalier of the hills, he hastened
into her presence when the summons came for him
to descend.   He dropped to his knee and kissed her
hand, determined to play the game, notwithstanding
his doubts.   As he arose she glanced for a flitting

second into his dark eyes, and her own long lashes drooped.

" Your highness! " he said gratefully.

" How well and strong you look," she said hurriedly. " Some of the tan is gone, but you look as though you had never been ill. Are you quite recovered? "

" They say I am as good as new," he smilingly answered. " A trifle weak and uncertain in my lower extremities, but a few days of exercise in the mountains will overcome all that. Is all well with you and Graustark? They will give me no news here, by whose order I do not know."

" Turn about is fair play, sir. It is a well-established fact that you will give *them* no news. Yes, all is well with me and mine. Were you beginning to think that I had deserted you? It has been two weeks, hasn't it? "

" Ah, your highness, I realize that you have had much more important things to do than to think of poor Baldos. I am exceedingly grateful for this sign of interest in my welfare. Your visit is the brightest experience of my life."

" Be seated! " she cried suddenly. " You are too ill to stand."

" Were I dying I should refuse to be seated while your highness stands," said he simply. His shoulders seemed to square themselves involuntarily and his left hand twitched as though accustomed to the habit of touching a sword-hilt. Beverly sat down instantly;

with his usual easy grace, he took a chair near by.
They were alone in the ante-chamber.

" Even though you were on your last legs? " she
murmured, and then wondered how she could have
uttered anything so inane.   Somehow, she was beginning to fear that he was not the ordinary person she
had judged him to be.   " You are to be discharged
from the hospital to-morrow," she added hastily.

" To-morrow? " he cried, his eyes lighting with joy.
" I may go then? "

" I have decided to take you to Edelweiss with me,"
she said, very much as if that were all there was to
it.   He stared at her for a full minute as though
doubting his ears.

" No! " he said, at last, his jaws settling, his eyes
glistening.   It was a terrible setback for Beverly's
confidence.   " Your highness forgets that I have your
promise of absolute freedom."

" But you are to be free," she protested: " You
have nothing to fear.   It is not compulsory, you
know.   You don't have to go unless you really want
to.   But my heart is set on having you in — in the
castle guard."   His bitter, mocking laugh surprised
and wounded her, which he was quick to see, for his
contrition was immediate.

" Pardon, your highness.   I am a rude, ungrateful
wretch, and I deserve punishment instead of reward.
The proposal was so astounding that I forgot myself
completely," he said.

Whereupon, catching him in this contrite mood, she
began a determined assault against his resolution.

For an hour she devoted her whole heart and soul to the task of overcoming his prejudices, fears and objections, meeting his protestations firmly and logically, unconscious of the fact that her very enthusiasm was betraying her to him. The first signs of weakening inspired her afresh and at last she was riding over him rough-shod, a happy victor. She made promises that Yetive herself could not have made; she offered inducements that never could be carried out, although in her zeal she did not know it to be so; she painted such pictures of ease, comfort and pleasure that he wondered why royalty did not exchange places with its servants. In the end, overcome by the spirit of adventure and a desire to be near her, he agreed to enter the service for six months, at the expiration of which time he was to be released from all obligations if he so desired.

" But my friends in the pass, your highness," he said in surrendering, " what is to become of them? They are waiting for me out there in the wilderness. I am not base enough to desert them."

" Can't you get word to them? " she asked eagerly. " Let them come into the city, too. We will provide for the poor fellows, believe me."

" That, at least, is impossible, your highness," he said, shaking his head sadly. " You will have to slay them before you can bring them within the city gates. My only hope is that Franz may be here to-night. He has permission to enter, and I am expecting him to-day or to-morrow."

" You can send word to them that you are sound

and safe and you can tell them that Graustark soldiers shall be instructed to pay no attention to them whatever. They shall not be disturbed." He laughed outright at her enthusiasm. Many times during her eager conversation with Baldos she had almost betrayed the fact that she was not the princess. Some of her expressions were distinctly unregal and some of her slips were hopeless, as she viewed them in retrospect.

"What am I? Only the humble goat-hunter, hunted to death and eager for a short respite. Do with me as you like, your highness. You shall be my princess and sovereign for six months, at least," he said, sighing. "Perhaps it is for the best."

"You are the strangest man I've ever seen," she remarked, puzzled beyond expression.

That night Franz appeared at the hospital and was left alone with Baldos for an hour or more. What passed between them, no outsider knew, though there were tears in the eyes of both at the parting. But Franz did not start for the pass that night, as they had expected. Strange news had come to the ears of the faithful old follower and he hung about Ganlook until morning came, eager to catch the ear of his leader before it was too late.

The coach was drawn up in front of the hospital at eight o'clock, Beverly triumphant in command. Baldos came down the steps slowly, carefully, favoring the newly healed ligaments in his legs. She smiled cheerily at him and he swung his rakish hat low. There was no sign of the black patch. Suddenly he started and peered intently into the little knot of people near the coach. A look of anxiety crossed his face. From the crowd advanced a grizzled old beggar who boldly extended his hand. Baldos grasped the proffered hand and then stepped into the coach. No one saw the bit of white paper that passed from Franz's palm into the possession of Baldos. Then the coach was off for Edelweiss, the people of Ganlook enjoying the unusual spectacle of a mysterious and apparently undistinguished stranger sitting in luxurious ease beside a fair lady in the royal coach of Graustark.

CHAPTER XII

IN SERVICE

T was a drowsy day, and, besides, Baldos was not in a communicative frame of mind. Beverly put forth her best efforts during the forenoon, but after the basket luncheon had been disposed of in the shade at the roadside, she was content to give up the struggle and surrender to the soothing importunities of the coach as it bowled along. She dozed peacefully, conscious to the last that he was a most ungracious creature and more worthy of resentment than of benefaction. Baldos was not intentionally disagreeable; he was morose and unhappy because he could not help it. Was he not leaving his friends to wander alone in the wilderness while he drifted weakly into the comforts and pleasures of an enviable service? His heart was not in full sympathy with the present turn of affairs, and he could not deny that a selfish motive was responsible for his action. He had the all too human eagerness to serve beauty; the blood and fire of youth were strong in this wayward nobleman of the hills.

Lying back in the seat, he pensively studied the face

of the sleeping girl whose dark-brown head was pillowed against the corner cushions of the coach. Her hat had been removed for the sake of comfort. The dark lashes fell like a soft curtain over her eyes, obscuring the merry gray that had overcome his apprehensions. Her breathing was deep and regular and peaceful. One little gloved hand rested carelessly in her lap, the other upon her breast near the delicate throat. The heart of Baldos was troubled. The picture he looked upon was entrancing, uplifting; he rose from the lowly state in which she had found him to the position of admirer in secret to a princess, real or assumed. He found himself again wondering if she were really Yetive, and with that fear in his heart he was envying Grenfall Lorry, the lord and master of this exquisite creature, envying with all the helplessness of one whose hope is blasted at birth.

The note which had been surreptitiously passed to him in Ganlook lay crumpled and forgotten inside his coat pocket, where he had dropped it the moment it had come into his possession, supposing that the message contained information which had been forgotten by Franz, and was by no means of a nature to demand immediate attention. Had he read it at once his suspicions would have been confirmed, and it is barely possible that he would have refused to enter the city.

Late in the afternoon the walls of Edelweiss were sighted. For the first time he looked upon the distant housetops of the principal city of Graustark. Up in the clouds, on the summit of the mountain peak over-

looking the city, stood the famed monastery of Saint
Valentine.   Stretching up the gradual incline were
the homes of citizens, accessible only by footpaths and
donkey roads.   Beverly was awake and impatient to
reach the journey's end.   He had proved a most disappointing companion, polite, but with a baffling
indifference that irritated her considerably.   There
was a set expression of defiance in his strong, clean-
cut face, the look of a soldier advancing to meet a
powerful foe.

" I do hope he'll not always act this way," she was
complaining in her thoughts.   " He was so charm-
ingly impudent out in the hills, so deliciously human.
Now he is like a clam.   Yetive will think I am such a
fool if he doesn't live up to the reputation I've given
him! "

" Here are the gates," he said, half to himself.
" What is there in store for me beyond those walls? "

" Oh, I wish you wouldn't be so dismal," she cried
in despair.   " It seems just like a funeral."

" A thousand apologies, your highness," he murmured, with a sudden lightness of speech and manner.   " Henceforth I shall be a most amiable jester,
to please you."

Beverly and the faithful Aunt Fanny were driven
to the castle, where the former bade farewell to her
new knight until the following morning, when he was
to appear before her for personal instructions.   Colonel Quinnox escorted him to the barracks of the guard,
where he was to share a room with young Haddan, a
corporal in the service.

"The wild, untamed gentleman from the hills came without a word, I see," said Lorry, who had watched the approach. He and Yetive stood in the window overlooking the grounds from the princess's boudoir. Beverly had just entered and thrown herself upon a divan.

"Yes, he's here," she said shortly.

"How long do you, with all your cleverness, expect to hoodwink him into the belief that you are the princess?" asked Yetive, amused but anxious.

"He's a great fool for being hoodwinked at all," said Beverly, very much at odds with her protégé. "In an hour from now he will know the truth and will be howling like a madman for his freedom."

"Not so soon as that, Beverly," said Lorry consolingly. "The guards and officers have their instructions to keep him in the dark as long as possible."

"Well, I'm tired and mad and hungry and everything else that isn't compatible. Let's talk about the war," said Beverly, the sunshine in her face momentarily eclipsed by the dark cloud of disappointment.

Baldos was notified that duty would be assigned to him in the morning. He went through the formalities which bound him to the service for six months, listening indifferently to the words that foretold the fate of a traitor. It was not until his new uniform and equipment came into his possession that he remembered the note resting in his pocket. He drew it out and began to read it with the slight interest of one who has anticipated the effect. But not for long was

he to remain apathetic.   The first few lines brought a
look of understanding to his eyes; then he laughed
the easy laugh of one who has cast care and confidence
to the winds.   This is what he read:

"She is nòt the princess.   We have been duped.   Last night I
learned the truth.   She is Miss Calhoun, an American, going to
be a guest at the castle.   Refuse to go with her into Edelweiss.
It may be a trap and may mean death.   Question her boldly
before committing yourself."

There came the natural impulse to make a dash for
the outside world, fighting his way through if necessary.   Looking back over the ground, he wondered
how he could have been deceived at all by the unconventional American.   In the clear light of retrospec-
tion he now saw how impossible it was for her to have
been the princess.   Every act, every word, every look
should have told him the truth.   Every flaw in her
masquerading now presented itself to him and he was
compelled to laugh at his own simplicity.   Caution,
after all, was the largest component part of his make-
up; the craftiness of the hunted was deeply rooted
in his being.   He saw a very serious side to the adventure.   Stretching himself upon the cot in the corner
of the room he gave himself over to plotting, planning, thinking.

In the midst of his thoughts a sudden light burst
in upon him.   His eyes gleamed with a new fire, his
heart leaped with new animation, his blood ran warm
again.   Leaping to his feet he ran to the window to
re-read the note from old Franz.   Then he settled
back and laughed with a fervor that cleared the brain
of a thousand vague misgivings.

" She is Miss Calhoun, an American going to be a guest at the castle," — not the princess, but *Miss* Calhoun. Once more the memory of the clear gray eyes leaped into life; again he saw her asleep in the coach on the road from Ganlook; again he recalled the fervent throbs his guilty heart had felt as he looked upon this fair creature, at one time the supposed treasure of another man. Now she was Miss Calhoun, and her gray eyes, her entrancing smile, her wondrous vivacity were not for one man alone. It was marvelous what a change this sudden realization wrought in the view ahead of him. The whole situation seemed to be transformed into something more desirable than ever before. His face cleared, his spirits leaped higher and higher with the buoyancy of fresh relief, his confidence in himself crept back into existence. And all because the fair deceiver, the slim girl with the brave gray eyes who had drawn him into a net, was not a princess!

Something told him that she had not drawn him into his present position with any desire to injure or with the slightest sense of malice. To her it had been a merry jest, a pleasant comedy. Underneath all he saw the goodness of her motive in taking him from the old life, and putting him into his present position of trust. He had helped her, and she was ready to help him to the limit of her power. His position in Edelweiss was clearly enough defined. The more he thought of it, the more justifiable it seemed as viewed from her point of observation. How long she hoped to keep him in the dark he could not tell. The outcome would be entertaining; her efforts to deceive, if she kept them up, would be amusing. Altogether, he was ready, with the leisure and joy of youth, to await developments and to enjoy the comedy from a point of view which she could not at once suspect.

His subtle efforts to draw Haddan into a discussion of the princess and her household resulted unsatisfactorily. The young guard was annoyingly unresponsive. He had his secret instructions and could not be inveigled into betraying himself. Baldos went to sleep that night with his mind confused by doubts. His talk with Haddan had left him quite undecided as to the value of old Franz's warning. Either Franz was mistaken, or Haddan was a most skilful dissembler. It struck him as utterly beyond the pale of reason that the entire castle guard should have been enlisted in the scheme to deceive him. When sleep came, he was contenting himself with the thought that morning doubtless would give him clearer insight to the situation.

Both he and Beverly Calhoun were ignorant of the true conditions that attached themselves to the new recruit. Baron Dangloss alone knew that Haddan was a trusted agent of the secret service, with instructions to shadow the newcomer day and night. That there was a mystery surrounding the character of Baldos, the goat-hunter, Dangloss did not question for an instant: and in spite of the instructions received at the outset, he was using all his skill to unravel it.

Baldos was not summoned to the castle until noon. His serene indifference to the outcome of the visit was calculated to deceive the friendly but watchful Haddan. Dressed carefully in the close-fitting uniform of the royal guard, taller than most of his fellows, handsomer by far than any, he was the most noticeable figure in and about the barracks. Haddan coached him in the way he was to approach the princess, Baldos listening with exaggerated intentness and with deep regard for detail.

Beverly was in the small audience-room off the main reception hall when he was ushered into her presence. The servants and ladies-in-waiting disappeared at a signal from her. She arose to greet him and he knelt to kiss her hand. For a moment her tongue was bound. The keen eyes of the new guard had looked into hers with a directness that seemed to penetrate her brain. That this scene was to be one of the most interesting in the little comedy was proved by the fact that two eager young women were hidden behind a heavy curtain in a corner of the room. The Princess Yetive and the Countess Dagmar were there to enjoy Beverly's first hour of authority, and she was aware of their presence.

" Have they told you that you are to act as my especial guard and escort? " she asked, with a queer flutter in her voice. Somehow this tall fellow with the broad shoulders was not the same as the ragged goat-hunter she had known at first.

" No, your highness," said he, easily. " I have come for instructions. It pleases me to know that I am to have a place of honor and trust such as this."

" General Marlanx has told me that a vacancy

exists, and I have selected you to fill it. The compensation will be attended to by the proper persons, and your duties will be explained to you by one of the officers. This afternoon, I believe, you are to accompany me on my visit to the fortress, which I am to inspect."

"Very well, your highness," he respectfully said. He was thinking of Miss Calhoun, an American girl, although he called her "your highness." "May I be permitted to ask for instructions that can come only from your highness?"

"Certainly," she replied. His manner was more deferential than she had ever known it to be, but he threw a bomb into her fine composure with his next remark. He addressed her in the Graustark language:

"Is it your desire that I shall continue to address you in English?"

Beverly's face turned a bit red and her eyes wavered. By a wonderful effort she retained her self-control, stammering ever so faintly when she said in English:

"I wish you would speak English," unwittingly giving answer to his question. "I shall insist upon that. Your English is too good to be spoiled."

Then he made a bold test, his first having failed. He spoke once more in the native tongue, this time softly and earnestly.

"As you wish, your highness, but I think it is a most ridiculous practice," he said, and his heart lost none of its courage. Beverly looked at him almost pathetically. She knew that behind the curtain two young women were enjoying her discomfiture. Something told her that they were stifling their mirth with dainty lace-bordered handkerchiefs.

"That will do, sir," she managed to say firmly. "It's very nice of you, but after this pay your homage in English," she went on, taking a long chance on his remark. It must have been complimentary, she reasoned. As for Baldos, the faintest sign of a smile touched his lips and his eyes were twinkling as he bent his head quickly. Franz was right; she did not know a word of the Graustark language.

"I have entered the service for six months, your highness," he said in English. "You have honored me, and I give my heart as well as my arm to your cause."

Beverly, breathing easier, was properly impressed by this promise of fealty. She was looking with pride upon the figure of her stalwart protégé.

"I hope you have destroyed that horrid black patch," she said.

"It has gone to keep company with other devoted but deserted friends," he said, a tinge of bitterness in his voice.

"The uniform is vastly becoming," she went on, realizing helplessly that she was providing intense amusement for the unseen auditors.

"It shames the rags in which you found me."

"I shall never forget them, Baldos," she said, with a strange earnestness in her voice.

"May I presume to inquire after the health of your good Aunt Fanny and — although I did not see him — your Uncle Sam? " he asked, with a face as straight and sincere as that of a judge. Beverly swallowed suddenly and checked a laugh with some difficulty.

" Aunt Fanny is never ill. Some day I shall tell you more of Uncle Sam. It will interest you."

" Another question, if it please your highness. Do you expect to return to America soon? "

This was the unexpected, but she met it with admirable composure.

" It depends upon the time when Prince Dantan resumes the throne in Dawsbergen," she said.

" And that day may never come," said he, such mocking regret in his voice that she looked upon him with newer interest.

" Why, I really believe you want to go to America," she cried.

The eyes of Baldos had been furtively drawn to the curtain more than once during the last few minutes. An occasional movement of the long oriental hangings attracted his attention. It dawned upon him that the little play was being overheard, whether by spies or conspirators he knew not. Resentment sprang up in his breast and gave birth to a daring that was as spectacular as it was confounding. With long, noiseless strides, he reached the door before Beverly could interpose. She half started from her chair, her eyes wide with dismay, her lips parted, but his hand was already clutching the curtain. He drew it aside relentlessly.

Two startled women stood exposed to view, smiles

"Your Highness," he said clearly, coolly, "I
fear we have spies and eavesdroppers here."

dying on their amazed faces. Their backs were against the closed door and two hands clutching handkerchiefs dropped from a most significant altitude. One of them flashed an imperious glance at the bold discoverer, and he knew he was looking upon the real princess of Graustark. He did not lose his composure. Without a tremor he turned to the American girl.

"Your highness," he said clearly, coolly, "I fear we have spies and eavesdroppers here. Is your court made up of — I should say, they are doubtless a pair of curious ladies-in-waiting. Shall I begin my service, your highness, by escorting them to yonder door?"

CHAPTER XIII

THE THREE PRINCES

EVERLY gasped. The countess stared blankly at the new guard. Yetive flushed deeply, bit her lip in hopeless chagrin, and dropped her eyes. A pretty turn, indeed, the play had taken! Not a word was uttered for a full half-minute; nor did the guilty witnesses venture forth from their retreat. Baldos stood tall and impassive, holding the curtain aside. At last the shadow of a smile crept into the face of the princess, but her tones were full of deep humility when she spoke.

"We crave permission to retire, your highness," she said, and there was virtuous appeal in her eyes. "I pray forgiveness for this indiscretion and implore you to be lenient with two miserable creatures who love you so well that they forget their dignity."

"I am amazed and shocked," was all that Beverly could say. "You may go, but return to me within an hour. I will then hear what you have to say."

Slowly, even humbly, the ruler of Graustark and her cousin passed beneath the upraised arm of the new guard. He opened a door on the opposite side of

144

the room, and they went out, to all appearance thoroughly crestfallen. The steady features of the guard did not relax for the fraction of a second, but his heart was thumping disgracefully.

" Come here, Baldos," commanded Beverly, a bit pale, but recovering her wits with admirable promptness. " This is a matter which I shall dispose of privately. It is to go no further, you are to understand."

" Yes, your highness."

" You may go now. Colonel Quinnox will explain everything," she said hurriedly. She was eager to be rid of him. As he turned away she observed a faint but peculiar smile at the corner of his mouth.

" Come here, sir! " she exclaimed hotly. He paused, his face as sombre as an owl's. " What do you mean by laughing like that? " she demanded. He caught the fierce note in her voice, but gave it the proper interpretation.

" Laughing, your highness? " he said in deep surprise. " You must be mistaken. I am sure that I could not have laughed in the presence of a princess."

" It must have been a — a shadow, then," she retracted, somewhat startled by his rejoinder. " Very well, then; you are dismissed."

As he was about to open the door through which he had entered the room, it swung wide and Count Marlanx strode in. Baldos paused irresolutely, and then proceeded on his way without paying the slightest attention to the commander of the army. Marlanx came to an amazed stop and his face flamed with resentment.

"Halt, sir!" he exclaimed harshly.   "Don't you know enough to salute me, sir?"

Baldos turned instantly, his figure straightening like a flash.   His eyes met those of the Iron Count and did not waver, although his face went white with passion.

"And who are you, sir?" he asked in cold, steely tones.   The count almost reeled.

"Your superior officer — that should be enough for you!" he half hissed with deadly levelness.

"Oh, then I see no reason why I should not salute you, sir," said Baldos, with one of his rare smiles.   He saluted his superior officer a shade too elaborately and turned away.   Marlanx's eyes glistened.

"Stop! Have I said you could go, sir? I have a bit of advice to —— "

"My command to go comes from *your* superior, sir," said Baldos, with irritating blandness.

"Be patient, general," cried Beverly in deep distress.   "He does not know any better.   I will stand sponsor for him."   And Baldos went away with a light step, his blood singing, his devil-may-care heart satisfied.   The look in her eyes was very sustaining. As he left the castle he said aloud to himself with an easy disregard of the consequences:

"Well, it seems that I am to be associated with the devil as well as with angels.   Heavens!   June is a glorious month."

"Now, you promised you'd be nice to him, General

Marlanx," cried Beverly the instant Baldos was out of the room. " He's new at this sort of thing, you know, and besides, you didn't address him very politely for an utter stranger."

" The insolent dog," snarled Marlanx, his self-control returning slowly. " He shall be taught well and thoroughly, never fear, Miss Calhoun. There is a way to train such recruits as he, and they never forget what they have learned."

" Oh, please don't be harsh with him," she pleaded. The smile of the Iron Count was not at all reassuring. " I know he will be sorry for what he has done, and you —— "

" I am quite sure he will be sorry," said he, with a most agreeable bow in submission to her appeal.

" Do you want to see Mr. Lorry? " she asked quickly. " I will send for him, general." She was at the door, impatient to be with the banished culprits.

" My business with Mr. Lorry can wait," he began, with a smile meant to be inviting, but which did not impress her at all pleasantly.

" Well, anyway, I'll tell him you're here," she said, her hand on the door-knob. " Will you wait here? Good-bye! " And then she was racing off through the long halls and up broad stair-cases toward the boudoir of the princess. There is no telling how long the ruffled count remained in the ante-room, for the excited Beverly forgot to tell Lorry that he was there.

There were half a dozen people in the room when Beverly entered eagerly. She was panting with ex-

"He positively refuses to let me dig," explained Beverly. "I tried, you know, but he — he — well, he squelched me."

"Well, after all is said and done, he caught us peeping to-day, and I am filled with shame," said the princess. "It doesn't matter who he is, he must certainly have a must unflattering opinion as to *what* we are."

"And he is sure to know us sooner or later," said the young countess, momentarily serious.

"Oh, if it ever comes to that I shall be in a splendid position to explain it all to him," said Beverly. "Don't you see, I'll have to do a lot of explaining myself?"

"Baron Dangloss!" announced the guard of the upper hall, throwing open the door for the doughty little chief of police.

"Your highness sent for me?" asked he, advancing after the formal salutation. The princess exhibited genuine amazement.

"I did, Baron Dangloss, but you must have come with the wings of an eagle. It is really not more than three minutes since I gave the order to Colonel Quinnox." The baron smiled mysteriously, but volunteered no solution. The truth is, he was entering the castle doors as the messenger left them, but he was much too fond of effect to spoil a good situation by explanations. It was a long two miles to his office in the Tower. "Something has just happened that impels me to ask a few questions concerning Baldos, the new guard."

" May I first ask what has happened? " Dangloss was at a loss for the meaning of the general smile that went around.

" It is quite personal and of no consequence. What do you know of him? My curiosity is aroused. Now, be quiet, Beverly; you are as eager to know as the rest of us."

" Well, your highness, I may as well confess that the man is a puzzle to me. He comes here a vagabond, but he certainly does not act like one. He admits that he is being hunted, but takes no one into his confidence. For that, he cannot be blamed."

" Have you any reason to suspect who he is? " asked Lorry.

" My instructions were to refrain from questioning him," complained Dangloss, with a pathetic look at the original plotters. " Still, I have made investigations along other lines."

" And who is he? " cried Beverly, eagerly.

" I don't know," was the disappointing answer. " We are confronted by a queer set of circumstances. Doubtless you all know that young Prince Dantan is flying from the wrath of his half-brother, our lamented friend Gabriel. He is supposed to be in our hills with a half-starved body of followers. It seems impossible that he could have reached our northern boundaries without our outposts catching a glimpse of him at some time. The trouble is that his face is unknown to most of us, I among the others. I have been going on the presumption that Baldos is in

reality Prince Dantan. But last night the belief received a severe shock."

"Yes?" came from several eager lips.

"My men who are watching the Dawsbergen frontier came in last night and reported that Dantan had
been seen by mountaineers no later than Sunday, three
days ago. These mountaineers were in sympathy
with him, and refused to tell whither he went. We
only know that he was in the southern part of Graustark three days ago. Our new guard speaks many
languages, but he has never been heard to use that of
Dawsbergen. That fact in itself is not surprising,
for, of all things, he would avoid his mother tongue.
Dantan is part English by birth and wholly so by
cultivation. In that he evidently finds a mate in
this Baldos."

"Then, he really isn't Prince Dantan?" cried
Beverly, as though a cherished ideal had been shattered.

"Not if we are to believe the tales from the south.
Here is another complication, however. There is, as
you know, Count Halfont, and perhaps all of you,
for that matter, a pretender to the throne of Axphain,
the fugitive Prince Frederic. He is described as
young, good looking, a scholar and the next thing to
a pauper."

"Baldos a mere pretender," cried Beverly in real
distress. "Never!"

"At any rate, he is not what he pretends to be,"
said the baron, with a wise smile.

" Then, you think he may be Prince Frederic? " asked Lorry, deeply interested.

" I am inclined to think so, although another complication has arisen. May it please your highness, I am in an amazingly tangled state of mind," admitted the baron, passing his hand over his brow.

" Do you mean that another mysterious prince has come to life? " asked Yetive, her eyes sparkling with interest in the revelations.

" Early this morning a despatch came to me from the Grand Duke Michael of Rapp-Thorberg, a duchy in western Europe, informing me that the duke's eldest son had fled from home and is known to have come to the far east, possibly to Graustark."

" Great Scott! " exclaimed Anguish. " It never rains but it hails, so here's hail to the princes three."

" We are the Mecca for runaway royalty, it seems," said Count Halfont.

" Go on with the story, Baron Dangloss," cried the princess. " It is like a book."

" A description of the young man accompanies the offer of a large reward for information that may lead to his return home for reconciliation. And —— " here the baron paused dramatically.

" And what? " interjected Beverly, who could not wait.

" The description fits our friend Baldos perfectly! "

" You don't mean it? " exclaimed Lorry. " Then, he may be any one of the three you have mentioned? "

" Let me tell you what the grand duke's secretary

says. I have the official notice, but left it in my desk. The runaway son of the grand duke is called Christobal. He is twenty-seven years of age, speaks English fluently, besides French and our own language. It seems that he attended an English college with Prince Dantan and some of our own young men who are still in England. Six weeks ago he disappeared from his father's home. At the same time a dozen wild and venturous retainers left the grand duchy. The party was seen in Vienna a week later, and the young duke boldly announced that he was off to the east to help his friend Dantan in the fight for his throne. Going on the theory that Baldos is this same Christobal, we have only to provide a reason for his preferring the wilds to the comforts of our cities. In the first place, he knows there is a large reward for his apprehension and he fears — our police. In the second place, he does not care to direct the attention of Prince Dantan's foes to himself. He missed Dantan in the hills and doubtless was lost for weeks. But the true reason for his flight is made plain in the story that was printed recently in Paris and Berlin newspapers. According to them, Christobal rebelled against his father's right to select a wife for him. The grand duke had chosen a noble and wealthy bride, and the son had selected a beautiful girl from the lower walks of life. Father and son quarreled and neither would give an inch. Christobal would not marry his father's choice, and the grand duke would not sanction his union with the fair plebeian."

Here Beverly exclaimed proudly, her face glowing: "He doesn't look like the sort of man who could be bullied into marrying anybody if he didn't want to."

"And he strikes me as the sort who would marry any one he set his heart upon having," added the princess, with a taunting glance at Miss Calhoun.

"Umph!" sniffed Beverly defiantly. The baron went on with his narrative, exhibiting signs of excitement.

"To lend color to the matter, Christobal's sweetheart, the daughter of a game-warden, was murdered the night before her lover fled. I know nothing of the circumstances attending the crime, but it is my understanding that Christobal is not suspected. It is possible that he is ignorant even now of the girl's fate."

"Well, by the gods, we have a goodly lot of heroes about us," exclaimed Lorry.

"But, after all," ventured the Countess Halfont, "Baldos may be none of these men."

"Good heavens, Aunt Yvonne, don't suggest anything so distressing," said Yetive. "He *must* be one of them."

"I suggest a speedy way of determining the matter," said Anguish. "Let us send for Baldos and ask him point blank who he is. I think it is up to him to clear away the mystery."

"No!" cried Beverly, starting to her feet.

"It seems to be the only way," said Lorry.

"But I promised him that no questions should be

asked," said Beverly, almost tearfully but quite resolutely. "Didn't I, Yet — your highness?"

"Alas, yes!" said the princess, with a pathetic little smile of resignation, but with loyalty in the clasp of her hand.

CHAPTER XIV.

A VISIT AND ITS CONSEQUENCES

HAT same afternoon Baldos, blissfully ignorant of the stir he had created in certain circles, rode out for the first time as a member of the Castle Guard. He and Haddan were detailed by Colonel Quinnox to act as private escort to Miss Calhoun until otherwise ordered. If Haddan thought himself wiser than Baldos in knowing that their charge was not the princess, he was very much mistaken; if he enjoyed the trick that was being played on his fellow guardsman, his enjoyment was as nothing as compared to the pleasure Baldos was deriving from the situation. The royal victoria was driven to the fortress, conveying the supposed princess and the Countess Dagmar to the home of Count Marlanx. The two guards rode bravely behind the equipage, resplendent in brilliant new uniforms. Baldos was mildly surprised and puzzled by the homage paid the young American girl. It struck him as preposterous that the entire population of Edelweiss could be in the game to deceive him.

"Who is the princess's companion?" he inquired of Haddan, as they left the castle grounds.

" The Countess Dagmar, cousin to her highness. She is the wife of Mr. Anguish."

" I have seen her before," said Baldos, a strange smile on his face.

The Countess Dagmar found it difficult at first to meet the eye of the new guard, but he was so punctiliously oblivious that her courage was restored. She even went so far as to whisper in Beverly's ear that he did not remember her face, and probably would not recognize Yetive as one of the eavesdroppers. The princess had flatly refused to accompany them on the visit to the fortress because of Baldos. Struck by a sudden impulse, Beverly called Baldos to the side of the vehicle.

" Baldos, you behaved very nicely yesterday in exposing the duplicity of those young women," she said.

" I am happy to have pleased your highness," he said steadily.

" It may interest you to know that they ceased to be ladies-in-waiting after that exposure."

" Yes, your highness, it certainly is interesting," he said, as he fell back into position beside Haddan. During the remainder of the ride he caught himself time after time gazing reflectively at the back of her proud little head, possessed of an almost uncontrollable desire to touch the soft brown hair.

" You can't fool that excellent young man much longer, my dear," said the countess, recalling the look in his dark eyes. The same thought had been afflicting Beverly with its probabilities for twenty-four hours and more.

Count Marlanx welcomed his visitors with a graciousness that awoke wonder in the minds of his staff. His marked preference for the American girl did not escape attention. Some of the bolder young officers indulged in surreptitious grimaces, and all looked with more or less compassion upon the happy-faced beauty from over the sea. Marlanx surveyed Baldos steadily and coldly, deep disapproval in his sinister eyes. He had not forgotten the encounter of the day before.

"I see the favorite is on guard," he said blandly. "Has he told you of the lesson in manners he enjoyed last night?" He was leading his guests toward the quarters, Baldos and Haddan following. The new guard could not help hearing the sarcastic remark.

"You didn't have him beaten?" cried Beverly, stopping short.

"No, but I imagine it would have been preferable. I *talked* with him for half an hour," said the general, laughing significantly.

When the party stopped at the drinking-fountain in the center of the fort, Baldos halted near by. His face was as impassive as marble, his eyes set straight before him, his figure erect and soldierly. An occasional sarcastic remark by the Iron Count, meant for his ears, made no impression upon the deadly composure of the new guard who had had his *lesson*. Miss Calhoun was conscious of a vague feeling that she had served Baldos an ill-turn when she put him into this position.

The count provided a light luncheon in his quarters after the ladies had gone over the fortress. Beverly Calhoun, with all of a woman's indifference to things material, could not but see how poorly equipped the fort was as compared to the ones she had seen in the United States. She and the countess visited the armory, the arsenal, and the repair shops before luncheon, reserving the pleasures of the clubhouse, the officers' quarters, and the parade-ground until afterwards. Count Marlanx's home was in the southeast corner of the enclosure, near the gates. Several of the officers lunched with him and the young ladies. Marlanx was assiduous in his attention to Beverly Calhoun — so much so, in fact, that the countess teased her afterwards about her conquest of the old and well-worn heart. Beverly thought him extremely silly and sentimental, much preferring him in the character of the harsh, implacable martinet.

At regular intervals she saw the straight, martial form of Baldos pass the window near which she sat. He was patrolling the narrow piazza which fronted the house. Toward the close of the rather trying luncheon she was almost unable to control the impulse to rush out and compel him to relax that imposing, machine-like stride. She hungered for a few minutes of the old-time freedom with him.

The Iron Count was showing her some rare antique bronzes he had collected in the south. The luncheon was over and the countess had strolled off toward the bastions with the young officers, leaving Beverly alone with the host. Servants came in to clear the tables, but the count harshly ordered them to wait until the guests had departed.

" It is the dearest thing I have seen," said Beverly, holding a rare old candlestick at arm's length and looking at it in as many ways as the wrist could turn. Her loose sleeves ended just below the elbows. The count's eyes followed the graceful curves of her white forearm with an eagerness that was annoying.

" I prize it more dearly than any other piece in my collection," he said. " It came from Rome; it has a history which I shall try to tell you some day, and which makes it almost invaluable. A German nobleman offered me a small fortune if I would part with it."

" And you wouldn't sell it? "

" I was saving it for an occasion, your highness," he said, his steely eyes glittering. " The glad hour has come when I can part with it for a recompense far greater than the baron's gold."

" Oh, isn't it lucky you kept it? " she cried. Then she turned her eyes away quickly, for his gaze seemed greedily endeavoring to pierce through the lace insertion covering her neck and shoulders. Outside the window the steady tramp of the tall guard went on monotonously.

" The recompense of a sweet smile, a tender blush and the unguarded thanks of a pretty woman. The candlestick is yours, Miss Calhoun,— if you will repay me for my sacrifice by accepting it without reservation."

Slowly Beverly Calhoun set the candlestick down

upon the table, her eyes meeting his with steady disdain.

" What a rare old jester you are, Count Marlanx,"
she said without a smile. " If I thought you were in
earnest I should scream with laughter. May I suggest that we join the countess? We must hurry
along, you know. She and I have promised to play
tennis with the princess at three o'clock." The
count's glare of disappointment lasted but a moment.
The diplomacy of egotism came to his relief, and he
held back the gift for another day, but not for another
woman.

" It grieves me to have you hurry away. My afternoon is to be a dull one, unless you permit me to
watch the tennis game," he said.

" I thought you were interested only in the game
of war," she said pointedly.

" I stand in greater awe of a tennis ball than I do
of a cannonball, if it is sent by such an arm as yours,"
and he not only laid his eyes but his hand upon her
bare arm. She started as if something had stung
her, and a cold shiver raced over her warm flesh. His
eyes for the moment held her spellbound. He was
drawing the hand to his lips when a shadow darkened the French window, and a saber rattled warn-
ingly.

Count Marlanx looked up instantly, a scowl on his
face. Baldos stood at the window in an attitude of
alert attention. Beverly drew her arm away spasmodically and took a step toward the window. The
guard saw by her eyes that she was frightened, but,

if his heart beat violently, his face was the picture of military stoniness.

"What are you doing there?" snarled the count.

"Did your highness call?" asked Baldos coolly.

"She did not call, fellow," said the count with deadly menace in his voice. "Report to me in half an hour. You still have something to learn, I see." Beverly was alarmed by the threat in his tones. She saw what was in store for Baldos, for she knew quite as well as Marlanx that the guard had deliberately intervened in her behalf.

"He cannot come in half an hour," she cried quickly. "I have something for him to do, Count Marlanx. Besides, I think I *did* call." Both men stared at her.

"My ears are excellent," said Marlanx stiffly.

"I fancy Baldos's must be even better, for he heard me," said Beverly, herself once more. The shadow of a smile crossed the face of the guard.

"He is impertinent, insolent, your highness. You will report to me to-morrow, sir, at nine o'clock in Colonel Quinnox's quarters. Now, go!" commanded the count.

"Wait a minute, Baldos. We are going out, too. Will you open that window for me?" Baldos gladly took it as a command and threw open the long French window. She gave him a grateful glance as she stepped through, and he could scarcely conceal the gleam of joy that shot into his own eyes. The dark scowl on the count's face made absolutely no impres-

sion upon him.   He closed the window and followed
ten paces behind the couple.

"Your guard is a priceless treasure," said the
count grimly.

"That's what you said about the candlestick," said
she sweetly.

She was disturbed by his threat to reprimand
Baldos.   For some time her mind had been struggling
with what the count had said about "the lesson."
It grew upon her that her friend had been bullied
and humiliated, perhaps in the presence of spectators.
Resentment fired her curiosity into action.   While the
general was explaining one of the new gun-carriages
to the countess, Beverly walked deliberately over to
where Baldos was standing.   Haddan's knowledge of
English was exceedingly limited, and he could understand but little of the rapid conversation.   Standing
squarely in front of Baldos, she questioned him in
low tones.

"What did he mean when he said he had given you
a lesson?" she demanded.   His eyes gleamed merrily.

"He meant to alarm your highness."

"Didn't he give you a talking to?"

"He coached me in ethics."

"You are evading the question, sir.   Was he mean
and nasty to you?   Tell me; I want to know."

"Well, he said things that a soldier must endure.
A civilian or an equal might have run him through
for it, your highness."   A flush rose to his cheeks
and his lips quivered ever so slightly.   But Beverly
saw and understood.   Her heart was in her eyes.

" That settles it," she said rigidly. " You are not to report to him at nine to-morrow."

" But he will have me shot, your highness," said he gladly.

" He will do nothing of the kind. You are *my* guard," and her eyes were gleaming dangerously. Then she rejoined the group, the members of which had been watching her curiously. " Count Marlanx," she said, with entrancing dimples, " will you report to me at nine to-morrow morning? "

" I have an appointment," he said slowly, but with understanding.

" But you will break it, I am sure," she asserted confidently. " I want to give you a lesson in — in lawn tennis."

Later on, when the victoria was well away from the fort, Dagmar took her companion to task for holding in public friendly discourse with a member of the guard, whoever he might be.

" It is altogether contrary to custom, and——" but Beverly put her hand over the critical lips and smiled like a guilty child.

" Now, don't scold," she pleaded, and the countess could go no further.

The following morning Count Marlanx reported at nine o'clock with much better grace than he had suspected himself capable of exercising. What she taught him of tennis on the royal courts, in the presence of an amused audience, was as nothing to what he learned of strategy as it can be practiced by a whimsical girl. Almost before he knew it she had won exemption for Baldos, that being the stake for the first set of singles. To his credit, the count was game. He took the wager, knowing that he, in his ignorance, could not win from the blithe young expert in petticoats. Then he offered to wager the brass candlestick against her bracelet. She considered for a moment and then, in a spirit of enthusiasm, accepted the proposition. After all, she coveted the candlestick. Half an hour later an orderly was riding to the fort with instructions to return at once with Miss Calhoun's candlestick. It is on record that they were "love" sets, which goes to prove that Beverly took no chances.

Count Marlanx, puffing and perspiring, his joints dismayed and his brain confused, rode away at noon with Baron Dangloss. Beverly, quite happy in her complete victory, enjoyed a nap of profound sweetness and then was ready for her walk with the princess. They were strolling leisurely about the beautiful grounds, safe in the shade of the trees from the heat of the July sun, when Baron Dangloss approached.

"Your royal highness," he began, with his fierce smile, "may I beg a moment's audience?"

"It has to do with Baldos, I'll take oath," said Beverly, with conviction.

"Yes, with your guard. Yesterday he visited the fortress. He went in an official capacity, it is true, but he was privileged to study the secrets of our defense with alarming freedom. It would not surprise me to find that this stranger has learned everything there is to know about the fort." His listeners were silent. The smiles left their faces. "I am not saying that he would betray us —— "

"No, no!" protested Beverly.

"—— but he is in a position to give the most valuable information to an enemy. An officer has just informed me that Baldos missed not a detail in regard to the armament, or the location of vital spots in the construction of the fortress."

"But he wouldn't be so base as to use his knowledge to our undoing," cried Yetive seriously.

"We only know that he is not one of us. It is not beyond reason that his allegiance is to another power, Dawsbergen, for instance. Count Marlanx is not at all in sympathy with him, you are aware. He is convinced that Baldos is a man of consequence, possibly one of our bitterest enemies, and he hates him. For my own part, I may say that I like the man. I believe he is to be trusted, but if he be an agent of Volga or Gabriel, his opportunity has come. He is in a position to make accurate maps of the fort and of all our masked fortifications along the city walls." Beyond a doubt, the baron was worried.

"Neither am I one of you," said Beverly stoutly. "Why shouldn't I prove to be a traitress?"

"You have no quarrel with us, Miss Calhoun," said Dangloss.

"If anything happens, then, I am to be blamed for it," she cried in deep distress. "I brought him to Edelweiss, and I believe in him."

"For his own sake, your highness, and Miss Calhoun, I suggest that no opportunity should be given him to communicate with the outside world. We cannot accuse him, of course, but we can *protect* him. I come to ask your permission to have him detailed for duty only in places where no suspicion can attach to any of his actions."

" You mean inside the city walls? " asked Yetive.

" Yes, your highness, and as far as possible from the fortress."

" I think it is a wise precaution. Don't be angry, Beverly," the princess said gently. " It is for his own sake, you see. I am acting on the presumption that he is wholly innocent of any desire to betray us."

" It would be easy for someone high in position to accuse and convict him," said Dangloss meaningly.

" And it would be just like someone, too," agreed Beverly, her thoughts, with the others', going toward none but one man " high in power."

Later in the day she called Baldos to her side as they were riding in the castle avenue. She was determined to try a little experiment of her own.

" Baldos, what do you think of the fortress? " she asked.

" I could overthrow it after half an hour's bombardment, your highness," he answered, without thinking. She started violently.

" Is it possible? Are there so many weak points? " she went on, catching her breath.

" There are three vital points of weakness, your highness. The magazine can be reached from the outside if one knows the lay of the land; the parade-ground exposes the ammunition building to certain disadvantages, and the big guns could be silenced in an hour if an enemy had the sense first to bombard from the elevation northeast of the city."

"Good heavens!" gasped poor Beverly. "Have you studied all this out?"

"I was once a *real* soldier, your highness," he said, simply. "It was impossible for me not to see the defects in your fort."

"You —— you haven't told anyone of this, have you?" she cried, white-faced and anxious.

"No one but your highness. You do not employ me as a tale-bearer, I trust."

"I did not mean to question your honor," she said. "Would you mind going before the heads of the war department and tell them just what you have told me? I mean about the weak spots."

"If it is your command, your highness," he said quietly, but he was surprised.

"You may expect to be summoned then, so hold yourself in readiness. And, Baldos —— ".

"Yes, your highness?"

"You need say nothing to them of our having talked the matter over beforehand — unless they pin you down to it, you know."

CHAPTER XV.

THE TESTING OF BALDOS

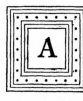FEW hours later, all was dark and silent within the castle. On the stone walks below, the steady tread of sentinels rose on the still air; in the hallways the trusted guardsmen glided about like spectres or stood like statues. An hour before the great edifice had been bright and full of animation; now it slumbered.

It was two o'clock. The breath of roses scented the air, the gurgle of fountains was the only music that touched the ear. Beverly Calhoun, dismissing Aunt Fanny, stepped from her window out upon the great stone balcony. A rich oriental dressing-gown, loose and comfortable, was her costume. Something told her that sleep would be a long time coming, and an hour in the warm, delightful atmosphere of the night was more attractive than the close, sleepless silence of her own room. Every window along the balcony was dark, proving that the entire household had retired to rest.

She was troubled. The fear had entered her head that the castle folk were regretting the advent of

Baldos, that everyone was questioning the wisdom of his being in the position he occupied through her devices. Her talk with him did much to upset her tranquillity. That he knew so much of the fortress bore out the subtle suspicions of Dangloss and perhaps others. She was troubled, not that she doubted him, but that if anything went wrong an accusation against him, however unjust, would be difficult to overcome. And she would be to blame, in a large degree.

For many minutes she sat in the dark shadow of a great pillar, her elbows upon the cool balustrade, staring dreamily into the star-studded vault above. Far away in the air she could see the tiny yellow lights of the monastery, lonely sentinel on the mountain top. From the heights near that abode of peace and penitence an enemy could destroy the fortress to the south. Had not Baldos told her so? One big gun would do the work if it could be taken to that altitude. Baldos could draw a perfect map of the fortress. He could tell precisely where the shells should fall. And already the chief men in Edelweiss were wondering who he was and to what end he might utilize his knowledge. They were watching him, they were warning her.

For the first time since she came to the castle, she felt a sense of loneliness, a certain unhappiness. She could not shake off the feeling that she was, after all, alone in her belief in Baldos. Her heart told her that the tall, straightforward fellow she had met in the hills was as honest as the day. She was deceiv-

ing him, she realized, but he was misleading no one.
Off in a distant part of the castle ground she could
see the long square shadow that marked the location
of the barracks and messroom. There he was sleeping, confidently believing in her and her power to
save him from all harm. Something in her soul cried
out to him that she would be staunch and true, and
that he might sleep without a tremor of apprehensive-
ness.

Suddenly she smiled nervously and drew back into
the shadow of the pillar. It occurred to her that he
might be looking across the moon-lit park, looking
directly at her through all that shadowy distance.
She was conscious of a strange glow in her cheeks and
a quickening of the blood as she pulled the folds of
her gown across her bare throat.

" Not the moon, nor the stars, nor the light in St.
Valentine's, but the black thing away off there on
the earth," said a soft voice behind her, and Beverly
started as if the supernatural had approached her.
She turned to face the princess, who stood almost
at her side.

" Yetive! How did you get here? "

" That is what you are looking at, dear," went on
Yetive, as if completing her charge. " Why are you
not in bed? "

" And you? I thought you were sound asleep long
ago," murmured Beverly, abominating the guilty
feeling that came over her. The princess threw her
arm about Beverly's shoulder.

" I have been watching you for half an hour,"

she said gently. " Can't two look at the moon and
stars as well as one? Isn't it my grim old castle?
Let us sit here together, dear, and dream awhile."

" You dear Yetive," and Beverly drew her down
beside her on the cushions. " But, listen: I want
you to get something out of your head. I was *not*
looking at anything in particular."

" Beverly, I believe you were thinking of Baldos,"
said the other, her fingers straying fondly across the
girl's soft hair.

" Ridiculous! " said Beverly, conscious for the first
time that he was seldom out of her thoughts. The
realization came like a blow, and her eyes grew very
wide out there in the darkness.

" And you are troubled on his account. I know
it, dear. You —— "

" Well, Yetive, why shouldn't I be worried? I
brought him here against his will," protested Beverly.
" If anything should happen to him —— " she shuddered involuntarily.

" Don't be afraid, Beverly. I have as much confidence in him as you have. His eyes are true. Grenfall believes in him, too, and so does Mr. Anguish.
Gren says he would swear by him, no matter who
he is."

" But the others? " Beverly whispered.

" Baron Dangloss is his friend, and so is Quinnox. They know a *man*. The count is different."

" I loathe that old wretch! "

" Hush! He has not wronged you in any way."

" But he *has* been unfair and mean to Baldos."

" It is a soldier's lot, my dear."

" But he may be Prince Dantan or Frederic or
the other one, don't you know," argued Beverly,
clenching her hands firmly.

" In that event, he would be an honorable soldier,
and we have nothing to fear in him.   Neither of them
is our enemy.   It is the possibility that he is not one
of them that makes his presence here look dangerous."

" I don't want to talk about him," said Beverly,
but she was disappointed when the princess oblig-
ingly changed the subject.

Baldos was not surprised, scarcely more than interested, when a day or two later, he was summoned to
appear before the board of strategy.   If anyone had
told him, however, that on a recent night a pair of
dreamy gray eyes had tried to find his window in the
great black shadow, he might have jumped in amazement and — delight.   For at that very hour he was
looking off toward the castle, and his thoughts were of
the girl who drew back into the shadow of the pillar.

The Graustark ministry had received news from
the southern frontier.   Messengers came in with the
alarming and significant report that Dawsbergen was
strengthening her fortifications in the passes and
moving war supplies northward.   It meant that
Gabriel and his people expected a fight and were preparing for it.   Count Halfont hastily called the
ministers together, and Lorry and the princess took
part in their deliberations.   General Marlanx represented the army; and it was he who finally asked to
have Baldos brought before the council.   The Iron

Count plainly intimated that the new guard was in a position to transmit valuable information to the enemy. Colonel Quinnox sent for him, and Baldos was soon standing in the presence of Yetive and her advisers. He looked about him with a singular smile. The one whom he was supposed to regard as the princess was not in the council chamber. Lorry opened the examination at the request of Count Halfont, the premier. Baldos quietly answered the questions concerning his present position, his age, his term of enlistment, and his interpretations of the obligations required of him.

"Ask him who he really is," suggested the Iron Count sarcastically.

"We can expect but one answer to that question," said Lorry, "and that is the one which he chooses to give."

"My name is Baldos — Paul Baldos," said the guard, but he said it in such a way that no one could mistake his appreciation of the fact that he could give one name as well as another and still serve his own purposes.

"That is lie number one," observed Marlanx loudly. Every eye was turned upon Baldos, but his face did not lose its half-mocking expression of serenity.

"Proceed with the examination, Mr. Lorry," said Count Halfont, interpreting a quick glance from Yetive.

"Are you willing to answer any and all questions we may ask in connection with your observations since

you became a member of the castle guard? " asked
Lorry.

" I am."

" Did you take especial care to study the interior
of the fortress when you were there several days
ago? "

" I did."

" Have you discussed your observations with anyone since that time? "

" I have."

" With whom? "

" With her highness, the princess," said Baldos,
without a quiver. There was a moment's silence, and
furtive looks were cast in the direction of Yetive,
whose face was a study. Almost instantaneously the
entire body of listeners understood that he referred
to Beverly Calhoun. Baldos felt that he had been
summoned before the board at the instigation of his
fair protectress.

" And your impressions have gone no further? "

" They have not, sir. It was most confidential."

" Could you accurately reproduce the plans of the
fortress? "

" I think so. It would be very simple."

" Have you studied engineering? "

" Yes."

" And you could scientifically enumerate the defects in the construction of the fort? "

" It would not be very difficult, sir."

" It has come to our ears that you consider the fortress weak in several particulars. Have you so stated at any time?"

"I told the princess that the fortress is deplorably weak. In fact, I think I mentioned that it could be taken with ease." He was not looking at Count Marlanx, but he knew that the old man's eyes were flaming. Then he proceeded to tell the board how he could overcome the fortress, elaborating on his remarks to Beverly. The ministers listened in wonder to the words of this calm, indifferent young man.

"Will you oblige us by making a rough draft of the fort's interior?" asked Lorry, after a solemn pause. Baldos took the paper and in remarkably quick time drew the exact lay of the fortress. The sketch went the rounds and apprehensive looks were exchanged by the ministers.

"It is accurate, by Jove," exclaimed Lorry. "I doubt if a dweller in the fort could do better. You must have been very observing."

"And very much interested," snarled Marlanx.

"Only so far as I imagined my observations might be of benefit to someone else," said Baldos coolly. Again the silence was like death.

"Do you know what you are saying, Baldos?" asked Lorry, after a moment.

"Certainly, Mr. Lorry. It is the duty of any servant of her highness to give her all that he has in him. If my observations can be of help to her, I feel in duty bound to make the best of them for her sake, not for my own."

"Perhaps you can suggest modifications in the

fort," snarled Marlanx. "Why don't you do it, sir, and let us have the benefit of your superior intelligence? No, gentlemen, all this prating of loyalty need not deceive us," he cried, springing to his feet. "The fellow is nothing more nor less than an infernal spy — and the Tower is the place for him! He can do no harm there."

"If it were my intention to do harm, gentlemen, do you imagine that I should withhold my information for days?" asked Baldos. "If I am a spy, you may rest assured that Count Marlanx's kindnesses should not have been so long disregarded. A spy does not believe in delays."

"My — my kindnesses?" cried Marlanx. "What do you mean, sir?"

"I mean this, Count Marlanx," said Baldos, looking steadily into the eyes of the head of the army. "It was kind and considerate of you to admit me to the fortress — no matter in what capacity, especially at a critical time like this. You did not know me, you had no way of telling whether my intentions were honest or otherwise, and yet I was permitted to go through the fort from end to end. No spy could wish for greater generosity than that."

An almost imperceptible smile went round the table, and every listener but one breathed more freely. The candor and boldness of the guard won the respect and confidence of all except Marlanx. The Iron Count was white with anger. He took the examination out of Lorry's hands, and plied the stranger with insulting questions, each calm answer making him

more furious than before. At last, in sheer impotence, he relapsed into silence, waving his hand
to Lorry to indicate that he might resume.

"You will understand, Baldos, that we have some
cause for apprehension," said Lorry, immensely gratified by the outcome of the tilt.   "You are a stranger;
and, whether you admit it or not, there is reason to
believe that you are not what you represent yourself
to be."

"I am a humble guard at present, sir, and a loyal
one. My life is yours should I prove otherwise."

Yetive whispered something in Lorry's ear at this
juncture. She was visibly pleased and excited. He
looked doubtful for an instant, and then apparently
followed her suggestion, regardless of consequences.

"Would you be willing to utilize your knowledge
as an engineer by suggesting means to strengthen
the fortress?"   The others stared in fresh amazement. Marlanx went as white as death.

"Never!" he blurted out hoarsely.

"I will do anything the princess commands me
to do," said Baldos easily.

"You mean that you serve her only?"

"I serve her first, sir. If she were here she could
command me to die, and there would be an end to
Baldos," and he smiled as he said it. The real princess looked at him with a new, eager expression, as if
something had just become clear to her. There was
a chorus of coughs and a round of sly looks.

"She could hardly ask you to die," said Yetive,
addressing him for the first time.

"A princess is like April weather, madam," said Baldos, with rare humor, and the laugh was general. Yetive resolved to talk privately with this excellent wit before the hour was over. She was confident that he knew her to be the princess.

"I would like to ask the fellow another question," said Marlanx, fingering his sword-hilt nervously. "You say you serve the princess. Do you mean by that that you imagine your duties as a soldier to comprise dancing polite attendance within the security of these walls?"

"I believe I enlisted as a member of the castle guard, sir. The duty of the guard is to protect the person of the ruler of Graustark, and to do that to the death."

"It is my belief that you are a spy. You can show evidence of good faith by enlisting to *fight* against Dawsbergen and by shooting to kill," said the count, with a sinister gleam in his eye.

"And if I decline to serve in any other capacity than the one I now —— "

"Then I shall brand you as a spy and a coward."

"You have already called me a spy, your excel·lency. It will not make it true, let me add, if you call me a coward. I refuse to take up arms against either Dawsbergen or Axphain."

The remark created a profound sensation.

"Then you are employed by both instead of one!" shouted the Iron Count gleefully.

"I am employed as a guard for her royal highness," said Baldos, with a square glance at Yetive, "and not as a fighter in the ranks. I will fight till death for her, but not for Graustark."

CHAPTER XVI

ON THE WAY TO ST. VALENTINE'S

Y Jove, I like that fellow's coolness," said Lorry to Harry Anguish, after the meeting. " He's after my own heart. Why, he treats us as though we were the suppliants, he the almsgiver. He is playing a game, I'll admit, but he does it with an assurance that delights me."

" He is right about that darned old fort," said Anguish. " His knowledge of such things proves conclusively that he is no ordinary person."

" Yetive had a bit of a talk with him just now," said Lorry, with a reflective smile. " She asked him point blank if he knew who she was. He did not hesitate a second. 'I remember seeing you in the audience chamber recently.' That was a facer for Yetive. 'I assure you that it was no fault of mine that you saw me,' she replied. 'Then it must have been your friend who rustled the curtains?' said the confounded bluffer. Yetive couldn't keep a straight face. She laughed and then he laughed. 'Some day you may learn more about me,' she said to him. 'I sincerely trust that I may, madam,' said he, and

181

I'll bet my hat he was enjoying it better than either of us. Of course, he knows Yetive is the princess. It's his intention to serve Beverly Calhoun, and he couldn't do it if he were to confess that he knows the truth. He's no fool."

Baldos was not long in preparing plans for the changes in the fortress. They embodied a temporary readjustment of the armament and alterations in the ammunition house. The gate leading to the river was closed and the refuse from the fort was taken to the barges by way of the main entrance. There were other changes suggested for immediate consideration, and then there was a general plan for the modernizing of the fortress at some more convenient time. Baldos laconically observed that the equipment was years behind the times. To the amazement of the officials, he was able to talk intelligently of forts in all parts of the world, revealing a wide and thorough knowledge and extensive inspection. He had seen American as well as European fortifications. The Graustark engineers went to work at once to perfect the simple changes he advised, leaving no stone unturned to strengthen the place before an attack could be made.

Two, three weeks went by and the new guard was becoming an old story to the castle and army folk. He rode with Beverly every fair day and he looked at her window by night from afar off in the sombre barracks. She could not dissipate the feeling that he knew her to be other than the princess, although he betrayed himself by no word or sign. She was en-

joying the fun of it too intensely to expose it to
the risk of destruction by revealing her true identity
to him. Logically, that would mean the end of
everything. No doubt he felt the same and kept his
counsel. But the game could not last forever, that
was certain. A month or two more, and Beverly
would have to think of the return to Washington.

His courage, his cool impudence, his subtle wit
charmed her more than she could express. Now she
was beginning to study him from a standpoint pecul-
iarly and selfishly her own. Where recently she had
sung his praises to Yetive and others, she now was
strangely reticent. She was to understand another
day why this change had come over her. Stories
of his cleverness came to her ears from Lorry and
Anguish and even from Dangloss. She was proud,
vastly proud of him in these days. The Iron Count
alone discredited the ability and the conscientiousness
of the " mountebank," as he named the man who had
put his nose out of joint. Beverly, seeing much of
Marlanx, made the mistake of chiding him frankly
and gaily about this aversion. She even argued
the guard's case before the head of the army, im-
prudently pointing out many of his superior quali-
ties in advocating his cause. The count was learn-
ing forbearance in his old age. He saw the wisdom
of procrastination. Baldos was in favor, but some
day there would come a time for his undoing.

In the barracks he was acquiring fame. Reports
went forth with unbiased freedom. He established
himself as the best swordsman in the service, as well

as the most efficient marksman. With the foils and
sabers he easily vanquished the foremost fencers in
high and low circles. He could ride like a Cossack
or like an American cowboy. Of them all, his warm-
est admirer was Haddan, the man set to watch him
for the secret service. It may be timely to state
that Haddan watched in vain.

The princess, humoring her own fancy as well as
Beverly's foibles, took to riding with her high-spir-
ited young guest on many a little jaunt to the hills.
She usually rode with Lorry or Anguish, cheerfully
assuming the subdued position befitting a lady-in-
waiting apparently restored to favor on probation. She enjoyed Beverly's unique position. In
order to maintain her attitude as princess, the fair
young deceiver was obliged to pose in the extremely
delectable attitude of being Lorry's wife.

" How can you expect the paragon to make love
to you, dear, if he thinks you are another man's
wife? " Yetive asked, her blue eyes beaming with the
fun of it all.

" Pooh! " sniffed Beverly. " You have only to
consult history to find the excuse. It's the dear old
habit of men to make love to queens and get beheaded
for it. Besides, he is not expected to make love to
me. How in the world did you get that into your
head? "

On a day soon after the return of Lorry and Anguish from a trip to the frontier, Beverly expressed
a desire to visit the monastery of St. Valentine, high
on the mountain top. It was a long ride over the

circuitous route by which the steep incline was avoided and it was necessary for the party to make an early start. Yetive rode with Harry Anguish and his wife the countess, while Beverly's companion was the gallant Colonel Quinnox. Baldos, relegated to the background, brought up the rear with Haddan.

For a week or more Beverly had been behaving toward Baldos in the most cavalier fashion. Her friends had been teasing her; and, to her own intense amazement, she resented it. The fact that she felt the sting of their sly taunts was sufficient to arouse in her the distressing conviction that he had become important enough to prove embarrassing. While confessing to herself that it was a bit treacherous and weak, she proceeded to ignore Baldos with astonishing persistency. Apart from the teasing, it seemed to her of late that he was growing a shade too confident.

He occasionally forgot his differential air, and relaxed into a very pleasing but highly reprehensible state of friendliness. A touch of the old jauntiness cropped out here and there, a tinge of the old irony marred his otherwise perfect mien as a soldier. His laugh was freer, his eyes less under subjugation, his entire personality more arrogant. It was time, thought she resentfully, that his temerity should meet some sort of check.

And, moreover, she had dreamed of him two nights in succession.

How well her plan succeeded may best be illustrated by saying that she now was in a most uncom-

fortable frame of mind.   Baldos refused to be properly depressed by his misfortune.   He retired to the
oblivion she provided and seemed disagreeably content.   Apparently, it made very little difference to
him whether he was in or out of favor.   Beverly
was in high dudgeon and low spirits.

The party rode forth at an early hour in the morning.   It was hot in the city, but it looked cold and
bleak on the heights.   Comfortable wraps were taken
along, and provision was made for luncheon at an
inn half way up the slope.   Quinnox regaled Beverly
with stories in which Grenfall Lorry was the hero and
Yetive the heroine.   He told her of the days when
Lorry, a fugitive with a price upon his head, charged
with the assassination of Prince Lorenz, then betrothed to the princess, lay hidden in the monastery
while Yetive's own soldiers hunted high and low for
him.   The narrator dwelt glowingly upon the trip
from the monastery to the city walls one dark night
when Lorry came down to surrender himself in order
to shield the woman he loved, and Quinnox himself
piloted him through the underground passage into
the very heart of the castle.   Then came the exciting scene in which Lorry presented himself as a
prisoner, with the denouement that saved the princess
and won for the gallant American the desire of his
heart.

"What a brave fellow he was!" cried Beverly, who
never tired of hearing the romantic story.

"Ah, he was wonderful, Miss Calhoun.   I fought
him to keep him from surrendering.   He beat me,

and I was virtually his prisoner when we appeared before the tribunal."

" It's no wonder she loved him and — married him."

" He deserved the best that life could give, Miss Calhoun."

" You had better not call me Miss Calhoun, Colonel Quinnox," said she, looking back apprehensively. " I am a highness once in a while, don't you know? "

" I implore your highness's pardon! " said he gaily.

The riders ahead had come to a standstill and were pointing off into the pass to their right. They were eight or ten miles from the city gates and more than half way up the winding road that ended at the monastery gates. Beverly and Quinnox came up with them and found all eyes centered on a small company of men encamped in the rocky defile a hundred yards from the main road.

It needed but a glance to tell her who comprised the unusual company. The very raggedness of their garments, the unforgetable disregard for consequences, the impudent ease with which they faced poverty and wealth alike, belonged to but one set of men — the vagabonds of the Hawk and Raven. Beverly went a shade whiter; her interest in everything else flagged, and she was lost in bewilderment. What freak of fortune had sent these men out of the fastnesses into this dangerously open place?

She recognized the ascetic Ravone, with his student's face and beggar's garb. Old Franz was there,

and so were others whose faces and heterogeneous garments had become so familiar to her in another day.
The tall leader with the red feather, the rakish hat
and the black patch alone was missing from the picture.

"It's the strangest-looking crew I've ever seen,"
said Anguish. "They look like pirates."

"Or gypsies," suggested Yetive. "Who are they,
Colonel Quinnox? What are they doing here?"
Quinnox was surveying the vagabonds with a critical,
suspicious eye.

"They are not robbers or they would be off like
rabbits," he said reflectively. "Your highness, there
are many roving bands in the hills, but I confess that
these men are unlike any I have heard about. With
your permission, I will ride down and question them."

"Do, Quinnox. I am most curious."

Beverly sat very still and tense. She was afraid
to look at Baldos, who rode up as Quinnox started
into the narrow defile, calling to the escort to follow. The keen eyes of the guard caught the situation at once. Miss Calhoun shot a quick glance at
him as he rode up beside her. His face was impassive, but she could see his hand clench the bridle-
rein, and there was an air of restraint in his whole
bearing.

"Remember your promise," he whispered hoarsely.
"No harm must come to them." Then he was off
into the defile. Anguish was not to be left behind.
He followed, and then Beverly, more venturesome and
vastly more interested than the others, rode recklessly

after.   Quinnox was questioning the laconic Ravone
when she drew rein.   The vagabonds seemed to evince
but little interest in the proceedings.   They stood
away in disdainful aloofness.   No sign of recogni-
tion passed between them and Baldos.

In broken, jerky sentences, Ravone explained to
the colonel that they were a party of actors on their
way to Edelweiss, but that they had been advised to
give the place a wide berth.   Now they were making
the best of a hard journey to Serros, where they
expected but little better success.   He produced certain papers of identification which Quinnox examined
and approved, much to Beverly's secret amazement.
The princess and the colonel exchanged glances and
afterwards a few words in subdued tones.   Yetive
looked furtively at Beverly and then at Baldos as if
to enquire whether these men were the goat-hunters
she had come to know by word of mouth.   The two
faces were hopelessly non-committal.

Suddenly Baldos's horse reared and began to
plunge as if in terror, so that the rider kept his seat
only by means of adept horsemanship.   Ravone
leaped forward and at the risk of injury clutched the
plunging steed by the bit.   Together they partially
subdued the animal and Baldos swung to the ground
at Ravone's side.   Miss Calhoun's horse in the meantime had caught the fever.   He pranced off to the
roadside before she could get him under control.

She was thus in a position to observe the two men
on the ground.   Shielded from view by the body of
the horse, they were able to put the finishing touches

to the trick Baldos had cleverly worked. Beverly distinctly saw the guard and the beggar exchange bits of paper, with glances that meant more than the words they were unable to utter.

Baldos pressed into Ravone's hand a note of some bulk and received in exchange a mere slip of paper. The papers disappeared as if by magic, and the guard was remounting his horse before he saw that the act had been detected. The expression of pain and despair in Beverly's face sent a cold chill over him from head to foot.

She turned sick with apprehension. Her faith had received a stunning blow. Mutely she watched the vagabonds withdraw in peace, free to go where they pleased. The excursionists turned to the main road. Baldos fell back to his accustomed place, his imploring look wasted. She was strangely, inexplicably depressed for the rest of the day.

CHAPTER XVII

A NOTE TRANSLATED

S HE was torn by conflicting emotions. That the two friends had surreptitiously exchanged messages, doubtless by an arrangement perfected since he had entered the service — possibly within the week — could not be disputed. When and how had they planned the accidental meeting? What had been their method of communication? And, above all, what were the contents of the messages exchanged? Were they of a purely personal nature, or did they comprehend injury to the principality of Graustark? Beverly could not, in her heart, feel that Baldos was doing anything inimical to the country he served, and yet her duty and loyalty to Yetive made it imperative that the transaction should be reported at once. A word to Quinnox and Ravone would be seized and searched for the mysterious paper. This, however, looked utterly unreasonable, for the vagabonds were armed and in force, while Yetive was accompanied by but three men who could be depended upon. Baldos, under the conditions, was not to be reckoned upon for support. On the other hand, if he meant no harm, it would be cruel, even fatal, to expose him to this charge of duplicity. And while she turned these troublesome alternatives over in her mind, the opportunity to act was lost. Ravone and his men were gone, and the harm, if any was intended, was done.

From time to time she glanced back at the guard. His face was imperturbable, even sphinx-like in its steadiness. She decided to hold him personally to account. At the earliest available moment she would demand an explanation of his conduct, threatening him if necessary. If he proved obdurate there was but one course left open to her. She would deliver him up to the justice he had outraged. Hour after hour went by, and Beverly suffered more than she could have told. The damage was done, and the chance to undo it was slipping farther and farther out of her grasp. She began to look upon herself as the vilest of traitors. There was no silver among the clouds that marred her thoughts that afternoon.

It was late in the day when the party returned to the castle, tired out. Beverly was the only one who had no longing to seek repose after the fatiguing trip. Her mind was full of unrest. It was necessary to question Baldos at once. There could be no peace for her until she learned the truth from him. The strain became so great that at last she sent word for him to attend her in the park. He was to accompany the men who carried the sedan chair in which she had learned to sit with a delightful feeling of being in the eighteenth century.

In a far corner of the grounds, now gray in the

early dusk, Beverly bade the bearers to set down her chair and leave her in quiet for a few minutes. The two men withdrew to a respectful distance, whereupon she called Baldos to her side. Her face was flushed with anxiety.

"You must tell me the truth about that transaction with Ravone," she said, coming straight to the point.

"I was expecting this, your highness," said he quietly. The shadows of night were falling, but she could distinguish the look of anxiety in his dark eyes.

"Well?" she insisted impatiently.

"You saw the notes exchanged?"

"Yes, yes, and I command you to tell me what they contained. It was the most daring thing I —— "

"You highness, I cannot tell you what passed between us. It would be treacherous," he said firmly. Beverly gasped in sheer amazement.

"Treacherous? Good heaven, sir, to whom do you owe allegiance — to me or to Ravone and that band of tramps?" she cried, with eyes afire.

"To both, your highness," he answered so fairly that she was for the moment abashed. "I am loyal to you — loyal to the heart's core, and yet I am loyal to that unhappy band of tramps, as you choose to call them. They are my friends. You are only my sovereign."

"And you won't tell me what passed between you?" she said, angered by this epigrammatic remark.

"I cannot and be true to myself."

"Oh, you are a glorious soldier," she exclaimed, with fierce sarcasm in her voice. "You speak of being true! I surprise you in the very act of ——"

"Stay, your highness!" he said coldly. "You are about to call me a spy and a traitor. Spare me, I implore you, that humiliation. I have sworn to serve you faithfully and loyally. I have not deceived you, and I shall not. Paul Baldos has wronged no man, no woman. What passed between Ravone and myself concerns us only. It had nothing to do with the affairs of Graustark."

"Of course you would say that. You wouldn't be fool enough to tell the truth," cried she hotly. "I am the fool! I have trusted you and if anything goes wrong I alone am to blame for exposing poor Graustark to danger. Oh, why didn't I cry out this afternoon?"

"I knew you would not," he said, with cool unconcern.

"Insolence! What do you mean by that?" she cried in confusion.

"In your heart you knew I was doing no wrong. You shielded me then as you have shielded me from the beginning."

"I don't see why I sit here and let you talk to me like that," she said, feeling the symptoms of collapse. "You have not been fair with me, Baldos. You are laughing at me now and calling me a witless little fool. You — you did something to-day that shakes my faith to the very bottom. I never can trust you again. Good heaven, I hate to confess to — to everyone that you are not honest."

"Your highness!" he implored, coming close to

the chair and bending over her. "Before God, I am honest with you. Believe me when I say that I have done nothing to injure Graustark. I cannot tell you what it was that passed between Ravone and me, but I swear on my soul that I have not been disloyal to my oath. Won't you trust me? Won't you believe?" His breath was fanning her ear, his voice was eager; she could feel the intensity of his eyes.

"Oh, I don't — don't know what to say to you," she murmured. "I have been so wrought up with fear and disappointment. You'll admit that it was very suspicious, won't you?" she cried, almost pleadingly.

"Yes, yes," he answered. His hand touched her arm, perhaps unconsciously. She threw back her head to give him a look of rebuke. Their eyes met, and after a moment both were full of pleading. Her lips parted, but the words would not come. She was afterwards more than thankful for this, because his eyes impelled her to give voice to amazing things that suddenly rushed to her head.

"I want to believe you," she whispered softly.

"You must — you do! I would give you my life. You have it now. It is in your keeping, and with it my honor. Trust me, I beseech you. I have trusted you."

"I brought you here ——" she began, defending him involuntarily. "But, Baldos, you forget that I am the princess!" She drew away in sudden shyness, her cheeks rosy once more, her eyes filling with the most distressingly unreasonable tears. He did not move for what seemed hours to her. She heard the sharp catch of his breath and felt the repression that was mastering some unwelcome emotion in him.

Lights were springing into existence in all parts of the park. Beverly saw the solitary window in the monastery far away, and her eyes fastened on it as if for sustenance in this crisis of her life — this moment of surprise — this moment when she felt *him* laying hands upon the heart she had not suspected of treason. Twilight was upon them; the sun had set and night was rushing up to lend unfair advantage to the forces against which they were struggling. The orchestra in the castle was playing something soft and tender — oh, so far away.

" I forget that I am a slave, your highness," he said at last, and his voice thrilled her through and through. She turned quickly and to her utter dismay found his face and eyes still close to hers, glowing in the darkness.

" Those men — over there," she whispered helplessly. " They are looking at you!"

" Now, I thank God eternally," he cried softly. " You do not punish me, you do not rebuke me. God, there is no night!"

" You — you must not talk like that," she cried, pulling herself together suddenly. " I cannot permit it, Baldos. You forget who you are, sir."

" Ah, yes, your highness," he said, before he stood erect. " I forget that I was a suspected traitor. Now I am guilty of *lèse majesté*." Beverly felt herself grow hot with confusion.

" What am I to do with you? " she cried in perplexity, her heart beating shamefully. " You swear
you are honest, and yet you won't tell me the truth.
Now, don't stand like that! You are as straight
as a ramrod, and I know your dignity is terribly
offended. I may be foolish, but I *do* believe you intend no harm to Graustark. You *cannot* be a
traitor."

" I will some day give my life to repay you for
those words, your highness," he said. Her hand was
resting on the side of the chair. Something warm
touched it, and then it was lifted resistlessly. Hot,
passionate lips burned themselves into the white fingers, and a glow went into every fiber of her body.

" Oh! " was all she could say. He gently released
the hand and threw up his chin resolutely.

" I am *almost* ready to die," he said. She laughed
for the first time since they entered the park.

" I don't know how to treat you," she said in a
helpless flutter. " You know a princess has many
trials in life."

" Not the least of which is womanhood."

" Baldos," she said after a long pause. Something
very disagreeable had just rushed into her brain.
" Have you been forgetting all this time that the
Princess Yetive is the wife of Grenfall Lorry? "

" It has never left my mind for an instant. From
the bottom of my heart I congratulate him. His
wife is an angel as well as a princess."

" Well, in the code of morals, is it quite proper to
be so *loyal* to another man's wife? " she asked, and

then she trembled. He was supposed to know her as the wife of Grenfall Lorry, and yet he had boldly shown his love for her.

"It depends altogether on the other man's wife," he said, and she looked up quickly. It was too dark to see his face, but something told her to press the point no further. Deep down in her heart she was beginning to rejoice in the belief that he had found her out. If he still believed her to be the real princess, then he was — but the subject of conversation, at least, had to be changed.

"You say your message to Ravone was of a purely personal nature," she said.

"Yes, your highness." She did not like the way in which he said "your highness." It sounded as if he meant it.

"How did you know that you were to see him to-day?"

"We have waited for this opportunity since last week. Franz was in the castle grounds last Thursday."

"Good heavens! You don't mean it!"

"Yes, your highness. He carried a message to me from Ravone. That is why Ravone and the others waited for me in the hills."

"You amaze me!"

"I have seen Franz often," he confessed easily. "He is an excellent messenger."

"So it would seem. We must keep a lookout for him. He is the go-between for you all, I see."

"Did you learn to say 'you all' in America?"

he asked. Her heart gave a great leap. There was
something so subtle in the query that she was vastly
relieved.

"Never mind about that, sir. You won't tell me
what you said in your note to Ravone."

"I cannot."

"Well, he gave you one in return. If you are perfectly sincere, Baldos, you will hand that note over
to me. It shall go no farther, I swear to you, if, as
you vow, it does not jeopardize Graustark. Now,
sir, prove your loyalty and your honesty."

He hesitated for a long time. Then from an inner
pocket he drew forth a bit of paper.

"I don't see why it has not been destroyed," he
said regretfully. "What a neglectful fool I have
been!"

"You might have said it had been destroyed," she
said, happy because he had not said it.

"But that would have been a lie. Read it, your
highness, and return it to me. It must be destroyed."

"It is too dark to read it here." Without a word
he handed the paper to her and called the chair bearers, to whom he gave instructions that brought her
speedily beneath one of the park lamps. She afterwards recalled the guilty impulse which forced her
to sit on the tell-tale note while the men were carrying her along in the driveway. When it was quite
safe she slyly opened the missive. His hand closed
over hers, and the note, and he bent close once more.

"My only fear is that the test will make it impossible for me to kiss your hand again," said he in a strained voice.   She looked up in surprise.

" Then it is really something disloyal? "

" I have called it a test, your highness," he responded enigmatically.

" Well, we'll see," she said, and forthwith turned her eyes to the all-important paper. A quick flush crossed her brow; her eyes blinked hopelessly. The note was written in the Graustark language!

" I'll read it later, Baldos. This is no place for me to be reading notes, don't you know? Really, it isn't. I'll give it back to you to-morrow," she was in haste to say.

An inscrutable smile came over his face.

" Ravone's information is correct, I am now convinced," he said slowly. " Pray, your highness, glance over it now, that I may destroy it at once," he persisted.

" The light isn't good."

" It seems excellent."

" And I never saw such a miserable scrawl as this. He must have written it on horseback and at full gallop."

" It is quite legible, your highness."

" I really cannot read the stuff. You know his handwriting. Read it to me. I'll trust you to read it carefully."

" This is embarrassing, your highness, but I obey, of course, if you command. Here is what Ravone says:

" 'We have fresh proof that she is not the princess, but the

American girl. Be exceedingly careful that she does not lead you into any admissions. The Americans are tricky. Have little to say to her, and guard your tongue well. We are all well and are hoping for the best.'"

CHAPTER XVIII

CONFESSIONS AND CONCESSIONS

EVERLY was speechless.

"Of course, your highness," said Baldos, deep apology in his voice, "Ravone is woefully misinformed. He is honest in his belief, and you should not misjudge his motives. How he could have been so blind as to confound you with that frisky American girl — but I beg your pardon. She is to be your guest. A thousand pardons, your highness."

She had been struck dumb by the wording of the note, but his apparently sincere apology for his friend set her every emotion into play once more. While he was speaking, her wits were forming themselves for conflict. She opened the campaign with a bold attack. "You — you believe me to be the princess, sure 'nough, don't you?" But with all her bravery, she was not able to look him in the face.

"How can you doubt it, your highness? Would I be serving you in the present capacity if I believed you to be anyone else?"

"Ravone's warning has not shaken your faith in me?"

"It has strengthened it. Nothing could alter the facts in the case. I have not, since we left Ganlook, been in doubt as to the identity of my benefactress."

"It seems to me that you are beating around the bush. I'll come straight to the point. How long have you known that I am not the princess of Graustark?"

"What!" he exclaimed, drawing back in well-assumed horror. "Do you mean — are you jesting? I beg of you, do not jest. It is very serious with me." His alarm was so genuine that she was completely deceived.

"I am not jesting," she half whispered, turning very cold. "Have you thought all along that I am the princess — that I am Grenfall Lorry's wife?"

"You told me that you were the princess."

"But I've never said that I was — was anyone's wife."

There was a piteous appeal in her voice and he was not slow to notice it and rejoice. Then his heart smote him.

"But what is to become of me if you are not the princess?" he asked after a long pause. "I can no longer serve you. This is my last day in the castle guard."

"You are to go on serving me — I mean you are to retain your place in the service," she hastened to say. "I shall keep my promise to you." How small and humble she was beginning to feel. It did not seem so entertaining, after all, this pretty deception of hers. Down in his heart, underneath the gal-

lant exterior, what was his opinion of her? Some·
thing was stinging her eyes fiercely, and she closed
them to keep back the tears of mortification.

"Miss Calhoun," he said, his manner changing
swiftly, "I have felt from the first that you are not
the princess of Graustark. I *knew* it an hour after I
entered Edelweiss. Franz gave me a note at Ganlook, but I did not read it until I was a member of the
guard."

"You have known it so long?" she cried joyously.
"And you have trusted me? You have not hated me
for deceiving you?"

"I have never ceased to regard you as *my*
sovereign," he said softly.

"But just a moment ago you spoke of me as a
frisky American girl," she said resentfully.

"I have used that term but once, while I have said
'your highness' a thousand times. Knowing that
you were Miss Calhoun, I could not have meant
either."

"I fancy I have no right to criticise you," she
humbly admitted. "After all, it does not surprise
me that you were not deceived. Only an imbecile
could have been fooled all these weeks. Everyone
said that you were no fool. It seems ridiculous that
it should have gone to this length, doesn't it?"

"Not at all, your highness. I am not ——"

"You have the habit, I see," she smiled.

"I have several months yet to serve as a member
of the guard. Besides, I am under orders to regard

you as the princess. General Marlanx has given me severe instructions in that respect."

"You are willing to play the game to the end?" she demanded, more gratified than she should have been.

"Assuredly, yes. It is the only safeguard I have. To alter my belief publicly would expose me to — to —— "

"To what, Baldos?"

"To ridicule, for one thing, and to the generous mercies of Count Marlanx. Besides, it would deprive me of the privilege I mentioned a moment ago — the right to kiss your hand, to be your slave and to do homage to the only sovereign I can recognize. Surely, you will not subject me to exile from the only joys that life holds for me. You have sought to deceive me, and I have tried to deceive you. Each has found the other out, so we are quits. May we not now combine forces in the very laudable effort to deceive the world? If the world doesn't know that we know, why, the comedy may be long drawn out and the climax be made the more amusing."

"I'm afraid there was a touch of your old-time sarcasm in that remark," she said. "Yes, I am willing to continue the comedy. It seems the safest way to protect you — especially from General Marlanx. No one must ever know, Baldos; it would be absolutely pitiful. I am glad, oh, so glad, that you have known all the time. It relieves my mind and my conscience tremendously."

"Yes," he said gently; "I have known all along

that you were not Mr. Lorry's wife." He had divined her thought and she flushed hotly. "You are still a princess, however. A poor goat-hunter can only look upon the rich American girl as a sovereign whom he must worship from far below."

"Oh, I'm not so rich as all that," she cried. "Besides, I think it is time for a general clearing-up of the mysteries. Are you Prince Dantan, Prince Frederic, or that other one — Christobal somebody? Come, be fair with me."

"It seems that all Edelweiss looks upon me as a prince in disguise. You found me in the hills ——"

"No; you found me. I have not forgotten, sir."

"I was a vagabond and a fugitive. My friends are hunted as I am. We have no home. Why everyone should suspect me of being a prince I cannot understand. Every roamer in the hills is not a prince. There is a price upon my head, and there is a reward for the capture of every man who was with me in the pass. My name is Paul Baldos, Miss Calhoun. There is no mystery in that. If you were to mention it in a certain city, you would quickly find that the name of Baldos is not unknown to the people who are searching for him. No, your highness, I regret exceedingly that I must destroy the absurd impression that I am of royal blood. Perhaps I am spoiling a pretty romance, but it cannot be helped. I was Baldos, the goat-hunter; I am now Baldos, the guard. Do you think that I would be serving as a Graustark guard if I were any one of the men you mention?"

Beverly listened in wonder and some disappointment, it must be confessed. Somehow a spark of hope was being forever extinguished by this straightforward denial. He was not to be the prince she had seen in dreams. "You are not like anyone else," she said. "That is why we thought of you as — as — as —— "

"As one of those unhappy creatures they call princes? Thank fortune, your highness, I am not yet reduced to such straits. My exile will come only when you send me away."

They were silent for a long time. Neither was thinking of the hour, or the fact that her absence in the castle could not be unnoticed. Night had fallen heavily upon the earth. The two faithful chair-bearers, respectful but with wonder in their souls, stood afar off and waited. Baldos and Beverly were alone in their own little world.

"I think I liked you better when you wore the red feather and that horrid patch of black," she said musingly.

"And was a heart-free vagabond," he added, something imploring in his voice.

"An independent courtier, if you please, sir," she said severely.

"Do you want me to go back to the hills? I have the patch and the feather, and my friends are —— "

"No! Don't suggest such a thing — yet." She began the protest eagerly and ended it in confusion.

"Alas, you mean that some day banishment is not unlikely?"

" You don't expect to be a guard all your life, do you? "

" Not to serve the princess of Graustark, I confess. My aim is much higher. If God lets me choose the crown I would serve, I shall enlist for life. The crown I would serve is wrought of love, the throne I would kneel before is a heart, the sceptre I would follow is in the slender hand of a woman. I could live and die in the service of my own choosing. But I am only the humble goat-hunter whose hopes are phantoms, whose ideals are conceived in impotence."

" That was beautiful," murmured Beverly, looking up, fascinated for the moment.

" Oh, that I had the courage to enlist," he cried, bending low once more. She felt the danger in his voice, half tremulous with something more than loyalty, and drew her hand away from a place of instant jeopardy. It was fire that she was playing with, she realized with a start of consciousness. Sweet as the spell had grown to be, she saw that it must be shattered.

" It is getting frightfully late," she sharply exclaimed. " They'll wonder where I've gone to. Why, it's actually dark."

" It has been dark for half an hour, your highness," said he, drawing himself up with sudden rigidness that distressed her. " Are you going to return to the castle? "

" Yes. They'll have out a searching party pretty soon if I don't appear."

" You have been good to me to-day," he said

"That was beautiful," murmured Beverly, looking up, fascinated for the moment.

thoughtfully. " I shall try to merit the kindness. Let me ——"

" Oh, please don't talk in that humble way! It's ridiculous! I'd rather have you absolutely imperti-nent, I declare upon my honor I would. Don't you remember how you talked when you wore the red feather? Well, I liked it."

Baldos laughed easily, happily. His heart was not very humble, though his voice and manner were.

" Red is the color of insolence, you mean."

" It's a good deal jauntier than blue," she declared.

" Before you call the bearers, Miss — your high-ness, I wish to retract something I said awhile ago," he said very seriously.

" I should think you would," she responded, utterly misinterpreting his intent.

" You asked me to tell you what my message to Ravone contained and I refused. Subsequently the extent of his message to me led us into a most thor-ough understanding. It is only just and right that you should know what I said to him."

" I trust you, Baldos," she protested simply.

" That is why I tell this to you. Yesterday, your highness, the castle guard received their month's pay. You may not know how well we are paid, so I will say that it is ten gavvos to each. The envelope which I gave to Ravone contained my wages for the past six weeks. They need it far more than I do. There was also a short note of good cheer to those poor comrades of mine, and the assurance that one day our luck may change and starvation be succeeded by plenty. And, still more, I told him that I knew you to be Miss Calhoun and that you were my angel of inspiration. That was all, your highness."

" Thank you, Baldos, for telling me," she said softly. " You have made me ashamed of myself."

" On the contrary, I fear that I have been indulging in mock heroics. Truth and egotism — like a salad — require a certain amount of dressing."

" Since you are Baldos, and not a fairy prince, I think you may instruct the men to carry me back, being without the magic tapestry which could transplant me in a whiff. Goodness, who's that? "

Within ten feet of the sedan chair and directly behind the tall guard stood a small group of people. He and Beverly, engrossed in each other, had not heard their approach. How long they had been silent spectators of the little scene only the intruders knew. The startled, abashed eyes of the girl in the chair were not long in distinguishing the newcomers. A pace in front of the others stood the gaunt, shadowy form of Count Marlanx.

Behind him were the Princess Yetive, the old prime minister, and Baron Dangloss.

CHAPTER XIX

THE NIGHT FIRES

HY, good evening. Is that you?" struggled somewhat hysterically through Beverly's lips. Not since the dear old days of the stolen jam and sugar-bits had she known the feelings of a culprit caught red-handed. The light from the park lamps revealed a merry, accusing smile on the face of Yetive, but the faces of the men were serious. Marlanx was the picture of suppressed fury.

"It is the relief expedition, your highness," said Yetive warmly. "We thought you were lost in the wilds of the jungle."

"She is much better protected than we could have imagined," said the Iron Count, malevolently mild and polite.

"Can't I venture into the park without being sent for?" asked Beverly, ready to fly into the proper rage. The pink had left her cheeks white. "I am proud to observe, however, that the relief expedition is composed of the most distinguished people in all Graustark. Is there any significance to be attached to the circumstance?"

"Can't we also go strolling in the park, my dear?" plaintively asked Yetive.

"It depends upon where we stroll, I fancy," suggested Marlanx derisively. Beverly flashed a fierce look at the head of the army. "By the way, Baron Dangloss, where is the incomparable Haddan?"

Baldos shot a startled glance at the two men and in an instant comprehension came to him. He knew the secret of Haddan's constant companionship. An expression of bitter scorn settled upon his mouth. Dangloss mumbled a reply, at which the Iron Count laughed sarcastically.

"I am returning to the castle," said Beverly coldly. "Pray don't let me interfere with your stroll. Or is it possible that you think it necessary to deliver me safely to my nurse, now that you have found me?"

"Don't be angry, dear," whispered Yetive, coming close to her side. "I will tell you all about it later on. It was all due to Count Marlanx."

"It was all done to humiliate me," replied Beverly, indignation surpassing confusion at last. "I hate all of you."

"Oh, Beverly!" whispered the princess, in distress.

"Well, perhaps *you* were led into it," retracted Beverly, half mollified. "Look at that old villain whispering over there. No wonder his wives up and died. They just *had* to do it. I hate all but you and Count Halfont and Baron Dangloss," which left but one condemned.

"And Baldos?" added Yetive, patting her hand.

"I wish you'd be sensible," cried Beverly, most un-

graciously, and Yetive's soft laugh ' irritated her.
" How long had you been listening to us? "

" Not so much as the tiniest part of a minute,"
said Yetive, recalling another disastrous eavesdropping. " I am much wiser than when Baldos first came
to serve you. We were quite a distance behind Count
Marlanx, I assure you."

" Then *he* heard something? " asked Beverly anxiously.

" He has been in a detestable mood ever since we
rejoined him. Could he have heard anything disagreeable? "

" No; on the contrary, it was quite agreeable."

All this time Baldos was standing at attention a few
paces off, a model soldier despite the angry shifting
of his black eyes. He saw that they had been caught
in a most unfortunate position. No amount of explaining could remove the impression that had been
forced upon the witnesses, voluntary or involuntary
as the case might be. Baldos could do nothing to
help her, while she was compelled to face the suspicions
of her best friends. At best it could be considered
nothing short of a clandestine meeting, the consequences of which she must suffer, not he. In his
heated brain he was beginning to picture scandal
with all the disgusting details that grow out of evil
misrepresentation.

Count Halfont separated himself from the group
of three and advanced to the sedan-chair. Marlanx
and Dangloss were arguing earnestly in low tones.

" Shall we return, your highness? " asked Halfont,

addressing both with one of his rarest smiles. " If
I remember aright, we were to dine *en famille* to-night,
and it is well upon the hour.   Besides, Count Marlanx
is a little distressed by your absent-mindedness, Miss
Beverly, and I fancy he is eager to have it out with
you."

" My absent-mindedness?   What is it that I have
forgotten? " asked Beverly, puckering her brow.

" That's the trouble, dear," said Yetive.   " You
forgot your promise to teach him how to play that
awful game called poker.   He has waited for you at
the castle since six o'clock.   It is now eight.   Is it
any wonder that he led the searching party?   He has
been on nettles for an hour and a half."

" Goodness, I'll wager he's in a temper! " exclaimed
Beverly, with no remorse, but some apprehension.

" It would be wisdom to apologize to him," suggested Yetive, and her uncle nodded earnestly.

" All right.   I think I can get him into good humor
without half trying.   Oh, Count Marlanx!   Come
here, please.   You aren't angry with me, are you?
Wasn't it awful for me to run away and leave you to
play solitaire instead of poker?   But, don't you know,
I was so wretchedly tired after the ride, and I knew
you wouldn't mind if I ——" and so she ran glibly
on, completely forestalling him, to the secret amusement of the others.   Nevertheless, she was nervous
and embarrassed over the situation.   There was every
reason to fear that the Iron Count had heard and
seen enough to form a pretty good opinion of what
had passed between herself and Baldos in this remote

corner of the park. A deep sense of shame was taking possession of her.

Marlanx, smiling significantly, looked into her brave little face, and permitted her to talk on until she had run out of breath and composure. Then he bowed with exaggerated gallantry and informed her that he was hers to command, and that it was not for him to forgive but to accept whatever was her gracious pleasure. He called upon the chair-bearers and they took up their burden. Beverly promptly changed her mind and concluded to walk to the castle. And so they started off, the chair going ahead as if out of commission forever. Despite her efforts to do so, the American girl (feeling very much abused, by the way), was unsuccessful in the attempt to keep the princess at her side. Yetive deliberately walked ahead with Halfont and Dangloss. It seemed to Beverly that they walked unnecessarily fast and that Marlanx was provokingly slow. Baldos was twenty paces behind, as was his custom.

"Is it necessary for me to ask you to double the number of lessons I am to have?" Marlanx asked. He was quite too close to her side to please Beverly.

"Can't you learn in one lesson? Most Americans think they know all about poker after the first game."

"I am not so quick-witted, your highness."

"Far be it from me to accelerate your wits, Count Marlanx. It might not be profitable."

"You might profit by losing, you know," he ventured, leaning still closer. "Poker is not the only game of chance. It was chance that gave me a winning hand this evening."

"I don't understand."

"It shall be my pleasure to teach you in return for instructions I am to have. I have tried to teach your excellent guard one phase of the game. He has not profited, I fear. He has been blind enough to pick a losing hand in spite of my advice. It is the game of hearts." Beverly could not but understand. She shrank away with a shudder. Her wits did not desert her, however.

"I know the game," she said steadily. "One's object is to cast off all the hearts. I have been very lucky at the game, Count Marlanx."

"Umph!" was his ironical comment. "Ah, isn't this a night for lovers?" he went on, changing tack suddenly. "To stroll in the shadows, where even the moon is blind, is a joy that love alone provides. Come, fair mistress, share this joy with me."

With that his hand closed over her soft arm above the elbow and she was drawn close to his side. Beverly's first shock of revulsion was succeeded by the distressing certainty that Baldos was a helpless witness of this indignity. She tried to jerk her arm away, but he held it tight.

"Release my arm, sir!" she cried, hoarse with passion.

"Call your champion, my lady. It will mean his death. I have evidence that will insure his conviction and execution within an hour. Nothing could save him. Call him, I say, and ——"

"I *will* call him. He is my sworn protector, and I will command him to knock you down if you don't go away," she flared, stopping decisively.

"At his peril——"

"Baldos!" she called, without a second's hesitation. The guard came up with a rush just as Marlanx released her arm and fell away with a muttered imprecation.

"Your highness!" cried Baldos, who had witnessed everything.

"Are you afraid to die?" she demanded briefly and clearly.

"No!"

"That is all," she said, suddenly calm. "I merely wanted to prove it to Count Marlanx." Tact had come to her relief most opportunely. Like a flash she saw that a conflict between the commander of the army and a guard could have but one result and that disastrous to the latter. One word from her would have ended everything for Baldos. She saw through the Iron Count's ruse as if by divine inspiration and profited where he least expected her to excel in shrewdness. Marlanx had deliberately invited the assault by the guard. His object had been to snare Baldos into his own undoing, and a horrible undoing it would have been. One blow would have secured the desired result. Nothing could have saved the guard who had struck his superior officer. But Beverly thought in time.

"To die is easy, your highness. You have but to ask it of me," said Baldos, whose face was white and drawn.

"She has no intention of demanding such a pleasant sacrifice," observed Count Marlanx, covering his failure skilfully. "Later on, perhaps, she may sign your death warrant. I am proud to hear, sir, that a member of my corps has the courage to face the inevitable, even though he be an alien and unwilling to die on the field of battle. You have my compliments, sir. You have been on irksome duty for several hours and must be fatigued as well as hungry. A soldier suffers many deprivations, not the least of which is starvation in pursuit of his calling. Mess is not an unwelcome relief to you after all these arduous hours. You may return to the barracks at once. The princess is under my care for the remainder of the campaign."

Baldos looked first at her and then at the sarcastic old general. Yetive and her companions were waiting for them at the fountain, a hundred yards ahead.

"You may go, Baldos," said Beverly in low tones.

"I am not fatigued nor ——" he began eagerly.

"Go!" snarled Marlanx. "Am I to repeat a command to you? Do you ignore the word of your mistress?" There was a significant sneer in the way he said it.

"Mistress?" gasped Baldos, his eye blazing, his arm half raised.

"Count Marlanx!" implored Beverly, drawing herself to her full height and staring at him like a wounded thing.

"I humbly implore you not to misconstrue the meaning of the term, your highness," said the Count affably. " Ah, you have dropped something. Permit he. It is a note of some description, I think."

He stooped quickly — too quickly — and recovered from the ground at her feet the bit of paper which had fallen from her hand. It was the note from Ravone to Baldos which Beverly had forgotten in the excitement of the encounter.

" Count Marlanx, give me that paper! " demanded Beverly breathlessly.

" Is it a love-letter? Perhaps it is intended for me. At any rate, your highness, it is safe against my heart for the time being. When we reach the castle I shall be happy to restore it. It is safer with me. Come, we go one way and — have you not gone, sir? " in his most sarcastic tone to the guard. Beverly was trembling.

" No, I have not; and I shall not go until I see you obey the command of her highness. She has asked you for that piece of paper," said Baldos, standing squarely in front of Marlanx.

" Insolent dog! Do you mean to question my ——"

" Give over that paper! "

" If you strike me, fellow, it will be ——"

" If I strike you it will be to kill, Count Marlanx. The paper, sir." Baldos towered over the Iron Count and there was danger in his dare-devil voice. " Surely, sir, I am but obeying your own instructions. ' Protect the princess and all that is hers, with your life,' you have said to me."

" Oh, I wish you hadn't done this, Baldos," cried Beverly, panic-stricken.

" You have threatened my life. I shall not forget it, fool. Here is the precious note, your highness, with my condolences to the writer." Marlanx passed the note to her and then looked triumphantly at the guard. " I daresay you have done all you can, sir. Do you wish to add anything more? "

" What can one do when dealing with his superior and finds him a despicable coward? " said Baldos, with cool irony. " You are reputed to be a brave soldier. I know that to be false or I would ask you to draw the sword you carry and ——" He was drawing his sword as he spoke.

" Baldos ! " implored Beverly. Her evident concern infuriated Marlanx. In his heart he knew Baldos to be a man of superior birth and a foeman not to be despised from his own station. Carried away by passion, he flashed his sword from its sheath.

" You have drawn on me, sir," he snarled. " I must defend myself against even such as you. You will find that I am no coward. Time is short for your gallant lover, madam."

Before she could utter a word of protest the blades had clashed and they were hungry for blood. It was dark in the shadows of the trees and the trio were quite alone with their tragedy. She heard Baldos laugh recklessly in response to Marlanx's cry of :

" Oh, the shame of fighting with such carrion as you ! "

" Don't jest at a time like this, count," said the guard, softly. " Remember that I lose, no matter which way it goes. If you kill me I lose, if I beat you I lose. Remember, you can still have me shot for insubordination and conduct unbecoming ——"

" Stop!" almost shrieked Beverly. At risk of personal injury she rushed between the two swordsmen. Both drew back and dropped their points. Not a dozen passes had been made.

" I beg your highness's pardon," murmured Baldos, but he did not sheathe his sword.

" He forced it upon me," cried Marlanx triumphantly. " You were witness to it all. I was a fool to let it go as far as this. Put up your sword until another day — if that day ever comes to you."

" He will have you shot for this, Baldos," cried Beverly in her terror. Baldos laughed bitterly.

" Tied and blindfolded, too, your highness, to prove that he is a brave man and not a coward. It was short but it was sweet. Would that you had let the play go on. There was a spice in it that made life worth living and death worth the dying. Have you other commands for me, your highness?" His manner was so cool and defiant that she felt the tears spring to her eyes.

" Only that you put up your sword and end this miserable affair by going to your — your room."

" It is punishment enough. To-morrow's execution can be no harder."

Marlanx had been thinking all this time. Into his soul came the thrill of triumph, the consciousness of a mighty power. He saw the chance to benefit by the sudden clash and he was not slow to seize it.

" Never fear, my man," he said easily, " it won't

be as bad as that. I can well afford to overlook your
indiscretion of to-night. There will be no execution,
as you call it. This was an affair between men, not
between man and the state. Our gracious referee is
to be our judge. It is for her to pardon and to con-
demn. It was very pretty while it lasted and you
are too good a swordsman to be shot. Go your way,
Baldos, and remember me as Marlanx the man, not
Marlanx the general. As your superior officer, I congratulate and commend you upon the manner in which
you serve the princess."

"You will always find me ready to fight and to
die for her," said Baldos gravely. "Do you think
you can remember that, Count Marlanx?"

"I have an excellent memory," said the count
steadily. With a graceful salute to Beverly, Baldos
turned and walked away in the darkness.

"A perfect gentleman, Miss Calhoun, but a
wretched soldier," said Marlanx grimly.

"He is a hero," she said quietly, a great calmness
coming over her. "Do you mean it when you say
you are not going to have him punished? He did
only what a man should do, and I glory in his folly."

"I may as well tell you point blank that you alone
can save him. He does not deserve leniency. It is
in my power and it is my province to have him
utterly destroyed, not only for this night's work, but
for other and better reasons. I have positive proof
that he is a spy. He knows I have this proof. That
is why he would have killed me just now. It is for
you to say whether he shall meet the fate of a spy

or go unscathed. You have but to exchange promises with me and the estimable guardsman goes free —
but he goes from Edelweiss forever. To-day he met
the enemy's scouts in the hills, as you know quite well.
Messages were exchanged, secretly, which you do
not know of, of course. Before another day is gone
I expect to see the results of his treachery. There may
be manifestations to-night. You do not believe me,
but wait and see if I am not right. He is one of
Gabriel's cleverest spies."

" I do not believe it. You shall not accuse him of
such things," she cried. " Besides, if he is a spy
why should you shield him for my sake? Don't you
owe it to Graustark to expose ——"

" Here is the princess," said he serenely. " Your
highness," addressing Yetive, " Miss Calhoun has a
note which she refuses to let anyone read but you.
Now, my dear young lady, you may give it directly
into the hands of her highness."

Beverly gave him a look of scorn, but without a second's hesitation placed the missive in Yetive's hand.
The Iron Count's jaw dropped, and he moistened his
lips with his tongue two or three times. Something
told him that a valuable chance had gone.

" I shall be only too happy to have your highness
read the result of my first lesson in the Graustark
language," she said, smiling gaily upon the count.

Two men in uniform came rushing up to the party,
manifestly excited. Saluting the general, both began
to speak at once.

" One at a time," commanded the count. " What is it? "

Other officers of the guard and a few noblemen from the castle came up, out of breath.

" We have discerned signal fires in the hills, your excellency," said one of the men from the fort. " There is a circle of fires and they mean something important. For half an hour they have been burning near the monastery; also in the valley below and on the mountains to the south."

There was an instant of deathly silence, as if the hearers awaited a crash. Marlanx looked steadily at Beverly's face and she saw the triumphant, accusing gleam in his eyes. Helplessly she stared into the crowd of faces. Her eyes fell upon Baldos, who suddenly appeared in the background. His face wore a hunted, imploring look. The next instant he disappeared among the shadows.

CHAPTER XX

GOSSIP OF SOME CONSEQUENCE

HERE is no time to be lost," exclaimed Count Marlanx. " Ask Colonel Braze to report to me at the eastern
gate with a detail of picked troopers
— a hundred of them. I will meet
him there in half an hour." He gave
other sharp, imperative commands, and in the twinkling of an eye the peaceful atmosphere was transformed into the turbulent, exciting rush of activity.
The significance of the fires seen in the hills could not
be cheaply held. Instant action was demanded. The
city was filled with the commotion of alarm; the army
was brought to its feet with a jerk that startled even
the most ambitious.

The first thing that General Marlanx did was to
instruct Quinnox to set a vigilant watch over Baldos.
He was not to be arrested, but it was understood that
the surveillance should be but little short of incarcera-
tion. He was found at the barracks shortly after the
report concerning the signal fires, and told in plain
words that General Marlanx had ordered a guard
placed over him for the time being, pending the result
of an investigation. Baldos had confidently expected

to be thrown into a dungeon for his affront. He did not know that Grenfall Lorry stood firm in his conviction that Baldos was no spy, and was supported by others in high authority.

Marlanx was bottling his wrath and holding back his revenge for a distinct purpose. Apart from the existence of a strong, healthy prejudice in the guard's favor, what the old general believed and what he could prove were two distinct propositions. He was crafty enough, however, to take advantage of a condition unknown to Beverly Calhoun, the innocent cause of all his bitterness toward Baldos.

As he hastened from the council chamber, his eyes swept the crowd of eager, excited women in the grand hall. From among them he picked Beverly and advanced upon her without regard for time and consequence. Despite her animation he was keen enough to see that she was sorely troubled. She did not shrink from him as he had half expected, but met him with bold disdain in her eyes.

" This is the work of your champion," he said in tones that did not reach ears other than her own. " I prophesied it, you must remember. Are you satisfied now that you have been deceived in him? "

" I have implicit confidence in him. I suppose you have ordered his arrest? " she asked with quiet scorn.

" He is under surveillance, at my suggestion. For your sake, and yours alone, I am giving him a chance. He is your protégé; you are responsible for his conduct. To accuse him would be to place you in an embarrassing position. There is a sickening rumor

in court circles that you have more than a merely kind
and friendly interest in the rascal. If I believed
that, Miss Calhoun, I fear my heart could not be kind
to him. But I know it is not true. You have a loft-
ier love to give. He is a clever scoundrel, and there
is no telling how much harm he has already done to
Graustark. His every move is to be watched and reported to me. It will be impossible for him to escape.
To save him from the vengeance of the army, I am
permitting him to remain in your service, ostensibly,
at least. His hours of duty have been changed, however. Henceforth he is in the night guard, from
midnight till dawn. I am telling you this, Miss
Calhoun, because I want you to know that in spite of
all the indignity I have suffered, you are more to me
than any other being in the world, more to me even
than my loyalty to Graustark. Do me the honor and
justice to remember this. I have suffered much for
you. I am a rough, hardened soldier, and you have
misconstrued my devotion. Forgive the harsh words
my passion may have inspired. Farewell! I must
off to undo the damage we all lay at the door of the
man you and I are protecting."

He was too wise to give her the chance to reply.
A moment later he was mounted and off for the eastern
gates, there to direct the movements of Colonel Braze
and his scouts. Beverly flew at once to Yetive with
her plea for Baldos. She was confronted by a rather
sober-faced sovereign. The news of the hour was not
comforting to the princess and her ministers.

"You don't believe he is a spy?" cried Beverly,

stopping just inside the door, presuming selfishly that Baldos alone was the cause for worry. She resolved to tell Yetive of the conflict in the park.

"Dear me, Beverly, I am not thinking of him. We've discussed him jointly and severally and every other way and he has been settled for the time being. You are the only one who is thinking of him, my dear child. We have weightier things to annoy us."

"Goodness, how you talk! He isn't annoying. Oh, forgive me, Yetive, for I am the silliest, addle-patedest goose in the kingdom. And you are so troubled. But do you know that he is being watched? They suspect him. So did I, at first, I'll admit it. But I don't — now. Have you read the note I gave to you out there?"

"Yes, dear. It's just as I expected. He has known from the beginning. He knew when he caught Dagmar and me spying behind that abominable curtain. But don't worry me any longer about him, please. Wait here with me until we have reports from the troops. I shall not sleep until I know what those fires meant. Forget Baldos for an hour or two, for my sake."

"You dear old princess, I'm an awful brute, sure 'nough. I'll forget him forever for your sake. It won't be hard, either. He's just a mere guard. Pooh! He's no prince."

Whereupon, reinforced by Mrs. Anguish and the Countess Halfont, she proceeded to devote herself to the task of soothing and amusing the distressed princess while the soldiers of Graustark ransacked the moonlit hills. The night passed, and the next day was far on its way to sunset before the scouts came in with tidings. No trace of the mysterious signalers had been found. The embers of the half-dozen fires were discovered, but their builders were gone. The search took in miles of territory, but it was unavailing. Not even a straggler was found. The so-called troupe of actors, around whom suspicion centered, had been swallowed by the capacious solitude of the hills. Riders from the frontier posts to the south came in with the report that all was quiet in the threatened district. Dawsbergen was lying quiescent, but with the readiness of a skulking dog.

There was absolutely no solution to the mystery connected with the fires on the mountain sides. Baldos was questioned privately and earnestly by Lorry and Dangloss. His reply was simple, but it furnished food for reflection and, at the same time, no little relief to the troubled leaders.

"It is my belief, Mr. Lorry, that the fires were built by brigands and not by your military foes. I have seen these fires in the north, near Axphain, and they were invariably meant to establish communication between separated squads of robbers, all belonging to one band. My friends and I on more than one occasion narrowly escaped disaster by prying into the affairs of these signalers. I take it that the squads have been operating in the south and were brought together last night by means of the fires. Doubtless they have some big project of their own sort on foot."

That night the city looked for a repetition of the

fires, but the mountains were black from dusk till
dawn.   Word reached the castle late in the evening,
from Ganlook, that an Axphainian nobleman and his
followers would reach Edelweiss the next day.   The
visit was a friendly but an important one.   The nobleman was no other than the young Duke of Mizrox,
intimate friend of the unfortunate Prince Lorenz who
met his death at the hand of Prince Gabriel, and
was the leader of the party which opposed the vengeful plans of Princess Volga.   His arrival in Edelweiss
was awaited with deep anxiety, for it was suspected
that his news would be of the most important character.

Beverly Calhoun sat on the balcony with the princess long after midnight.   The sky was black with
the clouds of an approaching storm; the air was heavy
with foreboding silence.   Twice, from their darkened
corner near the pillar, they saw Baldos as he paced
steadily past the castle on patrol, with Haddan at his
side.   Dreamily the watchers in the cool balcony
looked down upon the somber park and its occasional
guardsman.   Neither was in the mood to talk.   As
they rose at last to go to their rooms, something
whizzed through the air and dropped with a slight
thud in the center of the balcony.   The two young
women started back in alarm.   A faint light from
Beverly's window filtered across the stone floor.

" Don't touch it, Beverly," cried the princess, as
the girl started forward with an eager exclamation.
But Beverly had been thinking of the very object that
now quivered before her in the dull light, saucy, ag-

gressive and jaunty as it was the night when she saw it for the first time.

A long, slim red feather bobbed to and fro as if saluting her with soldierly fidelity. Its base was an orange, into which it had been stuck by the hand that tossed it from below. Beverly grasped it with more ecstasy than wisdom and then rushed to the stone railing, Yetive looking on in amazement. Diligently she searched the ground below for the man who had sent the red message, but he was nowhere in sight. Then came the sudden realization that she was revealing a most unmaidenly eagerness, to him as well as to the princess, for she did not doubt that he was watching from the shadows below. She withdrew from the rail in confusion and fled to her bed-chamber, followed by her curious companion. There were explanations — none of which struck speaker or listener as logical — and there were giggles which completely simplified the situation. Beverly thrust the slim red feather into her hair, and struck an attitude that would have set Baldos wild with joy if he could have seen it. The next day, when she appeared in the park, the feather stood up defiantly from the band of her sailor hat, though womanly perverseness impelled her to ignore Baldos when he passed her on his way to mess.

The Duke of Mizrox came into the city hours after the time set for his arrival. It was quite dark when the escort sent by Colonel Quinnox drew up at the castle gates with the visitor. The duke and his party had been robbed by brigands in the broad daylight and at a point not more than five miles from Edelweiss! And thus the mystery of the signal fires was explained. Count Marlanx did not soon forget the triumphant look he received from Beverly Calhoun when the duke's misfortunes were announced. Shameless as it may seem, she rejoiced exceedingly over the acts of the robbers.

Mizrox announced to the princess and her friends that he was not an emissary from the Axphainian government. Instead, he was but little less than a fugitive from the wrath of Volga and the crown adherents. Earlier in the week he had been summoned before Volga and informed that his absence for a few months, at least, from the principality was desirable. The privilege was allowed him of selecting the country which he desired to visit during that period, and he coolly chose Graustark. He was known to have friendly feelings for that state; but no objections were raised. This friendship also gave him a welcome in Edelweiss. Mizrox plainly stated his position to Yetive and the prime minister. He asked for protection, but declined to reveal any of the plans then maturing in his home country. This reluctance to become a traitor, even though he was not in sympathy with his sovereign, was respected by the princess. He announced his willingness to take up arms against Dawsbergen, but would in no way antagonize Axphain from an enemy's camp.

The duke admitted that the feeling in Axphain's upper circles was extremely bitter toward Graustark.

The old-time war spirit had not died down. Axphain despised her progressive neighbor.

"I may as well inform your highness that the regent holds another and a deeper grudge against Graustark," he said, in the audience chamber where were assembled many of the nobles of the state, late on the night of his arrival. "She insists that you are harboring and even shielding the pretender to our throne, Prince Frederic. It is known that he is in Graustark and, moreover, it is asserted that he is in direct touch with your government."

Yetive and her companions looked at one another with glances of comprehension. He spoke in English now for the benefit of Beverly Calhoun, an interested spectator, who felt her heart leap suddenly and swiftly into violent insurrection.

"Nothing could be more ridiculous," said Yetive after a pause. "We do not know Frederic, and we are not harboring him."

"I am only saying what is believed to be true by Axphain, your highness. It is reported that he joined you in the mountains in June and since has held a position of trust in your army."

"Would you know Prince Frederic if you were to see him?" quietly asked Lorry.

"I have not seen him since he was a very small boy, and then but for a moment — on the day when he and his mother were driven through the streets on their way to exile."

"We have a new man in the Castle Guard and there is a mystery attached to him. Would you mind looking at him and telling us if he is what Frederic might be in his manhood?" Lorry put the question and everyone present drew a deep breath of interest.

Mizrox readily consented and Baldos, intercepted on his rounds, was led unsuspecting into an outer chamber. The duke, accompanied by Lorry and Baron Dangloss, entered the room. They were gone from the assemblage but a few minutes, returning with smiles of uncertainty on their faces.

"It is impossible, your highness, for me to say whether or not it is Frederic," said the duke frankly. "He is what I imagine the pretender might be at his age, but it would be sheer folly for me to speculate. I do not know the man."

Beverly squeezed the Countess Dagmar's arm convulsively.

"Hurrah!" she whispered, in great relief. Dagmar looked at her in astonishment. She could not fathom the whimsical American.

"They have been keeping an incessant watch over the home of Frederic's cousin. He is to marry her when the time is propitious," volunteered the young duke. "She is the most beautiful girl in Axphain, and the family is one of the wealthiest. Her parents bitterly oppose the match. They were to have been secretly married some months ago, and there is a rumor to the effect that they did succeed in evading the vigilance of her people."

"You mean that they may be married?" asked Yetive, casting a quick glance at Beverly.

"It is not improbable, your highness. He is

known to be a daring young fellow, and he has never failed in a siege against the heart of woman. Report has it that he is the most invincible Lothario that ever donned love's armor." Beverly was conscious of furtive glances in her direction, and a faint pink stole into her temples. "Our fugitive princes are lucky in neither love nor war," went on the duke. "Poor Dantan, who is hiding from Gabriel, is betrothed to the daughter of the present prime minister of Dawsbergen, the beautiful Iolanda. I have seen her. She is glorious, your highness."

"I, too, have seen her," said Yetive, more gravely than she thought. "The report of their betrothal is true, then?"

"His sudden overthrow prevented the nuptials which were to have taken place in a month had not Gabriel returned. Her father, the Duke of Matz, wisely accepted the inevitable and became prime minister to Gabriel. Iolanda, it is said, remains true to him and sends messages to him as he wanders through the mountains."

Beverly's mind instantly reverted to the confessions of Baldos. He had admitted the sending and receiving of messages through Franz. Try as she would, she could not drive the thought from her mind that he was Dantan and now came the distressing fear that his secret messages were words of love from Iolanda. The audience lasted until late in the night, but she was so occupied with her own thoughts that she knew of but little that transpired.

Of one thing she was sure. She could not go to sleep that night.

CHAPTER XXI

THE ROSE

HE next morning Aunt Fanny had a hard time of it. Her mistress was petulant; there was no sunshine in the bright August day as it appeared to her. Toward dawn, after she had counted many millions of black sheep jumping backward over a fence, she had fallen asleep. Aunt Fanny obeyed her usual instructions on this luckless morning. It was Beverly's rule to be called every morning at seven o'clock. But how was her attendant to know that the graceful young creature who had kicked the counterpane to the foot of the bed and had mauled the pillow out of all shape, had slept for less than thirty minutes? How was she to know that the flushed face and frown were born in the course of a night of distressing perplexities? She knew only that the sleeping beauty who lay before her was the fairest creature in all the universe. For some minutes Aunt Fanny stood off and admired the rich youthful glory of the sleeper, prophetically reluctant to disturb her happiness. Then she obeyed the impulse of duty and spoke the summoning words.

236

"Wha — what time is it?" demanded the new-comer from the land of Nod, stretching her fine young body with a splendid but discontented yawn.

"Seben, Miss Bev'ly; wha' time do yo' s'pose hit is? Hit's d' reg'lah time, o' co'se. Did yo' all have a nice sleep, honey?" and Aunt Fanny went blissfully about the business of the hour.

"I didn't sleep a wink, confound it," grumbled Beverly, rubbing her eyes and turning on her back to glare up at the tapestry above the couch.

"Yo' wasn' winkin' any when Ah fust come into de room, lemme tell yo'," cackled Aunt Fanny with caustic freedom.

"See here, now, Aunt Fanny, I'm not going to stand any lecture from you this morning. When a fellow hasn't slept a —— "

"Who's a-lecturin' anybody, Ah'd lak to know? Ah'm jes' tellin' yo' what yo' was a-doin' when Ah came into de room. Yo' was a-sleepin' p'etty dog-gone tight, lemme tell yo'. Is yo' goin' out fo' yo' walk befo' b'eakfus, honey? 'Cause if yo' is, yo' all 'll be obleeged to climb out'n dat baid maghty quick-like. Yo' baf is ready, Miss Bev'ly."

Beverly splashed the water with unreasonable ferocity for a few minutes, trying to enjoy a diversion that had not failed her until this morning.

"Aunt Fanny," she announced, after looking darkly through her window into the mountains above, "if you can't brush my hair — ouch! — any easier than this, I'll have someone else do it, that's all. You're a regular old bear."

" Po' lil' honey," was all the complacent " bear "
said in reply, without altering her methods in the least.

" Well," said Beverly threateningly, with a shake
of her head, " be careful, that's all.   Have you heard
the news? "

" Wha' news, Miss Bev'ly? "

" We're going back to Washin'ton."

" Thank de Lawd!   When? "

" I don't know.   I've just this instant made up my
mind.   I think we'll start — let's see: this is the sixth
of August, isn't it?   Well, look and see, if you don't
know, stupid.   The tenth?   My goodness, where has
the time gone, anyway?   Well, we'll start sometime
between the eleventh and the twelfth."

" Of dis monf, Miss Bev'ly? "

" No; September.   I want you to look up a time-
table for me to-day.   We must see about the trains."

" Dey's on'y one leavin' heah daily, an' hit goes at
six in de mo'nin'.   One train a day!   Ain' 'at
scan'lous? "

" I'm sure, Aunt Fanny, it is their business — not
ours," said Beverly severely.

" P'raps dey mought be runnin' a excuhsion 'roun'
'baout Septembeh, Miss Bev'ly," speculated Aunt
Fanny consolingly.   " Dey gen'ly has 'em in Septembeh."

" You old goose," cried Beverly, in spite of herself.

" Ain' yo' habin' er good time, honey? "

" No, I am not."

" Fo' de lan's sake, Ah wouldn' s'picioned hit fo' a

minnit. Hit's de gayest place Ah mos' eveh saw —
'cept Wash'ton an' Lex'ton an' Vicksbu'g."

"Well, you don't know everything," said Beverly
crossly. "I wish you'd take that red feather out of
my hat — right away."

"Shall Ah frow hit away, Miss Bev'ly?"

"We — ll, no; you needn't do that," said Beverly.
"Put it on my dressing-table. I'll attend to it."

"Wha's become o' de gemman 'at wo' hit in the fust
place? Ah ain' seen him fo' two — three days."

"I'm sure I don't know. He's probably asleep.
That class of people never lose sleep over anything."

"'E's er pow'ful good-lookin' pusson," suggested
Aunt Fanny. Beverly's eyes brightened.

"Oh, do you think so?" she said, quite indifferently. "What are you doing with that hat?"

"Takin' out de featheh — jes' as ——"

"Well, leave it alone. Don't disturb my things,
Aunt Fanny. How many times must I tell
you ——"

"Good Lawd!" was all that Aunt Fanny could say.

"Don't forget about the time-tables," said Beverly, as she sallied forth for her walk in the park.

In the afternoon she went driving with Princess
Yetive and the young Duke of Mizrox, upon whose
innocent and sufficiently troubled head she was heap-
ing secret abuse because of the news he brought.
Later, Count Marlanx appeared at the castle for his
first lesson in poker. He looked so sure of himself
that Beverly hated him to the point of desperation.
At the same time she was eager to learn how matters

stood with Baldos. The count's threat still hung
over her head, veiled by its ridiculous shadow of
mercy. She knew him well enough by this time to
feel convinced that Baldos would have to account for
his temerity, sooner or later. It was like the cat and
the helpless mouse.

"It's too hot," she protested, when he announced
himself ready for the game. "Nobody plays poker
when it's 92 in the shade."

"But, your highness," complained the count, "war
may break out any day. I cannot concede delay."

"I think there's a game called ' shooting craps,' "
suggested she serenely. "It seems to me it would be
particularly good for warriors. You could be shooting something all the time."

He went away in a decidedly irascible frame of
mind. She did not know it, but Baldos was soon
afterward set to work in the garrison stables, a most
loathsome occupation, in addition to his duties as a
guard by night.

After mature deliberation Beverly set herself to the
task of writing home to her father. It was her
supreme intention to convince him that she would be
off for the States in an amazingly short time. The
major, upon receiving the letter three weeks later,
found nothing in it to warrant the belief that she was
ever coming home. He did observe, however, that
she had but little use for the army of Graustark, and
was especially disappointed in the set of men Yetive
retained as her private guard. For the life of her,
Beverly could not have told why she disapproved of

the guard in general or in particular, but she was
conscious of the fact, after the letter was posted, that
she had said many things that might have been left
unwritten. Besides, it was not Baldos's fault that
she could not sleep; it was distinctly her own. He
had nothing to do with it.

" I'll bet father will be glad to hear that I am coming home," she said to Yetive, after the letter was
gone.

" Oh, Beverly, dear, I hate to hear of your going,"
cried the princess. " When did you tell him you'd
start? "

" Why, oh,— er — let me see; when *did* I say?
Dash me — as Mr. Anguish would say — I don't believe I gave a date. It seems to me I said *soon*, that's
all."

" You don't know how relieved I am," exclaimed
Yetive rapturously, and Beverly was in high dudgeon
because of the implied reflection. " I believe you are
in a tiff with Baldos," went on Yetive airily.

" Goodness! How foolish you can be at times,
Yetive," was what Beverly gave back to her highness,
the Princess of Graustark.

Late in the evening couriers came in from the
Dawsbergen frontier with reports which created considerable excitement in castle and army circles.
Prince Gabriel himself had been seen in the northern
part of his domain, accompanied by a large detachment of picked soldiers. Lorry set out that very
night for the frontier, happy in the belief that something worth while was about to occur. General Mar-

lanx issued orders for the Edelweiss army corps to mass beyond the southern gates of the city the next morning. Commands were also sent to the outlying garrisons. There was to be a general movement of troops before the end of the week. Graustark was not to be caught napping.

Long after the departure of Lorry and Anguish, the princess sat on the balcony with Beverly and the Countess Dagmar. They did not talk much. The mission of these venturesome young American hus-hands was full of danger. Something in the air had told their wives that the first blows of war were to be struck before they looked again upon the men they loved.

" I think we have been betrayed by someone," said Dagmar, after an almost interminable silence. Her companion did not reply. " The couriers say that Gabriel knows where we are weakest at the front and that he knows our every movement. Yetive, there is a spy here, after all."

" And that spy has access to the very heart of our deliberations," added Beverly pointedly. " I say this in behalf of the man whom you evidently suspect, countess. *He* could not know these things."

" I do not say that he does know, Miss Calhoun, but it is not beyond reason that he may be the go-between, the means of transferring information from the main traitor to the messengers who await outside our walls."

" Oh, I don't believe it! " cried Beverly hotly.

" I wonder if these things would have happened if Baldos had never come to Edelweiss? " mused the princess. As though by common impulse, both of the Graustark women placed their arms about Beverly.

" It's because we have so much at stake, Beverly, dear," whispered Dagmar. " Forgive me if I have hurt you."

Of course, Beverly sobbed a little in the effort to convince them that she did not care whom they accused, if he proved to be the right man in the end. They left her alone on the balcony. For an hour after midnight she sat there and dreamed. Everyone was ready to turn against Baldos. Even she had been harsh toward him, for had she not seen him relegated to the most obnoxious of duties after promising him a far different life? And now what was he thinking of her? His descent from favor had followed upon the disclosures which made plain to each the identity of the other. No doubt he was attributing his degradation, in a sense, to the fact that she no longer relished his services, having seen a romantic little ideal shattered by his firm assertions. Of course, she knew that General Marlanx was alone instrumental in assigning him to the unpleasant duty he now observed, but how was Baldos to know that she was not the real power behind the Iron Count?

A light drizzle began to fall, cold and disagreeable. There were no stars, no moon. The ground below was black with shadows, but shimmering in spots touched by the feeble park lamps. She retreated through her window, determined to go to bed. Her rebellious brain, however, refused to banish him from her thoughts. She wondered if he were patroling the castle grounds in the rain, in all that lonely darkness. Seized by a sudden inspiration, she threw a gossamer about her, grasped an umbrella and ventured out upon the balcony once more. Guiltily she searched the night through the fine drizzling rain; her ears listened eagerly for the tread which was so well known to her.

At last he strode beneath a lamp not far away. He looked up, but, of course, could not see her against the dark wall. For a long time he stood motionless beneath the light. She could not help seeing that he was dejected, tired, unhappy. His shoulders drooped, and there was a general air of listlessness about the figure which had once been so full of courage and of hope. The post light fell directly upon his face. It was somber, despondent, strained. He wore the air of a prisoner. Her heart went out to him like a flash. The debonair knight of the black patch was no more; in his place there stood a sullen slave to discipline.

" Baldos! " she called softly, her voice penetrating the dripping air with the clearness of a bell. He must have been longing for the sound of it, for he started and looked eagerly in her direction. His tall form straightened as he passed his hand over his brow. It was but a voice from his dream, he thought. " Aren't you afraid you'll get wet? " asked the same low, sweet voice, with the suggestion of a laugh behind it. With long strides he crossed the pavement and stood almost directly beneath her.

" Your highness! " he exclaimed gently, joyously. " What are you doing out there? "

"Wondering, Baldos — wondering what you were thinking of as you stood under the lamp over there."

"I was thinking of your highness," he called up, softly.

"No, no!" she protested.

"I, too, was wondering — wondering what you were dreaming of as you slept, for you should be asleep at this hour, your highness, instead of standing out there in the rain."

"Baldos," she called down tremulously, "you don't like this work, do you?"

"It has nothing but darkness in it for me. I never see the light of your eyes. I never feel the ———"

"Sh! You must not talk like that. It's not proper, and besides someone may be listening. The night has a thousand ears — or is it eyes? But listen: to-morrow you shall be restored to your old duties. You surely cannot believe that I had anything to do with the order which compels you to work at this unholy hour."

"I was afraid you were punishing me for my boldness. My heart has been sore — you never can know how sore. I was disgraced, dismissed, forgotten ———"

"No, no — you *were* not! You must not say that. Go away now, Baldos. You will ride with me to-morrow," she cried nervously. "Please go to some place where you won't get dripping wet."

"You forget that I am on guard," he said with a laugh. "But you are a wise counsellor. Is the rain so pleasant to you?"

"I have an umbrella," she protested. "What are you doing?" she cried in alarm. He was coming hand over hand, up the trellis-work that enclosed the lower verandah.

"I am coming to a place where I won't get dripping wet," he called softly. There was a dangerous ring in his voice and she drew back in a panic.

"You must not!" she cried desperately. "This is madness! Go down, sir!"

"I am happy enough to fly, but cannot. So I do the next best thing — I climb to you." His arm was across the stone railing by this time and he was panting from the exertion, not two feet from where she crouched. "Just one minute of heaven before I go back to the shadows of earth. I am happy again. Marlanx told me you had dismissed me. I wonder what he holds in reserve for me. I knew he lied, but it is not until now that I rejoice. Come, you are to shield me from the rain."

"Oh, oh!" she gasped, overwhelmed by his daring passion. "I should die if anyone saw you here." Yet she spasmodically extended the umbrella so that it covered him and left her out in the drizzle.

"And so should I," responded he softly. "Listen to me. For hours and hours I have been longing for the dear old hills in which you found me. I wanted to crawl out of Edelweiss and lose myself forever in the rocks and crags. To-night when you saw me I was trying to say good-bye to you forever. I was trying to make up my mind to desert. I could not endure the new order of things. You had cast

me off. My friends out there were eager to have me
with them. In the city everyone is ready to call me a
spy — even you, I thought. Life was black and
drear. Now, my princess, it is as bright as heaven
itself."

"You must not talk like this," she whispered helplessly. "You are making me sorry I called to you."

"I should have heard you if you had only whispered, my rain princess. I have no right to talk of
love —— I am a vagabond; but I have a heart, and
it is a bold one. Perhaps I dream that I am here beside you — so near that I can touch your face — but
it is the sweetest of dreams. But for it I should have
left Edelweiss weeks ago. I shall never awaken from
this dream; you cannot rob me of the joys of dreaming."

Under the spell of his passion she drew nearer to
him as he clung strongly to the rail. The roses at
her throat came so close that he could bury his face
in them. Her hand touched his cheek, and he kissed
its palm again and again, his wet lips stinging her
blood to the tips of her toes.

"Go away, please," she implored faintly. "Don't
you see that you must not stay here — now?"

"A rose, my princess, — one rose to kiss all
through the long night," he whispered. She could
feel his eyes burning into her heart. With trembling,
hurried fingers she tore loose a rose. He could not
seize it with his hands because of the position he held,
and she laughed tantalizingly. Then she kissed it

first and pressed it against his mouth.   His lips and teeth closed over the stem and the rose was his.

" There are thorns," she whispered, ever so softly.

" They are the riches of the poor," he murmured with difficulty, but she understood.

" Now, go," she said, drawing resolutely away. An instant later his head disappeared below the rail. Peering over the side she saw his figure spring easily to the ground, and then came the rapid, steady tramp as he went away on his dreary patrol.

" I couldn't help it," she was whispering to herself between joy and shame.

Glancing instinctively out toward the solitary lamp she saw two men standing in its light.   One of them was General Marlanx; the other she knew to be the spy that watched Baldos.   Her heart sank like lead when she saw that the two were peering intently toward the balcony where she stood, and where Baldos had clung but a moment before.

CHAPTER XXII

A PROPOSAL

HE shrank back with a great dread in her heart. Marlanx, of all men! Why was he in the park at this hour of the night? There could be but one answer, and the very thought of it almost suffocated her. He was drawing the net with his own hands, he was spying with his own eyes. For a full minute it seemed to her that her heart would stop beating. How long had he been standing there? What had he seen or heard? Involuntarily she peered over the rail for a glimpse of Baldos. He had gone out into the darkness, missing the men at the lamp-post either by choice or through pure good fortune. A throb of thankfulness assailed her heart. She was not thinking of her position, but of his.

Again she drew stealthily away from the rail, possessed of a ridiculous feeling that her form was as plain to the vision as if it were broad daylight. The tread of a man impelled her to glance below once more before fleeing to her room. Marlanx was coming toward the verandah. She fled swiftly, pausing at the window to lower the friendly but forgotten um-

249

brella.   From below came the sibilant hiss of a man
seeking to attract her attention.   Once more she
stopped to listen.   The " hist " was repeated, and
then her own name was called softly but imperatively.
It was beyond the power of woman to keep from
laughing.   It struck her as irresistibly funny that
the Iron Count should be standing out there in the
rain, signaling to her like a love-sick boy.   Once she
was inside, however, it did not seem so amusing.
Still, it gave her an immense amount of satisfaction to
slam the windows loudly, as if in pure defiance.   Then
she closed the blinds, shutting out the night completely.

Turning up the light at her dressing-table, she sat
down in a state of sudden collapse.   For a long time
she stared at her face in the mirror.   She saw the
red of shame and embarrassment mount to her cheeks
and then she covered her eyes with her hands.

" Oh, what a fool you've been," she half sobbed,
shrinking from the mirror as if it were an accuser.

She prepared for bed with frantic haste.   Just as
she was about to scramble in and hide her face in the
pillows, a shocking thought came to her.   The next
instant she was at the windows and the slats were
closed with a rattle like a volley of firearms.   Then
she jumped into bed.   She wondered if the windows
were locked.   Out she sprang again like a flash, and
her little bare feet scurried across the room, first to
the windows and then to the door.

" Now, I reckon I'm safe," she murmured a moment
later, again getting into bed.   " I love to go to sleep

with the rain pattering outside like that. Oh, dear, I'm so sorry he has to walk all night in this rain. Poor fellow! I wonder where he is now. Goodness, it's raining cats and dogs!"

But in spite of the rain she could not go to sleep. Vague fears began to take possession of her. Something dreadful told her that Count Marlanx was on the balcony and at her window, notwithstanding the rainpour. The fear became oppressive, maddening. She felt the man's presence almost as strongly as if he were in plain view. He was there, she knew it.

The little revolver that had served her so valiantly at the Inn of the Hawk and Raven lay upon a stool near the bedside every night. Consumed by the fear that the window might open slowly at any moment, she reached forth and clutched the weapon. Then she shrank back in the bed, her eyes fixed upon the black space across the room. For hours she shivered and waited for the window to open, dozing away time and again only to come back to wakefulness with a start.

The next morning she confessed to herself that her fears had been silly. Her first act after breakfasting alone in her room was to seek out Colonel Quinnox, commander of the castle guard. In her mind she was greatly troubled over the fate of the bold visitor of the night before. There was a warm, red glow in her face and a quick beat in her heart as she crossed the parade-ground. Vagabond though he was, he had conquered where princes had failed. Her better judgment told her that she could be nothing to this debonair knight of the road, yet her heart stubbornly resisted all the arguments that her reason put forth.

Colonel Quinnox was pleasant, but he could give Beverly no promise of leniency in regard to Baldos. Instructions had come to him from General Marlanx, and he could not set them aside at will. Her plea that he might once more be assigned to old-time duties found the colonel regretfully obdurate. Baldos could not ride with her again until Marlanx withdrew the order which now obtained. Beverly swallowed her pride and resentment diplomatically, smiled her sweetest upon the distressed colonel, and marched defiantly back to the castle. Down in her rebellious, insulted heart she was concocting all sorts of plans for revenge. Chief among them was the terrible overthrow of the Iron Count. Her wide scope of vengeance even contemplated the destruction of Graustark if her end could be obtained in no other way.

Full of these bitter-sweet thoughts she came to the castle doors before she saw who was waiting for her upon the great verandah. As she mounted the steps, a preoccupied frown upon her fair brow, General Marlanx, lean, crafty and confident, advanced to greet her. The early hour was responsible for the bright solitude which marked the place. But few signs of life were in evidence about the castle.

She stopped with a sharp exclamation of surprise. Then scorn and indignation rushed in to fill the place of astonishment. She faced the smiling old man with anger in her eyes.

" Good morning," he said, extending his hand,

which she did not see. She was wondering how much he had seen and heard at midnight.

"I thought the troops were massing this morning," she said coldly. "Don't you mass, too?"

"There is time enough for that, my dear. I came to have a talk with you — in private," he said meaningly.

"It is sufficiently private here, Count Marlanx. What have you to say to me?"

"I want to talk about last night. You were very reckless to do what you did."

"Oh, you *were* playing the spy, then?" she asked scornfully.

"An involuntary observer, believe me — and a jealous one. I had hoped to win the affections of an innocent girl. What I saw last night shocked me beyond expression."

"Well, you shouldn't have looked," she retorted, tossing her chin; and the red feather in her hat bobbed angrily.

"I am surprised that one as clever as you are could have carried on an amour so incautiously," he said blandly.

"What do you mean?"

"I mean that I saw everything that occurred."

"Well, I'm not ashamed of it," obstinately. "Good-bye, Count Marlanx."

"One moment, please. I cannot let you off so easily. What right had you to take that man into your room, a place sacred in the palace of Graustark? Answer me, Miss Calhoun."

Beverly drew back in horror and bewilderment.

"Into my room?" she gasped.

"Let us waste no time in subterfuge. I saw him come from your window, and I saw all that passed between you in the balcony. Love's eyes are keen. What occurred in your chamber I can only ——"

"Stop! How dare you say such a thing to me?" she fiercely cried. "You miserable coward! You know he was not in my room. Take it back — take back every word of that lie!" She was white with passion, cold with terror.

"Bah! This is childish. I am not the only one who saw him, my dear. He was in your room — you were in his arms. It's useless to deny it. And to think that I have spared him from death to have it come to this! You need not look so horrified. Your secret is safe with me. I come to make terms with you. My silence in exchange for your beauty. It's worth it to you. One word from me, you are disgraced and Baldos dies. Come, my fair lady, give me your promise, it's a good bargain for both."

Beverly was trembling like a leaf. This phase of his villainy had not occurred to her. She was like a bird trying to avoid the charmed eye of the serpent.

"Oh, you — you miserable wretch!" she cried, hoarse with anger and despair. "What a cur you are! You know you are not speaking the truth. How can you say such things to me? I have never wronged you ——" She was almost in tears, impotent with shame and fear.

"It has been a pretty game of love for you and

the excellent Baldos. You have deceived those who
love you best and trust you most. What will the
princess say when she hears of last night's merry
escapade? What will she say when she learns who
was hostess to a common guardsman at the midnight
hour? It is no wonder that you look terrified. It is
for you to say whether she is to know or not. You
can bind me to silence. You have lost Baldos. Take
me and all that I can give you in his stead, and the
world never shall know the truth. You love him, I
know, and there is but one way to save him. Say the
word and he goes free to the hills; decline and his
life is not worth a breath of air."

"And pretending to believe this of me, you still
ask me to be your wife. What kind of a man are
you?" she demanded, scarcely able to speak.

"My wife?" he said harshly. "Oh, no. You are
not the wife of Baldos," he added significantly.

"Good God!" gasped Beverly, crushed by the
brutality of it all. "I would sooner die. Would to
heaven my father were here, he would shoot you as he
would a dog! Oh, how I loathe you! Don't you try
to stop me! I shall go to the princess myself. She
shall know what manner of beast you are."

She was racing up the steps, flaming with anger
and shame.

"Remember, I can prove what I have said. Be-
ware what you do. I love you so much that I now ask
you to become my wife. Think well over it. Your
honor and his life! It rests with you," he cried
eagerly, following her to the door.

"You disgusting old fool," she hissed, turning upon him as she pulled the big brass knocker on the door.

"I must have my answer to-night, or you know what will happen," he snarled, but he felt in his heart that he had lost through his eagerness.

She flew to Yetive's boudoir, consumed by rage and mortification. Between sobs and feminine maledictions she poured the whole story, in all its ugliness, into the ears of the princess.

"Now, Yetive, you have to stand by me in this," announced the narrator conclusively, her eyes beaming hopefully through her tears.

"I cannot prevent General Marlanx from preferring serious charges against Baldos, dear. I know he was not in your room last night. You did not have to tell me that, because I saw you both at the balcony rail." Beverly's face took on such a radiant look of rejoicing that Yetive was amply paid for the surprising and gratifying acknowledgment of a second period of eavesdropping. "You may depend upon me to protect you from Marlanx. He can make it very unpleasant for Baldos, but he shall pay dearly for this insult to you. He has gone too far."

"I don't think he has any proof against Baldos," said Beverly, thinking only of the guardsman.

"But it is so easy to manufacture evidence, my dear. The Iron Count has set his heart upon having you, and he is not the man to be turned aside easily."

"He seems to think he can get wives as easily as he gets rid of them, I observe. I was going back to

Washington soon, Yetive, but I'll stay on now and see
this thing to the end. He can't scare a Calhoun, no
sir-ee. I'll telegraph for my brother Dan to come
over here and punch his head to pieces."

"Now, now,— don't be so high and mighty, dear.
Let us see how rational we can be," said the princess
gently. Whereupon the hot-headed girl from Dixie
suspended hostilities and became a very demure young
woman. Before long she was confessing timidly,
then boldly, that she loved Baldos better than anything in all the world.

"I can't help it, Yetive. I know I oughtn't to,
but what is there to do when one can't help it? There
would be an awful row at home if I married him. Of
course, he hasn't asked me. Maybe he won't. In
fact, I'm sure he won't. I shan't give him a chance.
But if he does ask me I'll just keep putting him off.
I've done it before, you know. You see, for a long,
long time, I fancied he might be a prince, but he isn't
at all. I've had his word for it. He's just an ordinary person — like — like — well, like I am. Only
he doesn't look so ordinary. Isn't he handsome, Yetive? And, dear me, he is so impulsive! If he had
asked me to jump over the balcony rail with him last
night, I believe I would have done it. Wouldn't that
have surprised old Marlanx?" Beverly gave a merry
laugh. The troubles of the morning seemed to fade
away under the warmth of her humor. Yetive sat
back and marvelled at the manner in which this blithe
young American cast out the " blue devils."

" You must not do anything foolish, Beverly," she

cautioned. "Your parents would never forgive me if I allowed you to marry or even to fall in love with any Tom, Dick or Harry over here. Baldos may be the gallant, honest gentleman we believe him to be, but he also may be the worst of adventurers. One can never tell, dear. I wish now that I had not humored you in your plan to bring him to the castle. I'm afraid I have done wrong. You have seen too much of him and — oh, well, you *will* be sensible, won't you, dear?" There was real concern in the face of the princess. Beverly kissed her rapturously.

"Don't worry about me, Yetive. I know how to take care of myself. Worry about your old Gabriel, if you like, but don't bother your head about me," she cried airily. "Now let's talk about the war. Marlanx won't do anything until he hears from me. What's the use worrying?"

Nightfall brought General Marlanx in from the camps outside the gates. He came direct to the castle and boldly sent word to Beverly that he must speak to her at once. She promptly answered that she did not want to see him and would not. Without a moment's hesitation he appealed for an audience with the princess, and it was granted.

He proceeded, with irate coolness, to ask how far she believed herself bound to protect the person of Baldos, the guard. He understood that she was under certain obligations to Miss Calhoun and he wanted to be perfectly sure of his position before taking a step which now seemed imperative. Baldos was a spy in the employ of Dawsbergen. He had sufficient proof to warrant his arrest and execution; there were documents, and there was positive knowledge that he had conferred with strangers from time to time, even within the walls of the castle grounds. Marlanx cited instances in which Baldos had been seen talking to a strange old man inside the grounds, and professed to have proof that he had gone so far as to steal away by night to meet men beyond the city walls. He was now ready to seize the guard, but would not do so until he had conferred with his sovereign.

"Miss Calhoun tells me that you have made certain proposals to her, Count Marlanx," said Yetive coldly, her eyes upon his hawkish face.

"I have asked her to be my wife, your highness."

"You have threatened her, Count Marlanx."

"She has exposed herself to you? I would not have told what I saw last night."

"Would it interest you to know that I saw everything that passed on the balcony last night? You will allow me to say, general, that you have behaved in a most outrageous manner in approaching my guest with such foul proposals. Stop, sir! She has told me everything and I believe her. I believe my own eyes. There is no need to discuss the matter further. You have lost the right to be called a man. For the present I have only to say that you shall be relieved of the command of my army. The man who makes war on women is not fit to serve one. As for Baldos, you are at liberty to prefer the charges. He shall have a fair trial, rest assured."

"Your highness, hear me," implored Marlanx, white to the roots of his hair.

"I will hear what you have to say when my husband is at my side."

"I can but stand condemned, then, your highness, without a hearing. My vindication will come, however. With your permission, I retire to contrive the arrest of this spy. You may depose me, but you cannot ask me to neglect my duty to Graustark. I have tried to save him for Miss Calhoun's sake —— " But her hand was pointing to the door.

Ten minutes later Beverly was hearing everything from the lips of the princess, and Marlanx was cursing his way toward the barracks, vengeance in his heart. But a swift messenger from the castle reached the guard-room ahead of him. Colonel Quinnox was reading an official note from the princess when Marlanx strode angrily into the room.

"Bring this fellow Baldos to me, Colonel Quinnox," he said, without greeting.

"I regret to say that I have but this instant received a message from her highness, commanding me to send him to the castle," said Quinnox, with a smile.

"The devil! What foolishness is this?" snarled the Iron Count.

"Have a care, sir," said Quinnox stiffly. "It is of the princess you speak."

"Bah! I am here to order the man's arrest. It is more important than —— "

"Nevertheless, sir, he goes to the castle first. This

note says that I am to disregard any command you may give until further notice."

Marlanx fell back amazed and stunned. At this juncture Baldos entered the room. Quinnox handed him an envelope, telling him that it was from the princess and that he was to repair at once to the castle. Baldos glanced at the handwriting, and his face lit up proudly.

"I am ready to go, sir," he said, passing the Iron Count with a most disconcerting smile on his face.

CHAPTER XXIII

A SHOT IN THE DARKNESS

ALDOS started off at once for the castle, his heart singing. In the darkness of the night he kissed the message which had come to him from "her highness." The envelope had been closed with the official seal of Yetive, Princess of Graustark, and was sacred to the eyes of anyone save the man to whom it was directed. The words it contained were burned deep in his brain:

"You are ordered to report for duty in the castle. Come at once. Her highness has sent an official command to Colonel Quinnox. Count Marlanx has been here. You are not expected to desert until you have seen me. There is an underground passage somewhere.— B."

Baldos went alone and swiftly. The note to Colonel Quinnox had been imperative. He was to serve as an inner guard until further orders. Someone, it was reported, had tried to enter Miss Calhoun's room from the outside during the rainstorm of the previous night, and a special guard was to be stationed near the door. All of this was unknown to Baldos, but he did not ask for any explanations.

He was half way to the castle when the sharp report of a gun startled him. A bullet whizzed close to his ear! Baldos broke into a crouching run, but did not change his course. He knew that the shot was intended for him, and that its mission was to prevent him from reaching the castle. The attendants at the castle door admitted him, panting and excited, and he was taken immediately to the enchanted boudoir of the princess which but few men were fortunate enough to enter. There were three women in the room.

"I am here to report, your highness," said he, bowing low before the real princess, with a smile upon his flushed face.

"You are prompt," said the princess. "What have you to report, sir?"

"That an attempt has just been made to kill a member of the castle guard," he coolly answered.

"Impossible!"

"I am quite certain of it, your highness. The bullet almost clipped my ear."

"Good heavens!" gasped the listeners. Then they eagerly plied him with more agitated questions than he could answer.

"And did you not pursue the wretch?" cried the princess.

"No, your highness. I was commanded to report to you at once. Only the success of the assassin could have made me — well, hesitate," said he calmly. "A soldier has but to obey."

"Do you think there was a deliberate attempt to kill you?" asked the Countess Dagmar. Beverly Calhoun was dumb with consternation.

" I cannot say, madame.   Possibly it was an accidental discharge.   One should not make accusations unsupported.   If you have no immediate need of my services, your highness, I will ask you to grant me leave of absence for half an hour.   I have a peculiar longing to investigate."   There was a determined gleam in his eyes.

" No, no!" cried Beverly.   " Don't you dare to go out there again.   You are to stay right here in the castle, sir.   We have something else for you to do. It was that awful old Marlanx who shot at you. He —— "

"I left General Marlanx in Colonel Quinnox's quarters, Miss Calhoun," interposed Baldos grimly. " He could not have fired the shot.   For two or three nights, your highness, I have been followed and dogged with humiliating persistence by two men wearing the uniforms of castle guards.   They do not sleep at the barracks.   May I ask what I have done to be submitted to such treatment? "   There was a trace of poorly concealed indignation in his voice.

" I assure you that this is news to me," said Yetive in amazement.

" I am being watched as if I were a common thief," he went on boldly.   " These men are not your agents; they are not the agents of Graustark.   May I be permitted to say that they are spies set upon me by a man who has an object in disgracing me?   Who that man is, I leave to your royal conjecture."

" Marlanx? "

" Yes, your highness.   He bears me a deadly

grudge and yet he fears me. I know full well that he and his agents have built a strong case against me. They are almost ready to close in upon me, and they will have false evidence so craftily prepared that even my truest friends may doubt my loyalty to you and to the cause I serve. Before God, I have been true to my oath. I am loyal to Graustark. It was a sorry day when I left the valley and —— "

" Oh! cried Beverly piteously. " Don't say that."

" Alas, Miss Calhoun, it is true," said he sadly. " I am penned up here where I cannot fight back. Treason is laid against me. But, beyond all this, I have permitted my loyalty to mislead my ambition. I have aspired to something I can cherish but never possess. Better that I never should have tasted of the unattainable than to have the cup withdrawn just as its sweetness begins to intoxicate."

He stood before them, pale with suppressed emotion. The women of Graustark looked involuntarily at Beverly, who sat cold and voiceless, staring at the face of the guard. She knew what he meant; she knew that something was expected of her. A word from her and he would understand that he had not tasted of the unattainable. In one brief moment she saw that she had deliberately led him on, that she had encouraged him, that she actually had proffered him the cup from which he had begun to sip the bitterness. Pride and love were waging a conflict in this hapless southern girl's heart. But she was silent. She could not say the word.

" I think I know what you mean, Baldos," said Ye
tive, seeing that Beverly would not intervene. " We
are sorry. No one trusts to your honor more than I
do. My husband believes in you. I will confess that
you are to be arrested as a spy to-morrow. To-night
you are to serve as a guard in the castle. This should
prove to you that I have unbounded faith in you.
Moreover, I believe in you to the extent that I should
not be afraid to trust you if you were to go out into
the world with every secret which we possess. You
came here under a peculiar stress of circumstances,
not wholly of your own volition. Believe me, I am
your friend."

" I shall revere your highness forever for those
words," said he simply. His eyes went hungrily
to Beverly's averted face, and then assumed a careless gleam which indicated that he had resigned himself to the inevitable.

" I am constrained to ask you one question, sir,"
went on the princess. " You are not the common
goat-hunter you assume. Will you tell me in confidence who you really are?" The others held their
breath. He hesitated for a moment.

" Will it suffice if I say that I am an unfortunate
friend and advocate of Prince Dantan? I have
risked everything for his sake and I fear I have lost
everything. I have failed to be of service to him,
but through no fault of mine. Fate has been against
me."

" You are Christobal," cried Dagmar eagerly.
He gave her a startled glance, but offered no denial.

Beverly's face was a study. If he were Christobal, then what of the game-warden's daughter?

"We shall question you no further," said Yetive. You enlisted to serve Miss Calhoun. It is for her to command you while you are here. May God be with you to the end. Miss Calhoun, will you tell him what his duties are for to-night? Come, my dear."

Yetive and Dagmar walked slowly from the room, leaving Beverly and her guard alone.

"I am at your service, Miss Calhoun," he said easily. His apparent indifference stung her into womanly revolt.

"I was a fool last night," she said abruptly.

"No; I was the fool. I have been the fool from the beginning. You shall not blame yourself, for I do not blame you. It has been a sweet comedy, a summer pastime. Forget what I may have said to you last night, forget what my eyes may have said for weeks and weeks."

"I shall never forget," said she. "You deserve the best in the world. Would that I could give it to you. You have braved many dangers for my sake. I shall not forget. Do you know that we were watched last night?"

"Watched?" he cried incredulously. "Oh, fool that I am! I might have known. And I have subjected you to — to — don't tell me that harsh things have been said to you, Miss Calhoun!" He was deeply disturbed.

"General Marlanx saw you. He has threatened me, Baldos,—— "

"I will kill him! What do I care for the consequences? He shall pay dearly for —— "

"Stop! Where are you going? You are to remain here, sir, and take your commands from me. I
don't want you to kill him. They'd hang you or
something just as bad. He's going to be punished,
never fear!" Baldos smiled in spite of his dismay.
It was impossible to face this confident young champion in petticoats without catching her enthusiasm.
"What have you done with — with that rose?" she
asked suddenly, flushing and diffident. Her eyes
glistened with embarrassment.

"It lies next my heart. I love it," he said bravely.

"I think I'll command you to return it to me,"
vaguely.

"A command to be disobeyed. It is in exchange
for my feather," he smiled confidently.

"Well, of course, if you are going to be mean
about — Now, let me see," she said confusedly;
"what are your duties for to-night? You are to
stand guard in the corridor. Once in awhile you will
go out upon the balcony and take a look. You see, I
am afraid of someone. Oh, Baldos, what's the use
of my trifling like this? You are to escape from
Edelweiss to-night. That is the whole plan — the
whole idea in a nutshell. Don't look like that. Don't
you want to go?" Now she was trembling with excitement.

"I do not want to leave you," he cried eagerly.
"It would be cowardly. Marlanx would understand
that you gave aid and sanction. You would be left to

face the charges he would make. Don't you see, Beverly? You would be implicated — you would be accused. Why did you not let me kill him? No; I will not go!" Neither noticed the name by which he had called her.

"But I insist," she cried weakly. "You must go away from me. I — I command you to — "

"Is it because you want to drive me out of your life forever?" he demanded, sudden understanding coming to him.

"Don't put it that way," she murmured.

"Is it because you care for me that you want me to go?" he insisted, drawing near. "Is it because you fear the love I bear for you?"

"Love? You don't really — Stop! Remember where you are, sir! You must not go on with it, Baldos. Don't come a step nearer. Do go to-night! It is for the best. I have been awfully wicked in letting it run on as it has. Forgive me, please forgive me," she pleaded. He drew back, pale and hurt. A great dignity settled upon his face. His dark eyes crushed her with their quiet scorn.

"I understand, Miss Calhoun. The play is over. You will find the luckless vagabond a gentleman, after all. You ask me to desert the cause I serve. That is enough. I shall go to-night."

The girl was near to surrender. Had it not been for the persistent fear that her proud old father might suffer from her wilfulness, she would have thrown down the barrier and risked everything in the choice.

Her heart was crying out hungrily for the love of this tall, mysterious soldier of fortune.

"It is best," she murmured finally. Later on she was to know the meaning of the peculiar smile he gave her.

"I go because you dismiss me, not because I fear an enemy. If you choose to remember me at all, be just enough to believe that I am not a shameless coward."

"You are brave and true and good, and I am a miserable, deceitful wretch," she lamented. "You will seek Ravone and the others?"

"Yes. They are my friends. They love my poverty. And now, may it please your highness, when am I to go forth and in what garb? I should no longer wear the honest uniform of a Graustark guard."

"Leave it to me. Everything shall be arranged. You will be discreet? No one is to know that I am your — "

"Rest assured, Miss Calhoun. I have a close mouth," and he smiled contemptuously.

"I agree with you," said she regretfully. "You know how to hold your tongue." He laughed harshly. "For once in a way, will you answer a question?"

"I will not promise."

"You say that you are Dantan's friend. Is it true that he is to marry the daughter of the Duke of Matz, Countess Iolanda?"

"It has been so reported."

" Is she beautiful? "

" Yes; exceedingly."

" But is he to marry her? " she insisted, she knew not why.

" How should I know, your highness? "

" If you call me ' your highness ' again I'll despise you," she flared miserably. " Another question. Is it true that the young Duke Christobal fled because his father objected to his marriage with a game-warden's daughter? "

" I have never heard so," with a touch of hauteur.

" Does he know that the girl is dead? " she asked cruelly. Baldos did not answer for a long time. He stared at her steadily, his eyes expressing no emotion from which she could judge him.

" I think he is ignorant of that calamity, Miss Calhoun," he said. " With your permission, I shall withdraw. There is nothing to be gained by delay." It was such a palpable affront that she shrank within herself and could have cried.

Without answering, she walked unsteadily to the window and looked out into the night. A mist came into her eyes. For many minutes she remained there, striving to regain control of her emotions. All this time she knew that he was standing just where she had left him, like a statue, awaiting her command. At last she faced him resolutely.

" You will receive instructions as to your duties here from the guard at the stairs. When you hear the hall clock strike the hour of two in the morning go into the chapel, but do not let anyone see you or suspect. You know where it is. The door will be unlocked."

"Am I not to see you again?" he asked, and she did not think him properly depressed.

"Yes," she answered, after a pause that seemed like an eternity, and he went quietly, silently away.

CHAPTER XXIV

BENEATH THE GROUND

HILE Baldos was standing guard in the long, lofty hallway the Iron Count was busy with the machinations which were calculated to result in a startling upheaval with the break of a new day. He prepared and swore to the charges preferred against Baldos. They were despatched to the princess for her perusal in the morning. Then he set about preparing the vilest accusations against Beverly Calhoun. In his own handwriting and over his own signature he charged her with complicity in the betrayal of Graustark, influenced by the desires of the lover who masqueraded as her protégé. At some length he dwelt upon the well-laid plot of the spy and his accomplice. He told of their secret meetings, their outrages against the dignity of the court, and their unmistakable animosity toward Graustark. For each and every count in his vicious indictment against the girl he professed to have absolute proof by means of more than one reputable witness.

It was not the design of Marlanx to present this document to the princess and her cabinet. He knew

273

full well that it would meet the fate it deserved. It
was intended for the eyes of Beverly Calhoun alone.
By means of the vile accusations, false though they
were, he hoped to terrorize her into submission.
He longed to possess this lithe, beautiful creature
from over the sea. In all his life he had not hungered
for anything as he now craved Beverly Calhoun. He
saw that his position in the army was rendered inse-
cure by the events of the last day. A bold, vicious
stroke was his only means for securing the prize he
longed for more than he longed for honor and fame.

Restless and enraged, consumed by jealousy and
fear, he hung about the castle grounds long after he
had drawn the diabolical charges. He knew that
Baldos was inside the castle, favored, while he, a
noble of the realm, was relegated to ignominy and the
promise of degradation. Encamped outside the city
walls the army lay without a leader. Each hour saw
the numbers augmented by the arrival of reserves
from the districts of the principality. His place was
out there with the staff. Yet he could not drag himself away from the charmed circle in which his prey
was sleeping. Morose and grim, he anxiously paced
to and fro in an obscure corner of the grounds.

"What keeps the scoundrel?" he said to himself
angrily.

Presently, a villainous looking man dressed in the
uniform of the guards, stealthily approached. "I
missed him, general, but I will get him the next time,"
growled the man.

"Curse you for a fool!" hissed Marlanx through

his teeth. As another hireling came up. "What have you got to say?"

The man reported that Baldos had been seen on the balcony alone, evidently on watch.

Marlanx ground his teeth and his blood stormed his reason. "The job must be done to-night. You have your instructions. Capture him if possible; but if necessary, kill him. You know your fate, if you fail." Marlanx actually grinned at the thought of the punishment he would mete out to them. "Now be off!"

Rashly he made his way to the castle front. A bright moon cast its mellow glow over the mass of stone outlined against the western sky. For an hour he glowered in the shade of the trees, giving but slight heed to the guards who passed from time to time. His eyes never left the enchanted balcony.

At last he saw the man. Baldos came from the door at the end of the balcony, paced the full length in the moonlight, paused for a moment near Beverly Calhoun's window and then disappeared through the same door that had afforded him egress.

Inside the dark castle the clock at the end of the hall melodiously boomed the hour of two. Dead quiet followed the soft echoes of the gong. A tall figure stealthily opened the door to Yetive's chapel and stepped inside. There was a streak of moonlight through the clear window at the far end of the room. Baldos, his heart beating rapidly, stood still for a moment, awaiting the next move in the game. The ghost-like figure of a woman suddenly stood before him in the path of the moonbeam, a hooded figure in dark robes. He started as if confronted by the supernatural.

"Come," came in an agitated whisper, and he stepped to the side of the phantom. She turned and the moonlight fell upon the face of Beverly Calhoun. "Don't speak. Follow me as quickly as you can."

He grasped her arm, bringing her to a standstill.

"I have changed my mind," he whispered in her ear. "Do you think I will run away and leave you to shoulder the blame for all this? On the balcony near your window an hour ago I —— "

"It doesn't make any difference," she argued. "You have to go. I want you to go. If you knew just how I feel toward you you would go without a murmur."

"You mean that you hate me," he groaned.

"I wouldn't be so unkind as to say that," she fluttered. "I don't know who you are. Come; we can't delay a minute. I have a key to the gate at the other end of the passage and I know where the secret panel is located. Hush! It doesn't matter where I got the key. See! See how easy it is?"

He felt her tense little fingers in the darkness searching for his. Their hands were icy cold when the clasp came. Together they stood in a niche of the wall near the chancel rail. It was dark and a cold draft of air blew across their faces. He could not see, but there was proof enough that she had opened the secret panel in the wall, and that the damp, chill air came from the underground passage, which led to a point outside the city walls.

"You go first," she whispered nervously. "I'm afraid. There is a lantern on the steps and I have some matches. We'll light it as soon as — Oh, what was that?"

"Don't be frightened," he said. "I think it was a rat."

"Good gracious!" she gasped. "I wouldn't go in there for the world."

"Do you mean to say that you intended to do so?" he asked eagerly.

"Certainly. Someone has to return the key to the outer gate. Oh, I suppose I'll have to go in. You'll keep them off, won't you?" plaintively. He was smiling in the darkness, thinking what a dear, whimsical thing she was.

"With my life," he said softly.

"They're ten times worse than lions," she announced.

"You must not forget that you return alone," he said triumphantly.

"But I'll have the lantern going full blast," she said, and then allowed him to lead her into the narrow passageway. She closed the panel and then felt about with her foot until it located the lantern. In a minute they had a light. "Now, don't be afraid," she said encouragingly. He laughed in pure delight; she misunderstood his mirth and was conscious of a new and an almost unendurable pang. He was filled with exhilaration over the prospect of escape! Somehow she felt an impulse to throw her arms about him and drag him back into the chapel, in spite of the ghost of the game-warden's daughter.

"What is to prevent me from taking you with me?" he said intensely, a mighty longing in his breast. She laughed but drew back uneasily.

"And live unhappily ever afterward?" said she. "Oh, dear me! Isn't this a funny proceeding? Just think of me, Beverly Calhoun, being mixed up in schemes and plots and intrigues and all that. It seems like a great big dream. And that reminds me: you will find a raincoat at the foot of the steps. I couldn't get other clothes for you, so you'll have to wear the uniform. There's a stiff hat of Mr. Lorry's also. You've no idea how difficult it is for a girl to collect clothes for a man. There doesn't seem to be any real excuse for it, you know. Goodness, it looks black ahead there, doesn't it? I hate underground things. They're so damp and all that. How far is it, do you suppose, to the door in the wall?" She was chattering on, simply to keep up her courage and to make her fairest show of composure.

"It's a little more than three hundred yards," he replied. They were advancing through the low, narrow stone-lined passage. She steadfastly ignored the hand he held back for support. It was not a pleasant place, this underground way to the outside world. The walls were damp and mouldy; the odor of the rank earth assailed the nostrils; the air was chill and deathlike.

"How do you know?" she demanded quickly.

"I have traversed the passage before, Miss Calhoun," he replied. She stopped like one paralyzed, her eyes wide and incredulous. "Franz was my guide from the outer gate into the chapel. It is easy enough to get outside the walls, but extremely difficult to return," he went on easily.

"You mean to say that you have been in and out by way of this passage? Then, what was your object, sir?" she demanded sternly.

"My desire to communicate with friends who could not enter the city. Will it interest you if I say that the particular object of my concern was a young woman?"

She gasped and was stubbornly silent for a long time. Bitter resentment filled her soul, bitter disappointment in this young man. "A young woman!" he had said, oh, so insolently. There could be but one inference, one conclusion. The realization of it settled one point in her mind forever.

"It wouldn't interest me in the least. I don't even care who she was. Permit me to wish you much joy with her. Why don't you go on?" irritably, forgetting that it was she who delayed progress. His smile was invisible in the blackness above the lantern. There were no words spoken until after they had reached the little door in the wall.

Here the passage was wider. There were casks and chests on the floor, evidently containing articles that required instant removal from Edelweiss in case of an emergency.

" Who was that woman ? " she asked at last.   The
key to the door was in the nervous little hand.

" One very near and dear to me, Miss Calhoun.
That's all I can say at this time."

" Well, this is the only time you will have the
chance," she cried loftily.   " Here we part.
Hush ! " she whispered, involuntarily grasping his
arm.   " I think I heard a step.   Can anyone be following us ? "   They stopped and listened.   It was as
still as a tomb.

" It must be the same old rat," he answered jok-
ingly.   She was too nervous for any pleasantries, and
releasing her hold on his arm, said timidly, " Good-
bye ! "

" Am I to go in this manner ?   Have you no kind
word for me ?   I love you better than my soul.   It is
of small consequence to you, I know, but I crave one
forgiving word.   It may be the last."   He clasped
her hand and she did not withdraw it.   Her lips were
trembling, but her eyes were brave and obstinate.
Suddenly she sat down upon one of the chests.   If he
had not told her of the other woman !

" Forgive me instead, for all that I have brought
you to," she murmured.   " It was all my fault.   I
shall never forget you or forgive myself.   I — I am
going back to Washin'ton immediately.   I can't bear
to stay here now.   Good-bye, and God bless you.   Do
— do you think we shall ever see each other again ? "
Unconsciously she was clinging to his hand.   There
were tears in the gray eyes that looked pathetically
up into his.   She was very dear and enchanting,

down there in the grewsome passageway with the fitful
rays of the lantern lighting her face. Only the
strictest self-control kept him from seizing her in his
arms, for something told him that she would have surrendered.

"This is the end, I fear," he said, with grim persistence. She caught her breath in half a sob. Then
she arose resolutely, although her knees trembled
shamelessly.

"Well, then, good-bye," she said very steadily.
"You are free to go where and to whom you like.
Think of me once in awhile, Baldos. Here's the key.
Hurry! I — I can't stand it much longer!" She
was ready to break down and he saw it, but he made
no sign.

Turning the key in the rusty lock, he cautiously
opened the door. The moonlit world lay beyond. A
warm, intoxicating breath of fresh air came in upon
them. He suddenly stooped and kissed her hand.

"Forgive me for having annoyed you with my poor
love," he said, as he stood in the door, looking into
the night beyond.

"All —— all right," she choked out as she started
to close the door after him.

"Halt! You are our prisoner!"

The words rang out sharply in the silence of the
night. Instinctively, Beverly made an attempt to
close the door; but she was too late. Two burly, villainous looking men, sword in hand, blocked the exit
and advanced upon them.

" Back! Back! " Baldos shouted to Beverly,
drawing his sword.

Like a flash, she picked up the lantern and sprang
out of his way. Capture or worse seemed certain;
but her heart did not fail her.

" Put up your sword! You are under arrest! "
came from the foremost of the two. He had heard
enough of Baldos's skill with the sword to hope that
the ruse might be successful and that he would surrender peaceably to numbers. The men's instructions
were to take their quarry alive if possible. The reward for the man, living, exceeded that for him dead.

Baldos instantly recognized them as spies employed by Marlanx. They had been dogging his
footsteps for days and even had tried to murder him.
The desire for vengeance was working like madness in
his blood. He was overjoyed at having them at the
point of his sword. Beverly's presence vouchsafed
that he would show little mercy.

" Arrest me, you cowardly curs! " he exclaimed.
" Never! " With a spring to one side, he quickly
overturned one of the casks and pushing it in front
of him, it served as a rolling bulwark, preventing a
joint attack.

" You first! " he cried coolly, as his sword met
that of the leader. The unhappy wretch was no
match for the finest swordsman in Graustark. He
made a few desperate attempts to ward off his inevitable fate, calling loudly for his comrade to aid
him. The latter was eager enough, but Baldos's
strategic roll of the cask effectively prevented him

from taking a hand. With a vicious thrust, the blade of the goat-hunter tore clean through the man's chest and touched the wall behind.

"One!" cried Baldos, gloating in the chance that had come to him. The man gasped and fell. He was none too quick in withdrawing his dripping weapon, for the second man was over the obstacle and upon him.

CHAPTER XXV

THE VALOR OF THE SOUTH

OLD the lantern higher, Bev —— "
In the fury of the fight, he remembered the risk and importance of not
mentioning her name, and stopped
short. He was fighting fast but
warily, for he realized that his present
adversary was no mean one. As the swords played
back and forth in fierce thrusts and parries, he spoke
assuringly to Beverly: "Don't be frightened! As
soon as I finish with this fellow, we will go on! Ah!
Bravo! Well parried, my man! How the deuce
could such a swordsman as you become a cutthroat
of Marlanx?"

Beverly had been standing still all this time holding the light high above her head, according to her
lover's orders, for she knew now that such he was and
that she loved him with all her heart. She was a
weird picture standing there as she watched Baldos
fighting for their lives, her beautiful face deathlike
in its pallor. Not a cry escaped her lips, as the
sword-blades swished and clashed; she could hear the
deep breathing of the combatants in that tomb-like
passage.

284

Suddenly she started and listened keenly. From behind her, back there in the darkness, hurried footsteps were unmistakably approaching. What she had heard, then, was not the scurrying of a rat. Some one was following them. A terrible anguish seized her. Louder and nearer came the heavy steps. "Oh, my God! Baldos!" she screamed in terror. "Another is coming!"

"Have no fear, dear one!" he sung out gaily. His voice was infinitely more cheerful than he felt, for he realized only too well the desperate situation; he was penned in and forced to meet an attack from front and rear. He fell upon his assailant with redoubled fury, aiming to finish him before the newcomer could give aid.

From out of the gloom came a fiendish laugh. Instantly, the dark figure of a man appeared, his face completely hidden by a broad slouch hat and the long cloak which enveloped him. A sardonic voice hissed, "Trapped at last! My lady and her lover thought to escape, did they!" The voice was unfamiliar, but the atmosphere seemed charged with Marlanx. "Kill him, Zem!" he shouted. "Don't let him escape you! I will take care of the little witch, never fear!" He clutched at the girl and tried to draw her to him.

"Marlanx! By all the gods!" cried Baldos in despair. He had wounded his man several times, though not seriously. He dared not turn to Beverly's aid.

The scene was thrilling, grewsome. Within this narrow, dimly-lighted underground passage, with its musty walls sweating with dampness and thick with the tangled meshes of the spider's web, a brave girl and her lover struggled and fought back to back.

To her dismay, Beverly saw the point of a sword at her throat.

" Out of the way, girl," the man in the cloak snarled, furious at her resistance. " You die as well as your lover unless you surrender. He cannot escape me."

" And if I refuse," cried the girl, trying desperately to gain time.

" I will drive my blade through your heart and tell the world it was the deed of your lover."

Baldos groaned. His adversary, encouraged by the change in the situation, pressed him sorely.

" Don't you dare to touch me, Count Marlanx. I know you!" she hissed. " I know what you would do with me. It is not for Graustark that you seek his life."

The sword came nearer. The words died in her throat. She grew faint. Terror paralyzed her. Suddenly, her heart gave a great thump of joy. The resourcefulness of the trapped was surging to her relief. The valor of the South leaped into life. The exhilaration of conflict beat down all her fears. " Take away that sword, then, please," she cried, her voice trembling, but not with terror now; it was exultation. " Will you promise to spare his life? Will you swear to let him go, if I —— "

" No, no, never! God forbid!" implored Baldos.

" Ha, ha!" chuckled the man in the cloak. " Spare

his life! Oh, yes; after my master has revelled in your charms. How do you like that, my handsome goat-hunter?"

"You infernal scoundrel! I'll settle you yet!" Baldos fairly fumed with rage. Gathering himself together for a final effort, he rushed madly on his rapidly-weakening antagonist.

"Baldos!" she cried hopelessly and in a tone of resignation. "I must do it! It is the only way!"

The man in the cloak as well as Baldos was deceived by the girl's cry. He immediately lowered his sword. The lantern dropped from Beverly's hands and clattered to the floor. At the same instant she drew from her pocket her revolver, which she had placed there before leaving the castle, and fired point blank at him. The report sounded like a thunder clap in their ears. It was followed quickly by a sharp cry and imprecation from the lips of her persecutor, who fell, striking his head with a terrible force on the stones.

Simultaneously, there was a groan and the noise of a limp body slipping to the ground, and, Baldos, victor at last, turned in fear and trembling to find Beverly standing unhurt staring at the black mass at her feet.

"Thank God! You are safe!" Grasping her hand he led her out of the darkness into the moonlight.

Not a word was spoken as they ran swiftly on until they reached a little clump of trees, not far from one of the gates. Here Baldos gently released her hand. She was panting for breath; but he realized she must not be allowed to risk a moment's delay. She must pass the sentry at once.

" Have you the watchword? " he eagerly asked.

" Watchword? " she repeated feebly.

" Yes, the countersign for the night. It is Ganlook. Keep your face well covered with your hood. Advance boldly to the gates and give the word. There will be no trouble. The guard is used to pleasure seekers returning at all hours of night."

" Is he dead? " she asked timorously, returning to the scene of horror.

" Only wounded, I think, as are the other men, though they all deserve death."

He went with her as close to the gate as he thought safe. Taking her hand he kissed it fervently. " Good-bye! It won't be for long! " and disappeared.

She stood still and lifeless, staring after him, for ages, it seemed. He was gone. Gone forever, no doubt. Her eyes grew wilder and wilder with the pity of it all. Pride fled incontinently. She longed to call him back. Then it occurred to her that he was hurrying off to that other woman. No, he said he would return. She must be brave, true to herself, whatever happened. She marched boldly up to the gate, gave the countersign and passed through, not heeding the curious glances cast upon her by the sentry; turned into the castle, up the grand staircase, and fled to the princess's bed-chamber.

Beverly, trembling and sobbing, threw herself in

the arms of the princess. Incoherently, she related all that had happened, then swooned.

After she had been restored, the promise of Yetive to protect her, whatever happened, comforted her somewhat.

"It must have been Marlanx," moaned Beverly.

"Who else could it have been?" replied the princess, who was visibly excited.

Summoning all her courage, she went on: "First, we must find out if he is badly hurt. We'll trust to luck. Cheer up!" She touched a bell. There came a knock at the door. A guard was told to enter. "Ellos," she exclaimed, "did you hear a shot fired a short time ago?"

"I thought I did, your highness, but was not sure."

"Baldos, the guard, was escaping by the secret passage," continued the princess, a wonderful inspiration coming to her rescue. "He passed through the chapel. Miss Calhoun was there. Alone, and single-handed, she tried to prevent him. It was her duty. He refused to obey her command to stop and she followed him into the tunnel and fired at him. I'm afraid you are too late to capture him, but you may ——, Oh, Beverly, how plucky you were to follow him! Go quickly, Ellos! Search the tunnel and report at once." As the guard saluted, with wonder, admiration and unbelief, he saw the two conspirators locked in each other's arms.

Presently he returned and reported that the guards could find no trace of anyone in the tunnel,

but that they found blood on the floor near the exit
and that the door was wide open.

The two girls looked at each other in amazement.
They were dumbfounded, but a great relief was glowing in their eyes.

"Ellos," inquired the princess, considerably less
agitated, "does any one else know of this?"

"No, your highness, there was no one on guard
but Max, Baldos, and myself."

"Well, for the present, no one else must know
of his flight. Do you understand? Not a word to
any one. I, myself, will explain when the proper time
comes. You and Max have been very careless, but I
suppose you should not be punished. He has tricked
us all. Send Max to me at once."

"Yes, your highness," said Ellos, and he went away
with his head swimming. Max, the other guard, received like orders and then the two young women
sank limply upon a divan.

"Oh, how clever you are, Yetive," came from the
American girl. "But what next?"

"We may expect to hear something disagreeable
from Count Marlanx, my dear," murmured the perplexed, but confident princess, "but I think we have
the game in our own hands, as you would say in
America."

CHAPTER XXVI

THE DEGRADATION OF MARLANX

UNT FANNY, what is that white thing sticking under the window?" demanded Beverly late the next morning. She was sitting with her face to the windows while the old negress dressed her hair.

"Looks lak a love letteh, Miss Bev'ly," was the answer, as Aunt Fanny gingerly placed an envelope in her mistress's hand. Beverly looked at it in amazement. It was unmistakably a letter, addressed to her, which had been left at her window some time in the night. Her heart gave a thump and she went red with anticipated pleasure. With eager fingers she tore open the envelope. The first glance at the contents brought disappointment to her face. The missive was from Count Marlanx; but it was a relief to find that he was very much alive and kicking. As she read on, there came a look of perplexity which was succeeded by burning indignation. The man in the cloak was preparing to strike.

"Your secret is mine. I know all that happened in the chapel and underground passage. You have betrayed Graustark in aiding this man to escape. The plot was cleverly

291

executed, but you counted without the jealous eye of love. You can save yourself and your honor, and perhaps your princess, but the conditions are mine. This time there can be no trifling. I want you to treat me fairly. God help you if you refuse. Give me the answer I want and your secret is safe. I will shield you with my life. At eleven o'clock I shall come to see you. I have in my possession a document that will influence you. You will do well to keep a close mouth until you have seen this paper."

This alarming note was all that was needed to restore fire to the lagging blood of the American girl. Its effect was decidedly contrary to that which Marlanx must have anticipated. Instead of collapsing, Beverly sprang to her feet with energy and life in every fiber. Her eyes were flashing brightly, her body quivering with the sensations of battle.

"That awful old wretch!" she cried, to Aunt Fanny's amazement. "He is the meanest human being in all the world. But he's making the mistake of his life, isn't he, Aunt Fanny? Oh, of course you don't know what it is, so never mind. We've got a surprise for him. I'll see him at eleven o'clock, and then —— " she smiled quite benignly at the thought of what she was going to say to him. Beverly felt very secure in the shadow of the princess.

A clatter of horses' hoofs on the parade-ground drew her to the balcony. What she saw brought joy to her heart. Lorry and Anguish, muddy and disheveled, were dismounting before the castle.

"Ah, this is joy! Now there are three good Americans here. I'm not afraid," she said bravely. Aunt Fanny nodded her head in approval, although she did not know what it was all about. Curiosity more than alarm made Beverly eager to see the document which old Marlanx held in reserve for her. She determined to met him at eleven.

A message from the princess announced the unexpected return of the two Americans. She said they were (to use Harry Anguish's own expression) " beastly near starvation " and clamored for substantial breakfasts. Beverly was urged to join them and to hear the latest news from the frontier.

Lorry and Anguish were full of the excitement on which they had lived for many hours. They had found evidence of raids by the Dawsbergen scouts and had even caught sight of a small band of fleeing horsemen. Lorry reluctantly admitted that Gabriel's army seemed loyal to him and that there was small hope of a conflict being averted, as he had surmised, through the defection of the people. He was surprised but not dismayed when Yetive told him certain portions of the story in regard to Marlanx; and, by no means averse to seeing the old man relegated to the background, heartily endorsed the step taken by his wife. He was fair enough, however, to promise the general a chance to speak in his own defense, if he so desired. He had this in view when he requested Marlanx to come to the castle at eleven o'clock for consultation.

" Gabriel is devoting most of his energy now to hunting that poor Dantan into his grave," said Anguish. " I believe he'd rather kill his half-brother than conquer Graustark. Why, the inhuman monster has set himself to the task of obliterating everything that reminds him of Dantan. We learned from spies down there that he issued an order for the death of Dantan's sister, a pretty young thing named Candace, because he believed she was secretly aiding her fugitive brother. She escaped from the palace in Serros a week ago, and no one knows what has become of her. There's a report that she was actually killed, and that the story of her flight is a mere blind on the part of Gabriel."

"He would do anything," cried Yetive. "Poor child; they say she is like her English mother and is charming."

"That would set Gabriel against her, I fancy," went on Anguish. "And, by the way, Miss Calhoun, we heard something definite about your friend, Prince Dantan. It is pretty well settled that he isn't Baldos of the guard. Dantan was seen two days ago by Captain Dangloss's men. He was in the Dawsbergen pass and they talked with him and his men. There was no mistake this time. The poor, half-starved chap confessed to being the prince and begged for food for himself and his followers."

"I tried to find him, and, failing in that, left word in the pass that if he would but cast his lot with us in this trouble we soon would restore him to his throne," said Lorry. "He may accept and we shall have him turning up here some day, hungry for revenge. And now, my dear Beverly, how are you progressing with the excellent Baldos, of whom we cannot make a prince, no matter how hard we try?"

Beverly and the princess exchanged glances in which consternation was difficult to conceal. It was clear to Beverly that Yetive had not told her husband of the escape.

"I don't know anything about Baldos," she answered steadily. "Last night someone shot at him in the park."

"The deuce you say!"

"In order to protect him until you returned, Gren, I had him transferred to guard duty inside the castle," explained the princess. "It really seemed necessary. General Marlanx expects to present formal charges against him this morning, so I suppose we shall have to put him in irons for a little while. It seems too bad, doesn't it, Gren?"

"Yes. He's as straight as a string, I'll swear," said Lorry emphatically.

"I'll bet he wishes he were safely out of this place," ventured Anguish, and two young women busied themselves suddenly with their coffee.

"The chance is he's sorry he ever came into it," said Lorry tantalizingly.

While they were waiting for Marlanx the young Duke of Mizrox was announced. The handsome Axphainian came with relief and dismay struggling for mastery in his face.

"Your highness," he said, after the greetings, "I am come to inform you that Graustark has one prince less to account for. Axphain has found her fugitive."

"When?" cried the princess and Beverly in one voice and with astonishing eagerness, not unmixed with dismay.

" Three days ago," was the reply.

" Oh," came in deep relief from Beverly as she sank back into her chair. The same fear had lodged in the hearts of the two fair conspirators — that they had freed Baldos only to have him fall into the hands of his deadliest foes.

" I have a message by courier from my uncle in Axphain," said Mizrox. " He says that Frederic was killed near Labbot by soldiers, after making a gallant fight, on last Sunday night. The Princess Volga is rejoicing, and has amply rewarded his slayers. Poor Frederic! He knew but little happiness in this life."

There was a full minute of reflection before any of his hearers expressed the thought that had framed itself in every mind.

" Well, since Dantan and Frederic are accounted for, Baldos is absolutely obliged to be Christobal," said Anguish resignedly.

" He's just Baldos," observed Beverly, snuffing out the faint hope that had lingered so long. Then she said to herself: " And I don't care, either. I only wish he were back here again. I'd be a good deal nicer to him."

Messengers flew back and forth, carrying orders from the castle to various quarters. The ministers were called to meet at twelve o'clock. Underneath all the bustle there was a tremendous impulse of American cunning, energy and resourcefulness. Everyone caught the fever. Reserved old diplomats were overwhelmed by their own enthusiasm; custom-bound soldiers forgot the hereditary caution and fell into the ways of the new leaders without a murmur. The city was wild with excitement, for all believed that the war was upon them. There was but one shadow overhanging the glorious optimism of Graustark — the ugly, menacing attitude of Axphain. Even the Duke of Mizrox could give no assurance that his country would remain neutral.

Colonel Quinnox came to the castle in haste and perturbation. It was he who propounded the question that Yetive and Beverly were expecting: " Where is Baldos? " Of course, the flight of the suspected guard was soon a matter of certainty. A single imploring glance from the princess, meant for the faithful Quinnox alone, told him as plainly as words could have said that she had given the man his freedom. And Quinnox would have died a thousand times to protect the secret of his sovereign, for had not twenty generations of Quinnoxes served the rulers of Graustark with unflinching loyalty? Baron Dangloss may have suspected the trick, but he did not so much as blink when the princess instructed him to hunt high and low for the fugitive.

Marlanx came at eleven. Under the defiant calmness of his bearing there was lurking a mighty fear. His brain was scourged by thoughts of impending disgrace. The princess had plainly threatened his degradation. After all these years, he was to tremble with shame and humiliation; he was to cringe where he had always boasted of domineering power. And besides all this, Marlanx had a bullet wound in his left shoulder! The world could not have known, for he knew how to conceal pain.

He approached the slender, imperious judge in the council-chamber with a defiant leer on his face. If he went down into the depths he would drag with him the fairest treasure he had coveted in all his years of lust and desire.

"A word with you," he said in an aside to Beverly, as she came from the council-chamber, in which she felt she should not sit. She stopped and faced him. Instinctively she looked to see if he bore evidence of a wound. She was positive that her bullet had struck him the night before, and that Marlanx was the man with the cloak.

"Well?" she said coldly. He read her thoughts and smiled, even as his shoulder burned with pain.

"I will give you the chance to save yourself. I love you. I want you. I must have you for my own," he was saying.

"Stop, sir! It may be your experience in life that women kneel to you when you command. It may be your habit to win what you set about to win. But you have a novel way of presenting your *devoirs*, I must say. Is this the way in which you won the five unfortunates whom you want me to succeed? Did you scare them into submission?"

"No, no! I cared nothing for them. You are the only one I ever loved —— "

"Really, Count Marlanx, you are most amusing," she interrupted, with a laugh that stung him to the quick. "You have been unique in your love-making.

I am not used to your methods. Besides, after having known them, I'll confess that I don't like them in the least. You may have been wonderfully successful in the past, but you were not dealing with an American girl. I have had enough of your insults. Go! Go in and face —— "

" Have a care, girl!" he snarled. " I have it in my power to crush you."

" Pooh! " came scornfully from her lips. " If you molest me further I shall call Mr. Lorry. Let me pass!"

" Just glance at this paper, my beauty. I fancy you'll change your tune. It goes before the eyes of the council, unless you —— " he paused significantly.

Beverly took the document and with dilated eyes read the revolting charges against her honor. Her cheeks grew white with anger, then flushed a deep crimson.

" You fiend! " she cried, glaring at him so fiercely that he instinctively shrank back, the vicious grin dying in his face. " I'll show you how much I fear you. I shall give this revolting thing to the princess. She may read it to the cabinet, for all I care. No one will believe you. They'll kill you for this! "

She turned and flew into the presence of the princess and her ministers. Speeding to the side of Yetive, she thrust the paper into her hands. Surprise and expectancy filled the eyes of all assembled.

" Count Marlanx officially charges me with — with — Read it, your highness," she cried distractedly.

Yetive read it, pale-faced and cold. A determined gleam appeared in her eyes as she passed the document to her husband.

" Allode," Lorry said to an attendant, after a brief glance at its revolting contents, " ask Count Marlanx to appear here instantly. He is outside the door."

Lorry's anger was hard to control. He clenched his hands and there was a fine suggestion of throttling in the way he did it. Marlanx, entering the room, saw that he was doomed. He had not expected Beverly to take this appalling step. The girl, tears in her eyes, rushed to a window, hiding her face from the wondering ministers. Her courage suddenly failed her. If the charges were read aloud before these men it seemed to her that she never could lift her eyes again. A mighty longing for Washington, her father and the big Calhoun boys, rushed to her heart as she stood there and awaited the crash. But Lorry was a true nobleman.

" Gentlemen," he said quietly, " Count Marlanx has seen fit to charge Miss Calhoun with complicity in the flight of Baldos. I will not read the charges to you. They are unworthy of one who has held the highest position in the army of Graustark. He has ―― "

" Read this, my husband, before you proceed further," said Yetive, thrusting into his hand a line she had written with feverish haste. Lorry smiled gravely before he read aloud the brief edict which removed General Marlanx from the command of the army of Graustark.

"Is this justice?" protested Marlanx angrily. "Will you not give me a hearing? I beseech —— "

"Silence!" commanded the princess. "What manner of hearing did you expect to give Miss Calhoun? It is enough, sir. There shall be no cowards in my army."

"Coward?" he faltered. "Have I not proved my courage on the field of battle? Am I to be called a —— "

"Bravery should not end when the soldier quits the field of battle. You have had a hearing, Count Marlanx. I heard the truth about you last night."

"From Miss Calhoun?" sneered he viciously. "I must be content to accept this dismissal, your highness. There is no hope for me. Some day you may pray God to forgive you for the wrong you have done your most loyal servant. There is no appeal from your decision; but as a subject of Graustark I insist that Miss Calhoun shall be punished for aiding in the escape of this spy and traitor. He is gone, and it was she who led him through the castle to the outer world. She cannot deny this, gentlemen. I defy her to say she did not accompany Baldos through the secret passage last night."

"It will do no harm to set herself right by denying this accusation," suggested Count Halfont solemnly. Every man in the cabinet and army had hated Marlanx for years. His degradation was not displeasing to them. They would ask no questions.

But Beverly Calhoun stood staring out of the window, out upon the castle park and its gay sunshine.

She did not answer, for she did not hear the premier's words. Her brain was whirling madly with other thoughts. She was trying to believe her eyes.

"The spy is gone," cried Marlanx, seeing a faint chance to redeem himself at her expense. "She cannot face my charge. Where is your friend, Miss Calhoun?"

Beverly faced them with a strange, subdued calmness in her face. Her heart was throbbing wildly in the shelter of this splendid disguise.

"I don't know what all this commotion is about," she said. "I only know that I have been dragged into it shamelessly by that old man over there. If you step to the window you may see Baldos himself. He has not fled. He is on duty!"

Baldos was striding steadily across the park in plain view of all.

CHAPTER XXVII

THE PRINCE OF DAWSBERGEN

OTH Yetive and Beverly expe-rienced an amazing sense of relief. They did not stop to consider why or how he had returned to the castle grounds. It was sufficient that he was actually there, sound, well, and apparently satisfied.

"I dare say Count Marlanx will withdraw his in-famous charge against our guest," said Lorry, with deadly directness. Marlanx was mopping his damp forehead. His eyes were fastened upon the figure of the guard, and there was something like awe in their steely depths. It seemed to him that the super-natural had been enlisted against him.

"He left the castle last night," he muttered, half to himself.

"There seems to be no doubt of that," agreed Gas-pon, the grand treasurer. "Colonel Quinnox reports his strange disappearance." Clearly the case was a puzzling one. Men looked at one another in wonder and uneasiness.

"I think I understand the situation," exclaimed Marlanx, suddenly triumphant. "It bears out all

303

that I have said.   Baldos left the castle last night, as
I have sworn, but not for the purpose of escaping.
He went forth to carry information to our enemies.
Can anyone doubt that he is a spy? Has he not
returned to carry out his work?   And now, gentlemen,
I ask you — would he return unless he felt secure of
protection here?"

It was a facer.   Yetive and Beverly felt as though
a steel trap suddenly had been closed down upon them.
Lorry and Anguish were undeniably disconcerted.
There was a restless, undecided movement among the
ministers.

"Colonel Quinnox, will you fetch Baldos to the
verandah at once?" asked Lorry, his quick American
perception telling him that immediate action was
necessary.   "It is cooler out there."   He gave Beverly a look of inquiry.   She flushed painfully, guiltily, and he was troubled in consequence.

"As a mere subject, I demand the arrest of this
man," Marlanx was saying excitedly.   "We must go
to the bottom of this hellish plot to injure Graustark."

"My dear count," said Anguish, standing over
him, "up to this time we have been unable to discern
any reasons for or signs of the treachery you preach
about.   I don't believe we have been betrayed at all."

"But I have absolute proof, sir," grated the count.

"I'd advise you to produce it. We must have
something to work on, you know."

"What right have you to give advice, sir?   You
are not one of us.   You are a meddler — an imperti-
nent alien.   Your heart is not with Graustark, as

mine is. How long must we endure the insolence of these Americans?"

The count was fuming with anger. As might have been expected, the easy-going Yankees laughed unreservedly at his taunt. The princess was pale with indignation.

"Count Marlanx, you will confine your remarks to the man whom you have charged with treachery," she said. "You have asked for his arrest, and you are to be his accuser. At the proper time you will produce the proof. I warn you now that if you do not sustain these charges, the displeasure of the crown will fall heavily upon you."

"I only ask your highness to order his arrest," he said, controlling himself. "He is of the castle guard and can be seized only on your command."

"Baldos is at the castle steps, your highness," said Colonel Quinnox from the doorway. The entire party left the council-chamber and passed out to the great stone porch. It must be confessed that the princess leaned rather heavily upon Lorry's arm. She and Beverly trembled with anxiety as they stood face to face with the tall guard who had come back to them so mysteriously.

Baldos stood at the foot of the stone steps, a guard on each side of him. One of these was the shame-faced Haddan, Dangloss's watchman, whose vigil had been a failure. The gaze of the suspected guard purposely avoided that of Beverly Calhoun. He knew that the slightest communication between them would be misunderstood and magnified by the witnesses.

"Baldos," said Lorry, from the top step, "it has come to our ears that you left the castle surreptitiously last night. Is it true that you were aided by Miss Calhoun?" Baldos looked thankful for this eminently leading question. In a flash it gave him the key to the situation. Secretly he was wondering what emotions possessed the slender accomplice who had said good-bye to him not so many hours before at the castle gate. He knew that she was amazed, puzzled by his sudden return; he wondered if she were glad. His quick wits saw that a crisis had arrived. The air was full of it. The dread of this very moment was the thing which had drawn him into the castle grounds at early dawn. He had watched for his chance to glide in unobserved, and had snatched a few hours' sleep in the shelter of the shrubbery near the park wall.

"It is not true," he said clearly, in answer to Lorry's question. Both Beverly and Marlanx started as the sharp falsehood fell from his lips. "Who made such an accusation?" he demanded.

"Count Marlanx is our informant."

"Then Count Marlanx lies," came coolly from the guard. A snarl of fury burst from the throat of the deposed general. His eyes were red and his tongue was half palsied by rage.

"Dog! Dog!" he shouted, running down the steps. "Infamous dog! I swear by my soul that he —— "

"Where is your proof, Count Marlanx?" sternly interrupted Lorry. "You have made a serious accusation against our honored guest. It cannot be overlooked."

Marlanx hesitated a moment, and then threw his bomb at the feet of the conspirators.

"I was in the chapel when she opened the secret panel for him."

Not a word was uttered for a full minute. It was Beverly Calhoun who spoke first. She was as calm as a spring morning.

"If all this be true, Count Marlanx, may I ask why you, the head of Graustark's army, did not intercept the spy when you had the chance?"

Marlanx flushed guiltily. The question had caught him unprepared. He dared not acknowledge his presence there with the hired assassins.

"I — I was not in a position to restrain him," he fumbled.

"You preferred to wait until he was safely gone before making the effort to protect Graustark from his evil designs. Is that it? What was your object in going to the chapel? To pray? Besides, what right had you to enter the castle in the night?" she asked ironically.

"Your highness, may I be heard?" asked Baldos easily. He was smiling up at Yetive from the bottom of the steps. She nodded her head a trifle uneasily. "It is quite true that I left the castle by means of your secret passage last night."

"There!" shrieked Marlanx. "He admits that he —— "

"But I wish to add that Count Marlanx is in error

when he says that Miss Calhoun was my accomplice. His eyes were not keen in the darkness of the sanctuary. Perhaps he is not accustomed to the light one finds in a chapel at the hour of two. Will your highness kindly look in the direction of the southern gate? Your august gaze may fall upon the reclining figure of a boy asleep, there in the shadow of the friendly cedar. If Count Marlanx had looked closely enough last night he might have seen that it was a boy who went with me and not —— "

" Fool! Don't you suppose I know a woman's skirts? " cried the Iron Count.

" Better than most men, I fancy," calmly responded Baldos. " My young friend wore the garments of a woman, let me add."

Lorry came down and grasped Baldos by the arm. His eyes were stern and accusing. Above, Yetive and Beverly had clasped hands and were looking on dumbly. What did Baldos mean?

" Then, you did go through the passage? And you were accompanied by this boy, a stranger? How comes this, sir? " demanded Lorry. Every eye was accusing the guard at this juncture. The men were descending the steps as if to surround him.

" It is not the first time that I have gone through the passage, sir," said Baldos, amused by the looks of consternation. " I'd advise you to close it. Its secret is known to more than one person. It is known, by the way, to Prince Gabriel of Dawsbergen. It is known to every member of the band with which Miss Calhoun found me when she was a princess.

Count Marlanx is quite right when he says that I have gone in and out of the castle grounds from time to time. He is right when he says that I have communicated with men inside and outside of these grounds. But he is wrong when he accuses Miss Calhoun of being responsible for or even aware of my reprehensible conduct. She knew nothing of all this, as you may judge by taking a look at her face at this instant."

Beverly's face was a study in emotions. She was looking at him with dilated eyes. Pain and disappointment were concentrated in their expressive gray depths; indignation was struggling to master the love and pity that had lurked in her face all along. It required but a single glance to convince the most skeptical that she was ignorant of these astounding movements on the part of her protégé. Again every eye was turned upon the bold, smiling guardsman.

" I have been bitterly deceived in you," said Lorry, genuine pain in his voice. "We trusted you implicitly. I didn't think it of you, Baldos. After all, it is honorable of you to expose so thoroughly your own infamy in order to acquit an innocent person who believed in you. You did not have to come back to the castle. You might have escaped punishment by using Miss Calhoun as a shield from her highness's wrath. But none the less you compel me to give countenance to all that Count Marlanx has said."

" I insist that it was Miss Calhoun who went through the panel with him," said Marlanx eagerly.

" If it was this boy who accompanied you, what was
his excuse in returning to the castle after you had
fled? "

" He came back to watch over Miss Calhoun while
she slept. It was my sworn duty to guard her from
the man who had accused her. This boy is a member
of the band to which I belong and he watched while
I went forth on a pretty business of my own. It
will be useless to ask what that business was. I will
not tell. Nor will the boy. You may kill us, but our
secrets die with us. This much I will say: we have
done nothing disloyal to Graustark. You may believe
me or not. It has been necessary for me to communicate with my friends, and I found the means soon
after my arrival here. All the foxes that live in
the hills have not four legs," he concluded significantly.

" You are a marvel! " exclaimed Lorry, and there
was real admiration in his voice. " I'm sorry you
were fool enough to come back and get caught like
this. Don't look surprised, gentlemen, for I believe
that in your hearts you admire him quite as much as
I do." The faint smile that went the rounds was
confirmation enough. Nearly every man there had
been trained in English-speaking lands and not a
word of the conversation had been missed.

" I expected to be arrested, Mr. Lorry," said
Baldos calmly. " I knew that the warrant awaited
me. I knew that my flight of last night was no
secret. I came back willingly, gladly, your highness,

and now I am ready to face my accuser. There is nothing for me to fear."

" And after you have confessed to all these actions? By George, I like your nerve," exclaimed Lorry.

" I have been amply vindicated," cried Marlanx. " Put him in irons — and that boy, too."

" We'll interview the boy," said Lorry, remembering the lad beneath the tree.

" See; he's sleeping so sweetly," said Baldos gently. " Poor lad, he has not known sleep for many hours. I suppose he'll have to be awakened, poor little beggar."

Colonel Quinnox and Haddan crossed the grounds to the big cedar. The boy sprang to his feet at their call and looked wildly about. Two big hands clasped his arms, and a moment later the slight figure came pathetically across the intervening space between the stalwart guards.

" Why has he remained here, certain of arrest? " demanded Lorry in surprise.

" He was safer with me than anywhere else, Mr. Lorry. You may shoot me a thousand times, but I implore you to deal gently with my unhappy friend. He has done no wrong. The clothes you see upon that trembling figure are torturing the poor heart more than you can know. The burning flush upon that cheek is the red of modesty. Your highness and gentlemen, I ask you to have pity on this gentle friend of mine." He threw his arm about the shoulder of the slight figure as it drooped against him. " Count

Marlanx was right. It was a woman he saw with me in the chapel last night."

The sensation created by this simple statement was staggering. The flushed face was unmistakably that of a young girl, a tender, modest thing that shrank before the eyes of a grim audience. Womanly instinct impelled Yetive to shield the timid masquerader. Her strange association with Baldos was not of enough consequence in the eyes of this tender ruler to check the impulse of gentleness that swept over her. That the girl was guiltless of any wrong-doing was plain to be seen. Her eyes, her face, her trembling figure furnished proof conclusive. The dark looks of the men were softened when the arm of the princess went about the stranger and drew her close.

"Bah! Some wanton or other!" sneered Marlanx. "But a pretty one, by the gods. Baldos has always shown his good taste."

Baldos glared at him like a tiger restrained.

"Before God, you will have those words to unsay," he hissed.

Yetive felt the slight body of the girl quiver and then grow tense.

The eyes of Baldos now were fixed on the white, drawn face of Beverly Calhoun, who stood quite alone at the top of the steps. She began to sway dizzily and he saw that she was about to fall. Springing away from the guards, he dashed up the steps to her side. His arm caught her as she swayed, and its touch restored strength to her — the strength of resentment and defiance.

"Don't!" she whispered hoarsely.

"Have courage," he murmured softly. "It will all be well. There is no danger."

"So this is the woman!" she cried bitterly.

"Yes. You alone are dearer to me than she," he uttered hurriedly.

"I can't believe a word you say."

"You will, Beverly. I love you. That is why I came back. I could not leave you to meet it alone. Was I not right? Let them put me into irons — let them kill me —— "

"Come!" cried Colonel Quinnox, reaching his side at this instant. "The girl will be cared for. You are a prisoner."

"Wait!" implored Beverly, light suddenly breaking in upon her. "Please wait, Colonel Quinnox." He hesitated, his broad shoulders between her and the gaping crowd below. She saw with grateful heart that Yetive and Lorry were holding the steps as if against a warlike foe. "Is she — is she your wife?"

"Good heavens, no!" gasped Baldos.

"Your sweetheart?" piteously.

"She is the sister of the man I serve so poorly," he whispered. Quinnox allowed them to walk a few paces down the flagging, away from the curious gaze of the persons below.

"Oh, Baldos!" she cried, her heart suddenly melting. "Is she Prince Dantan's sister?" Her hand clasped his convulsively, as he nodded assent. "Now I *do* love you."

"Thank God!" he whispered joyously. "I knew

it, but I was afraid you never would speak the words.
I am happy — I am wild with joy."

"But they may shoot you," she shuddered. "You
have condemned yourself. Oh, I cannot talk to you
as I want to — out here before all these people.
Don't move, Colonel Quinnox — they can't see
through you. Please stand still."

"They will not shoot me, Beverly, dear. I am not
a spy," said Baldos, looking down into the eyes of
the slender boyish figure who stood beside the princess.
"It is better that I should die, however," he went on
bitterly. "Life will not be worth living without you.
You would not give yourself to the lowly, humble
hunter, so I —— "

"I will marry you, Paul. I love you. Can't anything be done to —— "

"It is bound to come out all right in the end," he
cried, throwing up his head to drink in the new joy
of living. "They will find that I have done nothing
to injure Graustark. Wait, dearest, until the day
gives up its news. It will not be long in coming. Ah,
this promise of yours gives me new life, new joy. I
could shout it from the housetops!"

"But don't!" she cried nervously. "How does
she happen to be here with you? Tell me, Paul. Oh,
isn't she a dear?"

"You shall know everything in time. Watch over
her, dearest. I have lied to-day for you, but it was
a lie I loved. Care for her if you love me. When
I am free and in favor again you will — Ah!" he
broke off suddenly with an exclamation. His eyes

were bent eagerly on the circle of trees just beyond the parade-ground. Then his hand clasped hers in one spasmodic grip of relief. An instant later he was towering, with head bare, at the top of the steps, his hand pointed dramatically toward the trees.

Ravone, still in his ragged uniform, haggard but eager, was standing like a gaunt spectre in the sunlight that flooded the terrace. The vagabond, with the eyes of all upon him, raised and lowered his arms thrice, and the face of Baldos became radiant.

"Your highness," he cried to Yetive, waving his hand toward the stranger, "I have the honor to announce the Prince of Dawsbergen."

CHAPTER XXVIII

A BOY DISAPPEARS

HIS startling announcement threw the company into the greatest excitement. Baldos ran down the steps and to the side of the astonished princess.

"Prince Dantan!" she cried, unbelieving.

He pushed the boyish figure aside and whispered earnestly into Yetive's ear. She smiled warmly in response, and her eyes sparkled.

"And this, your highness, is his sister, the Princess Candace," he announced aloud, bowing low before the girl. At that instant she ceased to be the timid, cringing boy. Her chin went up in truly regal state as she calmly, even haughtily, responded to the dazed, half-earnest salutes of the men. With a rare smile — a knowing one in which mischief was paramount — she spoke to Baldos, giving him her hand to kiss.

"Ah, dear Baldos, you have achieved your sweetest triumph — the theatrical climax to all this time of plotting. My brother's sister loves you for all this. Your highness," and she turned to Yetive with a captivating smile, "is the luckless sister of Dantan wel-

316

come in your castle? May I rest here in peace? It has been a bitterly long year, this past week," she sighed. Fatigue shot back into her sweet face, and Yetive's love went out to her unreservedly. As she drew the slight figure up the steps she turned and· said to her ministers:

" I shall be glad to receive Prince Dantan in the throne-room, without delay. I am going to put the princess to bed."

" Your highness," said Baldos from below, " may I be the first to announce to you that there will be no war with Dawsbergen? "

This was too much. Even Marlanx looked at his enemy with something like collapse in his eyes.

" What do you mean? " cried Lorry, seizing him by the arm.

" I mean that Prince Dantan is here to announce the recapture of Gabriel, his half-brother. Before the hour is past your own men from the dungeon in the mountains will come to report the return of the fugitive. This announcement may explain in a measure the conduct that has earned for me the accusation which confronts me. The men who have retaken Gabriel are the members of that little band you have heard so much about. Once I was its captain, Prince Dantan's chief of staff — the commander of his ragged army of twelve. Miss Calhoun and fate brought me into Edelweiss, but my loyalty to the object espoused by our glorious little army has never wavered. Without me they have succeeded in tricking and trapping Gabriel. It is more than the great army of Graustark could do. Your highness will pardon the boast under the circumstances?"

"If this is true, you have accomplished a miracle," exclaimed Lorry, profoundly agitated. "But can it be true? I can't believe it. It is too good. It is too utterly improbable. Is that really Prince Dantan?"

"Assuming that it is Dantan, Grenfall," said Yetive, "I fancy it is not courteous in us to let him stand over there all alone and ignored. Go to him, please." With that she passed through the doors, accompanied by Beverly and the young princess. Lorry and others went to greet the emaciated visitor in rags and tags. Colonel Quinnox and Baron Dangloss looked at one another in doubt and uncertainty. What were they to do with Baldos, the prisoner?

"You are asking yourself what is to be done with me," said Baldos easily. "The order is for my arrest. Only the princess can annul it. She has retired on a mission of love and tenderness. I would not have her disturbed. There is nothing left for you to do but to place me in a cell. I am quite ready, Colonel Quinnox. You will be wise to put me in a place where I cannot hoodwink you further. You do not bear me a grudge?" He laughed so buoyantly, so fearlessly that Quinnox forgave him everything. Dangloss chuckled, an unheard-of condescension on his part. "We shall meet again, Count Marlanx. You were not far wrong in your accusations against me, but you have much to account for in another direction."

"This is all a clever trick," cried the Iron Count. "But you shall find me ready to accommodate you when the time comes."

At this juncture Lorry and Count Halfont came up with Ravone. Baldos would have knelt before his ruler had not the worn, sickly young man restrained him.

"Your hand, Captain Baldos," he said. "Most loyal of friends. You have won far more than the honor and love I can bestow upon you. They tell me you are a prisoner, a suspected traitor. It shall be my duty and joy to explain your motives and your actions. Have no fear. The hour will be short and the fruit much the sweeter for the bitterness."

"Thunder!" muttered Harry Anguish. "You don't intend to slap him into a cell, do you, Gren?" Baldos overheard the remark.

"I prefer that course, sir, until it has been clearly established that all I have said to you is the truth. Count Marlanx must be satisfied," said he.

"And, Baldos, is all well with her?" asked the one we have known as Ravone.

"She is being put to bed," said Baldos, with a laugh so jolly that Ravone's lean face was wreathed in a sympathetic smile. "I am ready, gentlemen." He marched gallantly away between the guards, followed by Dangloss and Colonel Quinnox.

Naturally the Graustark leaders were cautious, even skeptical. They awaited confirmation of the glorious news with varying emotions. The shock produced by the appearance of Prince Dantan in the person

of the ascetic Ravone was almost stupefying.   Even
Beverly, who knew the vagabond better than all the
others, had not dreamed of Ravone as the fugitive
prince.   Secretly she had hoped as long as she could
that Baldos would prove, after all, to be no other than
Dantan.   This hope had dwindled to nothing, however, and she was quite prepared for the revelation.
She now saw that he was just what he professed to
be — a brave but humble friend of the young
sovereign; and she was happy in the knowledge that
she loved him for what he was and not for what he
might have been.

"He is my truest friend," said Ravone, as they
led Baldos away.   "I am called Ravone, gentlemen,
and I am content to be known by that name until better fortune gives me the right to use another.   You
can hardly expect a thing in rags to be called a
prince.   There is much to be accomplished, much to
be forgiven, before there is a Prince Dantan of Dawsbergen again."

"You are faint and weak," said Lorry, suddenly
perceiving his plight.   "The hospitality of the castle
is yours.   The promise we made a few days ago holds
good.   Her highness will be proud to receive you
when you are ready to come to the throne-room.   I
am Grenfall Lorry.   Come, sir; rest and refresh yourself in our gladdened home.   An hour ago we were
making ready to rush into battle; but your astonishing but welcome news is calculated to change every
plan we have made."

"Undoubtedly, sir, it will.   Dawsbergen hardly

will make a fight to release Gabriel. He is safe in
your dungeons. If they want him now, they must
come to your strongholds. They will not do it, believe me," said Ravone simply. " Alas, I am faint
and sore, as you suspect. May I lie down for an
hour or two? In that time you will have heard from
your wardens and my story will be substantiated.
Then I shall be ready to accept your hospitality as it
is proffered. Outside your city gates my humble
followers lie starving. My only prayer is that you
will send them cheer and succor."

No time was lost in sending to the gates for the
strollers who had accomplished the marvel of the day.
The news of Gabriel's capture was kept from the
city's inhabitants until verification came from the
proper sources, but those in control of the affairs of
state were certain that Ravone's story was true. All
operations came to a standstill. The movements of
the army were checked. Everything lay quiescent
under the shock of this startling climax.

" Hang it," growled Anguish, with a quizzical grin,
as Ravone departed under the guidance of Count
Halfont himself, " this knocks me galley-west. I'd
like to have had a hand in it. It must have been
great. How the devil do you think that miserable
little gang of tramps pulled it off? "

" Harry," said Lorry disgustedly, " they taught
us a trick or two."

While the young princess was being cared for by
Yetive's own maids in one of the daintiest bed-
chambers of the castle, Beverly was engaged in writ-

ing a brief but pointed letter to her Aunt Josephine, who was still in St. Petersburg. She had persistently refused to visit Edelweiss, but had written many imperative letters commanding her niece to return to the Russian capital. Beverly now was recalling her scattered wits in the effort to appease her aunt and her father at the same time. Major Calhoun emphatically had ordered her to rejoin her aunt and start for America at once. Yesterday Beverly would have begun packing for the trip home. Now she was eager to remain in Graustark indefinitely. She was so thrilled by joy and excitement that she scarcely could hold the pen.

"Father says the United States papers are full of awful war scares from the Balkans. Are we a part of the Balkans, Yetive?" she asked of Yetive, with a puzzled frown, emphasizing the pronoun unconsciously. "He says I'm to come right off home. Says he'll not pay a nickel of ransom if the brigands catch me, as they did Miss Stone and that woman who had the baby. He says mother is worried half to death. I'm just going to cable him that it's all off. Because he says if war breaks out he's going to send my brother Dan over here to get me. I'm having Aunt Josephine send him this cablegram from St. Petersburg: 'They never fight in Balkans. Just scare each other. Skip headlines, father dear. Will be home soon. Beverly.' How does that sound? It will cost a lot, but he brought it upon his own head. And we're not in the Balkans, anyway. Aunt Joe

will have a fit.   Please call an A. D. T. boy, princess.
I want to send this message to St. Petersburg."

When Candace entered the princess's boudoir half
an hour later, she was far from being the timid youth
who first came to the notice of the Graustark cabinet.
She was now attired in one of Beverly's gowns, and it
was most becoming to her.   Her short curly brown
hair was done up properly; her pink and white com-
plexion was as clear as cream, now that the dust of the
road was gone; her dark eyes were glowing with the
wonder and interest of nineteen years, and she was,
all in all, a most enticing bit of femininity.

"You are much more of a princess now than when
I first saw you," smiled Yetive, drawing her down
upon the cushions of the window-seat beside her.   Candace was shy and diffident, despite her proper habili-
ments.

"But she was such a pretty boy," protested Dagmar.   "You don't know how attractive you were in
those —— "

Candace blushed.   "Oh, they were awful, but they
were comfortable.   One has to wear trousers if one
intends to be a vagabond.   I wore them for more than
a week."

"You shall tell us all about it," said Yetive, holding the girl's hand in hers.   "It must have been a
most interesting week for you."

"Oh, there is not much to tell, your highness," said
Candace, suddenly reticent and shy.   "My step-
brother — oh, how I hate him — had condemned me
to die because he thought I was helping Dantan.

And I *was* helping him, too,— all that I could.   Old
Bappo, master of the stables, who has loved me for
a hundred years, he says, helped me to escape from
the palace at night.   They were to have seized me the
next morning.   Bappo has been master of the stables
for more than forty years.   Dear old Bappo!   He
procured the boy's clothing for me and his two sons
accompanied me to the hills, where I soon found my
brother and his men.   We saw your scouts and talked
to them a day or two after I became a member of
the band.   Bappo's boys are with the band now.
But my brother Dantan shall tell you of that.   I was
so frightened I could not tell what was going on.   I
have lived in the open air for a week, but I love it.
Dantan's friends are all heroes.   You will love them.
Yesterday old Franz brought a message into the castle
grounds.   It told Captain Baldos of the plan to seize
Gabriel, who was in the hills near your city.   Didn't
you know of that?   Oh, we knew it two days ago.
Baldos knew it yesterday.   He met us at four o'clock
this morning — that is, part of us.   I was sent on
with Franz so that I should not see bloodshed if it
came to the worst.   We were near the city gates and
Baldos came straight to us.   Isn't it funny that you
never knew all these things?   Then at daybreak
Baldos insisted on bringing me here to await the news
from the pass.   It was safer, and besides, he said he
had another object in coming back at once."

Beverly flushed warmly.   The three women were
crowding about the narrator, eagerly drinking in her
naive story.

" We came in through one of the big gates and not through the underground passage. That was a fib," said Candace, looking from one to the other with a perfectly delicious twinkle in her eye. The conspirators gulped and smiled guiltily. " Baldos says there is a very mean old man here who is tormenting the fairy princess — not the real princess, you know. He came back to protect her, which was very brave of him, I am sure. Where is my brother? " she asked, suddenly anxious.

" He is with friends. Don't be alarmed, dear," said Yetive.

" He is changing clothes, too? He needs clothes worse than I needed these. Does he say positively that Gabriel has been captured? "

" Yes. Did you not know of it? "

" I was sure it would happen. You know I was not with them in the pass."

Yetive was reflecting, a soft smile in her eyes.

" I was thinking of the time when I wore men's clothes," she said. " Unlike yours, mine were most uncomfortable. It was when I aided Mr. Lorry in escaping from the tower. I wore a guard's uniform and rode miles with him in a dark carriage before he discovered the truth." She blushed at the remembrance of that trying hour.

" And I wore boy's clothes at a girl's party once — my brother Dan's," said Beverly. " The hostess's brothers came home unexpectedly and I had to sit behind a bookcase for an hour. I didn't see much fun in boy's clothes."

"You ought to wear them for a week," said Candace, wise in experience. "They are not so bad when you become accustomed to them — that is, if they're strong and not so tight that they ——"

"You all love Baldos, don't you?" interrupted Yetive. It was with difficulty that the listeners suppressed their smiles.

"Better than anyone else. He is our idol. Oh, your highness, if what he says is true that old man must be a fiend. Baldos a spy! Why, he has not slept day or night for fear that we would not capture Gabriel so that he might be cleared of the charge without appealing to — to my brother. He has always been loyal to you," the girl said with eager eloquence.

"I know, dear, and I have known all along. He will be honorably acquitted. Count Marlanx was overzealous. He has not been wholly wrong, I must say in justice to him ——"

"How can you uphold him, Yetive, after what he has said about me?" cried Beverly, with blazing eyes.

"Beverly, Beverly, you know I don't mean that. He has been a cowardly villain so far as you are concerned and he shall be punished, never fear. I cannot condone that one amazing piece of wickedness on his part."

"You, then, are the girl Baldos talks so much about?" cried Candace eagerly. "You are Miss Calhoun, the fairy princess? I am so glad to know you." The young princess clasped Beverly's hand and looked into her eyes with admiration and approval. Beverly could have crushed her in her arms.

The sounds of shouting came up to the windows from below. Outside, men were rushing to and fro and there were signs of mighty demonstrations at the gates.

"The people have heard of the capture," said Candace, as calmly as though she were asking one to have a cup of tea.

There was a pounding at the boudoir door. It flew open unceremoniously and in rushed Lorry, followed by Anguish. In the hallway beyond a group of noblemen conversed excitedly with the women of the castle.

"The report from the dungeons, Yetive," cried Lorry joyously. "The warden says that Gabriel is in his cell again! Here's to Prince Dantan!"

Ravone was standing in the door. Candace ran over and leaped into his arms.

CHAPTER XXIX

THE CAPTURE OF GABRIEL

R AVONE was handsome in his borrowed
clothes. He was now the clean, im-
maculate gentleman instead of the
wretched vagabond of the hills. Even
Beverly was surprised at the change
in him. His erstwhile sad and melan-
choly face was flushed and bright with happiness.
The kiss he bestowed upon the delighted Candace
was tender in the extreme. Then, putting her aside,
he strode over and gallantly kissed the hand of
Graustark's princess, beaming an ecstatic smile upon
the merry Beverly an instant later.

"Welcome, Prince Dantan," said Yetive. "A
thousand times welcome."

"All Graustark is your throne, most glorious
Yetive. That is why I have asked to be presented here
and not in the royal hall below," said Ravone.

"You will wait here with us, then, to hear the good
news from our warden," said the princess. "Send
the courier to me," she commanded. "Such sweet
news should be received in the place which is dearest
to me in all Graustark."

The ministers and the lords and ladies of the castle

were assembled in the room when Baron Dangloss appeared with the courier from the prison. Count Marlanx was missing. He was on his way to the fortress, a crushed, furious, impotent old man. In his quarters he was to sit and wait for the blow that he knew could not be averted. In fear and despair, hiding his pain and his shame, he was racking his brain for means to lessen the force of that blow. He could withdraw the charges against Baldos, but he could not soften the words he had said and written of Beverly Calhoun. He was not troubling himself with fear because of the adventures in the chapel and passage. He knew too well how Yetive could punish when her heart was bitter against an evil-doer. Graustark honored and protected its women.

The warden of the dungeons from which Gabriel had escaped months before reported to the princess that the prisoner was again in custody. Briefly he related that a party of men led by Prince Dantan had appeared early that day bringing the fugitive prince, uninjured, but crazed by rage and disappointment. They had tricked him into following them through the hills, intent upon slaying his brother Dantan. There could be no mistake as to Gabriel's identity. In conclusion, the warden implored her highness to send troops up to guard the prison in the mountain-side. He feared an attack in force by Gabriel's army.

"Your highness," said Lorry, "I have sent instructions to Colonel Braze, requiring him to take a large force of men into the pass to guard the prison.

Gabriel shall not escape again, though all Daws-bergen comes after him."

"You have but little to fear from Dawsbergen," said Ravone, who was seated near the princess, Candace at his side. "Messages have been brought to me from the leading nobles of Dawsbergen, assuring me that the populace is secretly eager for the old reign to be resumed. Only the desperate fear of Gabriel and a few of his bloody but loyal advisers holds them in check. Believe me, Dawsbergen's efforts to release Gabriel will be perfunctory and half-hearted in the extreme. He ruled like a madman. It was his intense, implacable desire to kill his brother that led to his undoing. Will it be strange, your highness, if Dawsbergen welcomes the return of Dantan in his stead?"

"The story! The story of his capture! Tell us the story," came eagerly from those assembled. Ravone leaned back languidly, his face tired and drawn once more, as if the mere recalling of the hardships past was hard to bear.

"First, your highness, may I advise you and your cabinet to send another ultimatum to the people of Dawsbergen?" he asked. "This time say to them that you hold two Dawsbergen princes in your hand. One cannot and will not be restored to them. The other will be released on demand. Let the embassy be directed to meet the Duke of Matz, the premier. He is now with the army, not far from your frontier. May it please your highness, I have myself taken the liberty of despatching three trusted followers with the news of Gabriel's capture. The two Bappos and Carl Vandos are now speeding to the frontier. Your embassy will find the Duke of Matz in possession of all the facts."

" The Duke of Matz, I am reliably informed, some day is to be father-in-law to Dawsbergen," smilingly said Yetive. " I shall not wonder if he responds most favorably to an ultimatum."

Ravone and Candace exchanged glances of amusement, the latter breaking into a deplorable little gurgle of laughter.

" I beg to inform you that the duke's daughter has disdained the offer from the crown," said Ravone. " She has married Lieutenant Alsanol, of the royal artillery, and is as happy as a butterfly. Captain Baldos could have told you how the wayward young woman defied her father and laughed at the beggar prince."

" Captain Baldos is an exceedingly discreet person," Beverly volunteered. " He has told no tales out of school."

" I am reminded of the fact that you gave your purse into my keeping one memorable day — the day when we parted from our best of friends at Ganlook's gates. I thought you were a princess, and you did not know that I understood English. That was a sore hour for us. Baldos was our life, the heart of our enterprise. Gabriel hates him as he hates his own brother. Steadfastly has Baldos refused to join us in the plot to seize Prince Gabriel. He once took an oath to kill him on sight, and I was so opposed to this that he had to be left out of the final adventures."

"Please tell us how you succeeded in capturing that — your half-brother," cried Beverly, forgetting that it was another's place to make the request. The audience drew near, eagerly attentive.

"At another time I shall rejoice in telling the story in detail. For the present let me ask you to be satisfied with the statement that we tricked him by means of letters into the insane hope that he could capture and slay his half-brother. Captain Baldos suggested the plan. Had he been arrested yesterday, I feel that it would have failed. Gabriel was and is insane. We led him a chase through the Graustark hills until the time was ripe for the final act. His small band of followers fled at our sudden attack, and he was taken almost without a struggle, not ten miles from the city of Edelweiss. In his mad ravings we learned that his chief desire was to kill his brother and sister and after that to carry out the plan that has long been in his mind. He was coming to Edelweiss for the sole purpose of entering the castle by the underground passage, with murder in his heart. Gabriel was coming to kill the Princess Yetive and Mr. Lorry. He has never forgotten the love he bore for the princess, nor the hatred he owes his rival. It was the duty of Captain Baldos to see that he did not enter the passage in the event that he eluded us in the hills."

Later in the day the Princess Yetive received from the gaunt, hawkish old man in the fortress a signed statement, withdrawing his charges against Baldos, the guard. Marlanx did not ask for leniency; it was not in him to plead. If the humble withdrawal of charges against Baldos could mitigate the punishment he knew Yetive would impose, all well and good. If it went for naught, he was prepared for the worst. Down there in his quarters, with wine before him, he sat and waited for the end. He knew that there was but one fate for the man, great or small, who attacked a woman in Graustark. His only hope was that the princess might make an exception in the case of one who had been the head of the army — but the hope was too small to cherish.

Baldos walked forth a free man, the plaudits of the people in his ears. Baron Dangloss and Colonel Quinnox were beside the tall guard as he came forward to receive the commendations and apologies of Graustark's ruler and the warm promises of reward from the man he served.

He knelt before the two rulers who were holding court on the veranda. The cheers of nobles, the shouts of soldiery, the exclamations of the ladies did not turn his confident head. He was the born knight. The look of triumph that he bestowed upon Beverly Calhoun, who lounged gracefully beside the stone balustrade, brought the red flying to her cheeks. He took something from his breast and held it gallantly to his lips, before all the assembled courtiers. Beverly knew that it was a faded rose!

CHAPTER XXX

IN THE GROTTO

 HE next morning a royal messenger came to Count Marlanx. He bore two sealed letters from the princess. One briefly informed him that General Braze was his successor as commander-in-chief of the army of Graustark. He hesitated long before opening the other. It was equally brief and to the point. The Iron Count's teeth came together with a savage snap as he read the signature of the princess at the end. There was no recourse. She had struck for Beverly Calhoun. He looked at his watch. It was eleven o'clock. The edict gave him twenty-four hours from the noon of that day. The gray old libertine despatched a messenger for his man of affairs, a lawyer of high standing in Edelweiss. Together they consulted until midnight. Shortly after daybreak the morning following, Count Marlanx was in the train for Vienna, never to set foot on Graustark's soil again. He was banished and his estates confiscated by the government.

The ministry in Edelweiss was not slow to reopen

334

negotiations with Dawsbergen. A proclamation was sent to the prime minister, setting forth the new order of affairs and suggesting the instant suspension of hostile preparations and the restoration of Prince Dantan. Accompanying this proclamation went a dignified message from Dantan, informing his people that he awaited their commands. He was ready to resume the throne that had been so desecrated. It would be his joy to restore Dawsbergen to its once peaceful and prosperous condition. In the meantime the Duke of Mizrox despatched the news to the Princess Volga of Axphain, who was forced to abandon — temporarily, at least — her desperate designs upon Graustark. The capture of Gabriel put an end to her transparent plans.

"But she is bound to break out against us sooner or later and on the slightest provocation," said Yetive.

"I daresay that a friendly alliance between Graustark and Dawsbergen will prove sufficient to check any ambitions she may have along that line," said Ravone significantly. "They are very near to each other now, your highness. Friends should stand together."

Beverly Calhoun was in suspense. Baldos had been sent off to the frontier by Prince Dantan, carrying the message which could be trusted to no other. He accompanied the Graustark ambassadors of peace as Dantan's special agent. He went in the night time and Beverly did not see him. The week which followed his departure was the longest she ever spent. She was troubled in her heart for fear that he might not return, despite the declaration she had made to him in one hysterical moment. It was difficult for her to keep up the show of cheerfulness that was expected of her. Reticence became her strongest characteristic. She persistently refused to be drawn into a discussion of her relations with, the absent one. Yetive was piqued by her manner at first, but wisely saw through the mask as time went on. She and Prince Dantan had many quiet and interesting chats concerning Beverly and the erstwhile guard. The prince took Lorry and the princess into his confidence. He told them all there was to tell about his dashing friend and companion.

Beverly and the young Princess Candace became fast and loving friends. The young girl's worship of her brother was beautiful to behold. She huddled close to him on every occasion, and her dark eyes bespoke adoration whenever his name was mentioned in her presence.

" If he doesn't come back pretty soon, I'll pack up and start for home," Beverly said to herself resentfully one day. " Then if he wants to see me he'll have to come all the way to Washin'ton. And I'm not sure that he can do it, either. He's too disgustingly poor."

" Wha's became o' dat Misteh Baldos, Miss Bev'ly ? " asked Aunt Fanny in the midst of these sorry cogitations. " Has he tuck hit int' his haid to desert us fo' good? Seems to me he'd oughteh ____ "

" Now, that will do, Aunt Fanny," reprimanded

her mistress sternly. "You are not supposed to know anything about affairs of state. So don't ask."

At last she no longer could curb her impatience and anxiety. She deliberately sought information from Prince Dantan. They were strolling in the park on the seventh day of her inquisition.

"Have you heard from Paul Baldos?" she asked, bravely plunging into deep water.

"He is expected here to-morrow or the next day, Miss Calhoun. I am almost as eager to see him as you are," he replied, with a very pointed smile.

"Almost? Well, yes, I'll confess that I am eager to see him. I never knew I could long for anyone as much as I — Oh, well, there's no use hiding it from you. I couldn't if I tried. I care very much for him. You don't think it sounds silly for me to say such a thing, do you? I've thought a great deal of him ever since the night at the Inn of the Hawk and Raven. In my imagination I have tried to strip you of your princely robes to place them upon him. But he is only Baldos, in spite of it all. He knows that I care for him, and I know that he cares for me. Perhaps he has told you."

"Yes, he has confessed that he loves you, Miss Calhoun, and he laments the fact that his love seems hopeless. Paul wonders in his heart if it would be right in him to ask you to give up all you have of wealth and pleasure to share a humble lot with him."

"I love him. Isn't that enough? There is no wealth so great as that. But," and she pursed her mouth in pathetic despair, " don't you think that you

can make a noble or something of him and give him
a station in life worthy of his ambitions? He has
done so much for you, you know."

" I have nothing that I can give to him, he says.
Paul Baldos asks only that he may be my champion
until these negotiations are ended. Then he desires
to be free to serve whom he will. All that I can do
is to let him have his way. He is a freelance and he
asks no favors, no help."

" Well, I think he's perfectly ridiculous about it,
don't you? And yet, that is the very thing I like
in him. I am only wondering how we — I mean, how
he is going to live, that's all."

" If I am correctly informed he still has several
months to serve in the service for which he enlisted.
You alone, I believe, have the power to discharge
him before his term expires," said he meaningly.

That night Baldos returned to Edelweiss, ahead of
the Graustark delegation which was coming the next
day with representatives from Dawsbergen. He
brought the most glorious news from the frontier.
The Duke of Matz and the leading dignitaries had
heard of Gabriel's capture, both through the Bappo
boys and through a few of his henchmen who had
staggered into camp after the disaster. The news
threw the Dawsbergen diplomats into a deplorable
state of uncertainty. Even the men high in authority,
while not especially depressed over the fall of their
sovereign, were in doubt as to what would be the next
move in their series of tragedies. Almost to a man
they regretted the folly which had drawn them into

the net with Gabriel. Baldos reported that the Duke
of Matz and a dozen of the most distinguished men
in Dawsbergen were on their way to Edelweiss to complete arrangements for peace and to lay their renun-
ciation of Gabriel before Dantan in a neutral court.
The people of Dawsbergen had been clamoring long
for Dantan's restoration, and Baldos was commis-
sioned to say that his return would be the signal for
great rejoicing. He was closeted until after midnight with Dantan and his sister, Lorry and Princess Yetive being called in at the end to hear and
approve of the manifesto prepared by the Prince of
Dawsbergen. The next morning the word went forth
that a great banquet was to be given in the castle that
night for Prince Dantan and the approaching noblemen. The prince expected to depart almost immediately thereafter to resume the throne in Serros.

Baldos was wandering through the park early in
the morning. His duties rested lightly upon his shoulders, but he was restless and dissatisfied. The longing in his heart urged him to turn his eyes ever and
anon toward the balcony and then to the obstinate-
looking castle doors. The uniform of a Graustark
guard still graced his splendid figure. At last a
graceful form was seen coming from the castle toward
the cedars. She walked bravely, but aimlessly. That
was plain to be seen. It was evident that she was
and was not looking for some one. Baldos observed
with a thrill of delight that a certain red feather stood
up defiantly from the band of her sailor hat. He

liked the way her dark-blue walking-skirt swished in harmony with her lithe, firm strides.

She was quite near before he advanced from his place among the trees. He did not expect her to exhibit surprise or confusion and he was not disappointed. She was as cool as a brisk spring morning. He did not offer his hand, but, with a fine smile of contentment, bowed low and with mock servility.

"I report for duty, your highness," he said. She caught the ring of gladness in his voice.

"Then I command you to shake hands with me," she said brightly. "You have been away, I believe?" with a delicious inflection.

"Yes, for a century or more, I'm sure." Constraint fell upon them suddenly. The hour had come for a definite understanding and both were conquered by its importance. For the first time in his life he knew the meaning of diffidence. It came over him as he looked helplessly into the clear, gray, earnest eyes. "I love you for wearing that red feather," he said simply.

"And I loved you for wearing it," she answered, her voice soft and thrilling. He caught his breath joyously.

"Beverly," as he bent over her, "you are my very life, my —— "

"Don't, Paul!" she whispered, drawing away with an embarrassed glance about the park. There were people to be seen on all sides. But he had forgotten them. He thought only of the girl who ruled his heart. Seeing the pain in his face, she hastily, even blushingly, said: "It is so public, dear."

He straightened himself with soldierly precision, but his voice trembled as he tried to speak calmly in defiance to his eyes. "There is the grotto — see! It is seclusion itself. Will you come with me? I must tell you all that is in my heart. It will burst if I do not."

Slowly they made their way to the fairy grotto deep in the thicket of trees. It was Yetive's favorite dreaming place. Dark and cool and musical with the rippling of waters, it was an ideal retreat. She dropped upon the rustic bench that stood against the moss-covered wall of boulders. With the gentle reserve of a man who reveres as well as loves, Baldos stood above her. He waited and she understood. How unlike most impatient lovers he was!

"You may sit beside me," she said with a wistful smile of acknowledgment. As he flung himself into the seat, his hand eagerly sought hers, his courtly reserve gone to the winds.

"Beverly, dearest one, you never can know how much I love you," he whispered into her ear. "It is a deathless love, unconquerable, unalterable. It is in my blood to love forever. Listen to me, dear one: I come of a race whose love is hot and enduring. My people from time immemorial have loved as no other people have loved. They have killed and slaughtered for the sake of the glorious passion. Love is the religion of my people. You must, you shall believe me when I say that I will love you better than my soul so long as that soul exists. I loved you the day I met you. It has been worship since that time."

His passion carried her resistlessly away as the great waves sweep the deck of a ship at sea. She was out in the ocean of love, far from all else that was dear to her, far from all harbors save the mysterious one to which his passion was piloting her through a storm of emotion.

"I have longed so to hold you in my arms, Beverly — even when you were a princess and I lay in the hospital at Ganlook, my fevered arms hungered for you. There never has been a moment that my heart has not been reaching out in search of yours. You have glorified me, dearest, by the promise you made a week ago. I know that you will not renounce that precious pledge. It is in your eyes now — the eyes I shall worship to the end of eternity. Tell me, though, with your own lips, your own voice, that you will be my wife, mine to hold forever."

For answer she placed her arms about his neck and buried her face against his shoulder. There were tears in her gray eyes and there was a sob in her throat. He held her close to his breast for an eternity, it seemed to both, neither giving voice to the song their hearts were singing. There was no other world than the fairy grotto.

"Sweetheart, I am asking you to make a great sacrifice," he said at last, his voice hoarse but tender. She looked up into his face serenely. "Can you give up the joys, the wealth, the comforts of that home across the sea to share a lowly cottage with me and

my love? Wait, dear,— do not speak until I am
through. You must think of what your friends will
say. The love and life I offer you now will not be
like that which you always have known. It will be
poverty and the dregs, not riches and wine. It
will be —— "

But she placed her hand upon his lips, shaking her
head emphatically. The picture he was painting was
the same one that she had studied for days and days.
Its every shadow was familiar to her, its every un-
wholesome corner was as plain as day.

"The rest of the world may think what it likes,
Paul," she said. "It will make no difference to me.
I have awakened from my dream. My dream prince
is gone, and I find that it's the real man that I love.
What would you have me do? Give you up because
you are poor? Or would you have me go up the lad-
der of fame and prosperity with you, a humble but
adoring burden? I know you, dear. You will not
always be poor. They may say what they like. I
have thought long and well, because I am not a fool.
It is the American girl who marries the titled foreigner
without love that is a fool. Marrying a poor man is
too serious a business to be handled by fools. I have
written to my father, telling him that I am going to
marry you," she announced. He gasped with unbelief.

"You have — already?" he cried.

"Of course. My mind has been made up for more
than a week. I told it to Aunt Fanny last night."

"And she?"

"She almost died, that's all," said she unblushingly. "I was afraid to cable the news to father. He might stop me if he knew it in time. A letter was much smarter."

"You dear, dear little sacrifice," he cried tenderly. "I will give all my life to make you happy."

"I am a soldier's daughter, and I can be a soldier's wife. I have tried hard to give you up, Paul, but I couldn't. You are love's soldier, dear, and it is a — a relief to surrender and have it over with."

They fell to discussing plans for the future. It all went smoothly and airily until he asked her when he should go to Washington to claim her as his wife. She gave him a startled, puzzled look.

"To Washin'ton?" she murmured, turning very cold and weak. "You — you won't have to go to Washin'ton, dear; I'll stay here."

"My dear Beverly, I can afford the trip," he laughed. "I am not an absolute pauper. Besides, it is right and just that your father should give you to me. It is the custom of our land." She was nervous and uncertain.

"But — but, Paul, there are many things to think of," she faltered.

"You mean that your father would not consent?"

"Well,— he — he might be unreasonable," she stammered. "And then there are my brothers, Keith and Dan. They are foolishly interested in me. Dan thinks no one is good enough for me. So does Keith. And father, too, for that matter,— and mother. You see, it's not just as if you were a grand

and wealthy nobleman. They may not understand.
We are southerners, you know. Some of them have
peculiar ideas about ——"

"Don't distress yourself so much, dearest," he said
with a laugh. "Though I see your position clearly
— and it is not an enviable one."

"We can go to Washin'ton just as soon as we are
married," she compromised. "Father has a great
deal of influence over there. With his help behind
you you will soon be a power in the United ——" but
his hearty laugh checked her eager plotting. "It's
nothing to laugh at, Paul," she said.

"I beg your pardon a thousand times. I was
thinking of the disappointment I must give you now.
I cannot live in the United States — never. My home
is here. I am not born for the strife of your land.
They have soldiers enough and better than I. It is
in the turbulent east that we shall live — you and I."
Tears came into her eyes.

"Am I not to — to go back to Washin'ton?" She
tried to smile.

"When Prince Dantan says we may, perhaps."

"Oh, he is my friend," she cried in great relief.
"I can get any favor I ask of him. Oh, Paul, Paul, I
know that my folks will think I'm an awful fool, but
I can't help it. I shall let you know that I intend
to be a blissful one, at least."

He kissed her time and again, out there in the dark,
soft light of the fairy grotto.

"Before we can be married, dearest, I have a journey of some importance to take," he announced, as they arose to leave the bower behind.

" A journey?   Where? "

" To Vienna.   I have an account to settle with a man who has just taken up his residence there."   His hand went to his sword-hilt and his dark eyes gleamed with the fire she loved.   " Count Marlanx and I have postponed business to attend to, dearest.   Have no fear for me.   My sword is honest and I shall bring it back to you myself."

She shuddered and knew that it would be as he said.

CHAPTER XXXI

CLEAR SKIES

HE Duke of Matz and his associates reached Edelweiss in the afternoon. Their attendants and servants carried luggage bearing the princely crest of Dawsbergen, and meant for Prince Dantan and his sister Candace. In the part of the castle set apart for the visitors an important consultation was held behind closed doors. There Dantan met his countrymen and permitted them to renew the pledge of fealty that had been shattered by the overpowering influence of his mad half-brother. What took place at this secret meeting the outside world never knew. Only the happy result was made known. Prince Dantan was to resume his reign over Dawsbergen, as if it never had been interrupted.

The castle, brilliant from bottom to top, filled with music and laughter, experienced a riot of happiness such as it had not known in years. The war clouds had lifted, the sunshine of contentment was breaking through the darkness, and there was rejoicing in the hearts of all. Bright and glorious were the colors that made up the harmony of peace. Men and women

347

of high degree came to the historic old walls, garbed
in the riches of royalty and nobility.   To Beverly
Calhoun it was the most enchanting sight she had
ever looked upon.   From the galleries she gazed down
into the halls glittering with the wealth of Graustark and was conscious of a strange feeling of glorifi-
cation.   She felt that she had a part in this jubilee.
With Candace she descended the grand staircase and
mingled with the resplendent crowd.

She was the center of attraction.   Dressed in a
simple, close-fitting gown of black velvet, without
an ornament, her white arms and shoulders gleaming
in the soft light from the chandeliers, she was an
enticing creature to be admired by men and women
alike.   Two stalwart Americans felt their hearts
bound with pride as they saw the conquest their coun-
trywoman was making.   Candace, her constant companion in these days, was consumed with delight.

" You are the prettiest thing in all this world,"
she ecstatically whispered into Beverly's ear.   " My
brother says so, too," she added conclusively.   Beverly was too true a woman not to revel in this subtle
flattery.

The great banquet hall was to be thrown open at
midnight.   There was dancing and song during the
hours leading up to this important event.   Beverly
was entranced.   She had seen brilliant affairs at
home, but none of them compared to this in regal
splendor.   It was the sensuous, overpowering splendor of the east.

Prince Dantan joined the throng just before midnight. He made his way direct to the little circle of which Beverly and Candace formed the center. His rich, full military costume gave him a new distinction that quite overcame Beverly. They fell into an animated conversation, exchanging shafts of wit that greatly amused those who could understand the language.

"You must remember," Beverly said in reply to one of Ravone's sallies, "that Americans are not in the least awed by Europe's greatness. It has come to the pass when we call Europe our playground. We now go to Europe as we go to the circus or the county fair at home. It isn't much more trouble, you know, and we must see the sights."

"Alas, poor Europe!" he laughed. As he strolled about with her and Candace he pointed out certain men to her, asking her to tax her memory in the effort to recall their faces if not their apparel. She readily recognized in the lean, tired faces the men she had met first at the Inn of the Hawk and Raven.

"They were vagabonds then, Miss Calhoun. Now they are noblemen. Does the transition startle you?"

"Isn't Baldos among them?" she asked, voicing the query that had been uppermost in her mind since the moment when she looked down from the galleries and failed to see him. She was wondering how he would appear in court costume.

"You forget that Baldos is only a guard," he said kindly.

"He is a courtier, nevertheless," she retorted.

She was vaguely disappointed because he was miss-

ing from the scene of splendor. It proved to her
that caste overcame all else in the rock-ribbed east.
The common man, no matter how valiant, had no place
in such affairs as these. Her pride was suffering.
She was as a queen among the noblest of the realm.
As the wife of Baldos she would live in another world
— on the outskirts of this one of splendor and arro-
gance. A stubborn, defiant little frown appeared on
her brow as she pictured herself in her mind's eye
standing afar off with " the man " Baldos, looking
at the opulence she could not reach. Her impetuous,
rebellious little heart was thumping bitterly as she
considered this single phase of the life to come. She
was ready to cry out against the injustice of it all.
The little frown was portentous of deep-laid designs.
She would break down this cruel barrier that kept
Baldos from the fields over which prejudice alone
held sway. Her love for him and her determina-
tion to be his wife were not in the least dulled by
these reflections.

The doors to the great banquet-hall were thrown
open at last and in the disorder that followed she wondered who was to lead her to the feasting. The Duke
of Mizrox claimed the Princess Candace.

" I am to have the honor," said someone at her side,
and the voice was the one she least expected to hear
utter the words. The speaker was the man who deserved the place beside Yetive — Prince Dantan
himself.

Bewildered, her heart palpitating with various emotions, she took his arm and allowed herself to be drawn

wonderingly through the massive doors. As they
entered, followed by the brilliant company, the superb
orchestra that Beverly had so often enjoyed, began
to play the stirring " Hands Across the Sea." The
musicians themselves seemed to have caught the uni-
versal feeling of joy and mirth that was in the air,
and played as if inspired, their leader bowing low to
the young American girl as she passed. It was his
affectionate tribute to her. Prince Dantan, to her
amazement, led her up the entire length of the banquet hall, to the head of the royal table, gorgeous
with the plate of a hundred Graustark rulers, placing
her on his left and next to the slightly raised
royal chairs. Candace was on his right, the picture
of happiness. Beverly felt dizzy, weak. She looked
helplessly at Prince Dantan. His smile was puzzling.
As if in a daze, she saw Grenfall Lorry with the
Countess Yvonne standing exactly opposite to her,
he with the others, awaiting the appearance of the
princess and the one who was to sit beside her.

The music ceased, there was a hush over the room,
and then Yetive came forward, magnificent in her
royal robes, smiling and happy. A tall man in the
uniform of an exalted army officer stood beside her,
gold braid and bejeweled things across his breast.
Beverly turned deathly white, her figure stiffened and
then relaxed.

It was Baldos!

She never knew how she dropped into the chair the
servant held for her. She only knew that his dark
eyes were smiling at her with love and mischief in

their depths. There was a vague, uncertain sound
of chattering; someone was talking eagerly to her,
but she heard him not; there was a standing toast to
the Prince of Dawsbergen; then the audacious ghost
of Baldos was proposing a ringing response to the
Princess Yetive; the orchestra was playing the Graustark and Dawsbergen national hymns. But it was
all as a dream to her. At last she heard Candace
calling to her, her face wreathed in smiles. Scores
of eyes seemed to be looking at her and all of them
were full of amusement.

"Now, say that a girl can't keep a secret," came
to her ears from the radiant sister of Dantan. Ravone, at her side, spoke to her, and she turned to him
dizzily.

"You first knew me as Ravone, Miss Calhoun," he
was saying genially. "Then it became necessary, by
royal command, for me to be Prince Dantan. May
I have the honor of introducing myself in the proper
person? I am Christobal of Rapp-Thorburg, and I
shall be no other than he hereafter. The friendship
that binds me to Prince Dantan, at last in his proper
place beside the Princess of Graustark, is to be
strengthened into a dearer relationship before many
days have passed."

"The Princess Candace ceases to be his sister,"
volunteered the Duke of Mizrox. "She is and long
has been his affianced wife."

Enchanted and confused over all that had occurred
in the last few moments, Beverly murmured her heart-
felt congratulations to the joyous couple. The or-

chestra had again ceased playing. All eyes turned to Baldos,— the real Prince Dantan,— who, glass in hand, rose to his feet.

" Your Royal Highness, Ladies and Gentlemen: Graustark and Dawsbergen are entering a new era. I pledge you my honor that never again shall the slightest misunderstanding exist between them. They shall go forth to their glorious destiny as one people. Your gracious ruler has seen fit to bestow her hand and affections upon an American gentleman, your esteemed prince consort. We all know how loyally the people have approved her choice. There is one present, a trusted friend of your beautiful princess, and lovingly called in your hearts, Beverly of Graustark. Whose example more worthy for me to follow than that of the Princess Yetive? With whom could I better share my throne and please you more than with your beloved American protégé. I ask you to drink a toast to my betrothed, Beverly Calhoun, the future Princess of Dawsbergen."

Every glass was raised and the toast drunk amidst ringing cheers. The military band crashed out the air so dear to all Americans, especially to southern hearts. Beverly was too overcome to speak.

" You all ——! " she exclaimed.

There was a tremendous commotion in the gallery. eople were standing in their seats half frightened id amused, their attention attracted by the unusual :ene. A portly negress totally unconscious of the nsation she was causing, her feet keeping time to :he lively strains of music, was frantically waving a

red and yellow bandanna handkerchief.   It was Aunt
Fanny, and in a voice that could be heard all over
the banquet hall, she shouted: " Good Lawd, honey,
ef der ain't playin' ' Away Down South in Dixie,'
Hooray! Hooray! "

*   *   *   *

Hours later Beverly was running, confused and
humbled, through the halls to her room, when a swifter
one than she came up and checked her flight.

" Beverly," cried an eager voice. She slackened
her pace and glanced over her shoulder. The smiling, triumphant face of Baldos met her gaze. The
upper hall was almost clear of people. She was
strangely frightened, distressingly diffident. Her
door was not far away, and she would have reached
it in an instant later had he not laid a restraining,
compelling hand upon her arm. Then she turned to
face him, her lips parted in protest. " Don't look
at me in that way," he cried imploringly. " Come,
dearest, come with me. We can be alone in the nook
at the end of the hall. Heavens, I am the happiest
being in all the world. It has turned out as I have
prayed it should."

She allowed him to lead her to the darkened nook.
In her soul she was wondering why her tongue was
so powerless. There were a hundred things she
wanted to say to him, but now that the moment had
come she was voiceless. She only could look helplessly at him. Joy seemed to be paralyzed within
her; it was as if she slept and could not be awakened.
As she sank upon the cushion he dropped to his knee

"I hated you to-night, I thought," she cried,
taking his face in her hands.

before her, his hand clasping hers with a fervor that thrilled her with life. As he spoke, her pulses quickened and the blood began to race furiously.

"I have won your love, Beverly, by the fairest means. There has never been an hour in which I have not been struggling for this glorious end. You gave yourself to me when you knew I could be nothing more than the humblest soldier. It was the sacrifice of love. You will forgive my presumption — my very insolence, dear one, when I tell you that my soul is the forfeit I pay. It is yours through all eternity. I love you. I can give you the riches of the world as well as the wealth of the heart. The vagabond dies; your poor humble follower gives way to the supplicating prince. You would have lived in a cot as the guardsman's wife; you will take the royal palace instead?"

Beverly was herself again. The spell was gone. Her eyes swam with happiness and love; the suffering her pride had sustained was swept into a heap labeled romance, and she was rejoicing.

"I hated you to-night, I thought," she cried, taking his face in her hands. "It looked as though you had played a trick on me. It was mean, dear. I couldn't help thinking that you had used me as a plaything and it — it made me furious. But it is different now. I see, oh, so plainly. And just as I had resigned myself to the thought of spending the rest of my life in a cottage, away outside the pale of this glorious life! Oh, it is like a fairy tale!"

"Ah, but it was not altogether a trick, dear one.

There was no assurance that I could regain the throne — not until the very last. Without it I should have been the beggar instead of the prince. We would have lived in a hovel, after all. Fortune was with me. I deceived you for months, Beverly — my Beverly, but it was for the best. In defense of my honor and dignity, however, I must tell you that the princess has known for many days that I am Dantan. I told her the truth when Christobal came that day with the news. It was all well enough for me to pass myself off as a vagabond, but it would have been unpardonable to foist him upon her as the prince."

" And she has known for a week? " cried Beverly in deep chagrin.

" And the whole court has known."

" I alone was blind? "

" As blind as the proverb. Thank God, I won your love as a vagabond. I can treasure it as the richest of my princely possessions. You have not said that you will go to my castle with me, dear."

She leaned forward unsteadily and he took her in his eager arms. Their lips met and their eyes closed in the ecstasy of bliss. After a long time she lifted her lids and her eyes of gray looked solemnly into his dark ones.

" I have much to ask you about, many explanations to demand, sir," she said threateningly.

" By the rose that shields my heart, you shall have the truth," he laughed back at her. " I am still your servant. My enlistment is endless. I shall always serve your highness."

" Your highness! " she murmured reflectively. Then a joyous smile of realization broke over her face. " Isn't it wonderful? "

" Do you think your brothers will let me come to Washington, now? " he asked teasingly.

" It does seem different, doesn't it? " she murmured, with a strange little smile. " You *will* come for me? "

" To the ends of the earth, your highness."

THE END

Printed in the United States
68452LVS00005B/122

9 780809 532018